I0846649

IN THE GARDEN AT MIDNIGHT

A Luxembourg War Story

This is a work of fiction. All characters, organizations, and events portrayed in this novel are either products of the author's imagination or used fictitiously.

In The Garden At Midnight

Copyright © 2026 by Tim Byers

Published by Gray Squirrel Press

A subsidiary of Gray Squirrel LLC

Manufactured in the United States of America

PAPERBACK ISBN 979-8-9912390-2-8

All rights reserved.

No portion of this book may be reproduced in any form without written permission from the publisher or author, except as permitted by U.S. copyright law.

For Chloe

CHAPTER ONE

Cologne, Germany, May 31, 1942, Near Midnight

For the first time since Willem left for the Eastern Front, Karin broke curfew on her own.

She slipped outside but pressed against the front door of their small house on Baumstrasse, her back tense against the cool wood. Willem's instructions came easily, as if he were beside her.

"Step one—look up."

She obeyed. The night sky stretched as a dark ribbon from one end of her narrow street to the next, dusted by breathtakingly bright stars, the only light above the blacked-out city. The beauty calmed her nerves and showed her the way to the park. She let out a slow breath and moved to the edge of the step.

Oh, how I've missed this.

Her foot hovered a moment before touching the brick path. At the end of the hedge, she stopped.

"Step two—listen and watch."

Out in the darkness, the Hitler Youth patrolled. Teenage boys in black shorts, brown shirts, and dark side caps, roamed the streets with the zeal of their older brothers in the Wehrmacht and SS, searching for blackout and curfew violators.

Karin turned back to check her house. Any crack of light could be seen from above—light that led bombers to their targets. All was dark. She had made sure.

"Walk ten steps. Stop. Listen. Look."

Willem was clever. One didn't just run for the park. Patrols had to be detected and evaded. Having been an active member himself, Willem warned her about their zeal. Roaming the streets after curfew was intoxicating, especially to the youngest. Karin scoffed once, but once Willem was gone, she understood. Paying attention was essential.

She began to move.

One, two, three, four...

At ten she stopped, her heart racing again. Trusting Willem had always been easy. Trusting herself was far harder. The stars were glorious, but the street still a dark channel.

She looked back at the house. She could retreat in but a few seconds.

Willem's words were waiting.

"The first ten steps are the hardest. Let your eyes adjust, relax, and keep going. Remember why you need this."

Willem was wise. She needed their night walks. In the weeks since he left, she had begun to forget. Wartime life pressed in from every side, from rationing to blackouts, propaganda and school. Everywhere listened to and watched. Tonight, Opa grumbled over thin soup and stale bread. And earlier, a telegram from Berlin:

Aus: Berlin 31 Mai 1942

Verlobt mit Heinrich

Mutti

Engaged to Heinrich, Mother

Just like Mother, Karin thought. Moving on and up in ten words or less.

She couldn't argue with a piece of paper, but she could have told Opa to keep his complaints to himself.

Instead, she broke curfew.

She took another ten steps, then twenty. The darkness softened. Shapes emerged—peaks of roofs, the edges of step overhangs, the dark globes of the streetlights jutting into the sky. Her frustration began to recede, too. She repeated the cadence Willem taught her: walk, pause, listen.

Baumstrasse ended at its junction with the wider Aachener Strasse. At the corner, Karin pressed against a tall iron lamp-post and looked right. Toward the city, the street narrowed into a canyon of black apartment blocks. To the left, it continued one more block before opening toward the great Ring Park, where the canopy of stars seemed to touch the horizon.

She pushed away from the post and walked faster. Her steps clopped without counting. Willem would not have been pleased with her carelessness, but she wasn't thinking of him now. Her heart surged, pulled by the wide-open space, the quiet. The freedom.

Beyond the shadows of the apartments, the familiar iron arch rose up, black against the stars.

She began to run.

Ring Park encircled old Cologne where medieval fortress walls had once stood, long ago torn down and transformed into lawns, gardens, and crushed-stone walkways lined with mature hardwood trees. Now, anti-aircraft guns lay shrouded beneath nets camouflaged with cut branches. If one believed the radio, the guns were simply a precaution. The mighty Luftwaffe would protect the city from bombs.

Karin chose to believe it. The park was her only escape.

Seeing the arch, her pace quickened. Each step loosened the grip of daily life. Home, once filled with Oma's gentle singing and the smell of fresh baking, now echoed with Opa's groans. School, where once she had loved to learn, was now a gauntlet of Nazi purity tests. Berlin, where Mother lived, was the epicenter of everything she hated.

The Park was the last place those things could not reach her.

She slipped beneath the arch. Willem had assured her that the Hitler Youth would never venture beyond it.

"They're afraid to go in there. It's too natural, too wild. Not enough pavement and concrete."

She smiled and let out a long breath. Mist swirled around her head, and she offered a silent prayer of thanks.

She had made it. She was free.

Long strides carried her into the park. The narrow streets of the Old City were left behind. Ahead lay a broad, rounded lawn, dotted by the silhouettes of trees. Beyond, the rooftops stretched low against the horizon. She was just a speck beneath the vast canopy of stars.

One night the previous summer, Karin had opened the blackout curtains, unable to sleep, and threw open the windows to the midnight air. Oma's garden, lush below her in the backyard, whispered in the night breeze. Karin climbed into the windowsill to stare at the stars. Moments later, a gentle hand touched her shoulder.

"The heavens declare the glory of God," Oma had said, quoting her favorite Psalm from the Bible. "It's the one blessing of the blackout."

Karin missed her grandmother more than ever.

Stone crunched beneath her feet. Above, the stars gleamed like the dust of diamonds. Freedom and fresh air combined to bring calm—perhaps even hope. She had been cooped up too long since Willem's departure. He was right. It was time to change. Could she start over? Make a friend at school?

The next thought startled her.

Could she even join the BDM?

The annual recruitment drive for membership in the Bund Deutsches Mädchen, the League of German Girls, was on. For two years she had managed to avoid it with carefully curated excuses. But loneliness had a sharp edge, too. Most of the Mädchen seemed happy enough, laughing and singing together in their uniforms. Not everyone was like Elfreda, who cared nothing for friendship and only for power and advancement. Unlike the Hitler Youth, preparing boys for the Wehrmacht, the BDM was about forming good German wives and mothers. Politics was everywhere, but the girls managed to have a lot of fun training on cooking, sewing, and caring for the sick and needy.

The idea seemed impossible, like a surprise tomato plant in the dead garden. Willem would not have been surprised. He knew what she was going to need when he was gone.

Fresh air. Open sky. Stars.

And tonight, a gift.

In the strip of damp grass along the hedge, a rabbit hopped out of the moon shadow. Karin smiled. If Willem could see her, he would smile too.

A shadow moved across the path. The rabbit retreated into the hedge.

A figure emerged from behind a lamppost and crunched to the center of the path.

"Do not move, fraulein."

The voice was confident. A boy—not yet a man—advanced with his arm held rigid, clutching a night stick. For a heartbeat, Karin thought of running. Did he have a dog?

He closed the distance too quickly. Slightly taller than she was, his features were lost in the darkness.

"Papers, bitte."

Karin froze.

CHAPTER TWO

Karin couldn't speak. Willem had not prepared her for this possibility. He had assured her the Hitler Youth would not venture into the park, and the voice sounded too young for Gestapo. Who was he? Could he demand to see her papers?

"Fraulein, I will see your papers. Now!" As his voice rose, shocked by what he took as defiance, he also took a step closer. Now Karin could see clearly the black shirt, belt across the waist and shoulder, close tucked cap, and high leather boots. Hitler Youth after all.

Karin fumbled at the small pouch strung inside her blue wool sweater. Like all Germans, she had learned to never be without identification. By fortune of habit, she had slipped it on in the foyer before leaving. She held out the card to him with a hand shaking with fear.

The boy snatched it away and slipped the stick in his belt. From his knapsack he retrieved a flashlight and, covering it mostly with his hand, examined the information. In the faint glow, she could see the outline of his face. He looked familiar, though she could not place him. His face was round, almost puffy, and glistened in the light.

He looked up.

"Fraulein Blik, why are you here?"

She pondered how best to answer, and thought to lie, but fear drove any creative options from her thoughts. She considered it a joke when Willem once said that if they were ever caught to let him do the talking because she was a terrible liar.

"Taking a walk," she answered.

He cocked his head sideways.

"A walk? At this time of night?"

"It's quiet and peaceful."

"It's against the law. I can have you arrested."

The declaration was not a surprise to Karin, though she noticed he mentioned arrest merely as a possibility, not a certainty. She was tempted to be angry with Willem. He had always assured her he knew what he was doing. He had protected her. He made it possible for her not to worry. His absence now became all the more terrifying.

"Please, I was only looking for some fresh air."

The Jugend didn't respond.

"Blik," he said, pondering. "Blik—I know that name."

Karin said nothing. The Jugend shined the light in her face. The bright light stung, and she drew back.

"Maximillian Blik," he said.

"My father."

"Ah yes, the great hero," he declared, with Karin wondering if his voice carried any hints of sarcasm. She remained silent.

"He served the Fatherland with distinction. Copenhagen, Paris, Luxembourg. I recall now. I pass under his portrait every week at Gestapo headquarters. A great man."

Karin knew that same portrait at home, a smaller version in a wooden frame on the table by the door. Father's sharp chin, sand-colored hair swept back, one eyebrow lifted just enough to signal confidence. Even in death, his eyes saw her going up the stairs, crossing the room, leaving the house.

I know your secrets, they seemed to say.

"You disgrace his memory, fraulein."

"You didn't know him," she replied.

As if interrupted by a new thought, he twisted his head slightly.

"Shhhhhh!" he hissed and took a step forward.

Karin froze, as a sudden, awful thought occurred to her about his purpose.

Before she could react, he had closed the distance between them and snatched her by the arm. His grip was strong and pinched the soft flesh above her elbow. He pushed her sideways off the path onto the strip of damp lawn, where beyond stretched a row of bushes. Karin's stomach turned over, and a sensation of fire rose in the back of her throat.

"You can't do this," she said, twisting, but unable to free herself from his grip. She was walking, stumbling backwards and terrified, suddenly, that she would fall.

"Let me go, or I'll scream."

The boy seemed not to hear her. He kept pulling her closer to the bushes. The panic rose inside her. She had heard of Hitler Youth assaulting girls this way. Her legs started to weaken. In the darkness grew white spots that spread across her vision. She opened her mouth to scream but couldn't breathe.

His head turned back, watching for something. In the next seconds, his gaze was fixed behind them on the path.

He dragged her on and kept glancing over his shoulder. Then, within a meter of the bushes, he stopped. His mood seemed to have changed. He stared at her, and a kind of recognition swept over his face. This was her chance.

"Don't flatter yourself," he said. "You're pretty enough, but what do you take me for?"

"Then what are you doing?"

"Perhaps you should tell me," he replied. "A girl doesn't break curfew on her own without a good reason."

She opened her mouth to repeat her explanation, but he cut her off.

"And a bit of fresh air is not much of a reason for risking arrest."

"It's the truth."

"Hardly. A pretty mädchen like you, who, according to your papers, is not a member of the BDM, breaks curfew for other reasons. Would you care to explain?"

"I don't know what you're talking about."

"You're here to meet someone."

"No."

"Perhaps not just someone, but a group."

Her arm was numb from the fierce clamp he kept on her arm. He jerked her closer. "Tell me what you know."

"You're hurting me! I don't know what you're talking about, I swear."

"Shhhhhhh!"

The boy dropped to a knee, yanking Karin hard in the process. She lost her balance and fell. Against her forearms, the grass was cool, wet, and sticky.

The boy looked back. Faint voices could be heard now above the rustle of leaves. Then, the outer edge of darkness seemed to move. From the far end of the line of bushes, just at the limit of their vision, three figures emerged, walking slowly toward them.

The boy pulled her close.

"Is *he* with them?"

"What are you talking about? Who do you mean?"

"The one they call Frei. You were meeting them, no?"

Absorbed by the approaching figures, Karin didn't answer. She had no idea who he was talking about. They kept coming, seemingly unaware of Karin and the Jugend's presence, although the trio walked not clumped together as one would expect with companions, but spread out in a kind of line, a few meters apart, as though they were on patrol.

"Halt! Hands up! All of you!" the Jugend called from his crouched position beside her. At the same time, the beam of his flashlight found the center figure, who stopped dead and drew back, blinded by the light.

Karin's eyes widened at the sight of the target—a thin, wiry skeleton of a boy, about her age, in a grossly oversized pin-striped suit. His face was narrow, with a sharp chin, bony cheeks and dark, sunken eyes. Even more peculiar, his hair was cropped close on one side but hung almost to his shoulder on the other in greasy black strands. He looked malnourished and frightening at the same time.

The Hitler Youth wasted no time. Taking advantage of the momentary effect of the blinding light, he swung the beam to the left. It couldn't help but find a huge hulk of a boy and cause the same reaction. This second one stood a head or more taller than the boy in the center. He had a broad face and flat nose that looked like it had been broken in the past. He wore a full-length military coat of gray wool that, despite his height and bulk, was still oversized and hung on him like a tent. He staggered back, swatting at the light like one would a swarm of bees.

Once more the Hitler Youth shifted his attack. The light sliced the opposite direction, past the boy in the center, and came to rest on a third figure—a girl. Her oversized coat confirmed the impression that they were more than just companions. These garments were a kind of uniform. Sprouting out above the up-turned collar and her ghost-white face were shoots of carrot-red hair tied in a black bandana. The heavy makeup, which set dark eyes against ghastly white cheeks, tempted Karin to think of the circus, had the girl not looked so ghoulish. And unlike the other two, to whom the light was like a flaming torch to wolves, she defied the Hitler Youth. She didn't flinch. A single hand was stretched forward, palm out, blocking the light as a traffic cop would block traffic. She refused to shrink back. To Karin, she was the most terrifying of the three.

"Not much of a weapon there, Jugend." The voice came from the shorter boy in the middle, the apparent leader.

The Hitler Youth swung the light back to the center. This time, perhaps inspired by the girl's defiance, the leader did not shrink back. The Jugend's light, focused on the boy's face, transformed that single eye, the one that was not shrouded by the long black strands, into a solitary black diamond.

"Your führer doesn't trust you with guns yet, does he?" he asked, his lip curling up in a snarl. "At least not until you are out of diapers."

His companions spit out laughs.

"Shut up!" the Jugend snapped. "Put your hands up, I said. You're under arrest."

The leader's snarl turned into a devilish grin.

"Funny for you to talk so strong when there's three of us and only two of you," he said. "And all you have is that tiny little light."

He snapped his finger and looked to the boy on his right. "Take him, Ziggy."

"Right-o, Daddy-O!" the taller boy said in English.

The phrase was foreign to Karin, but there was no time to consider it. The beam jumped to the taller boy and flashed against the blade of a knife. Karin twitched at the sight of it, but the Jugend's grip held firm.

The one called Ziggy took a step forward. The Jugend matched the move by directing the beam up to his eyes. Unlike with the other two, the light still had its effect on Ziggy. He stumbled and, like before, swatted at the light.

The Jugend thrust Karin forward.

"Steady now," he warned. "I've got one of yours."

The leader clucked his tongue, a signal. Ziggy stopped.

"One of ours? That girl?"

The Jugend brought the edge of the light to Karin's face. "Blik's the name. Karin Blik. She was careless. And unless you want to see her hurt, you'll stand back."

The words hung in the mist.

"But I'm not one of them!" Karin said.

"Get up!" the Jugend snorted, ignoring her protest with a hard yank. She clambered up. Wet grass clung to her bare knees and palms. The chill had penetrated to her core, causing her movements to stiffen. He pulled her forward. The tremors of cold rippled up and down her frame as she stared out ahead. The trio was closing in.

In the next instant, she realized what the Jugend was doing. He had forced her between himself and the boy with the knife—as a shield. The understanding, which should have terrified her even more, began instead as disbelief. The feeling turned quickly to anger. Her eyes remained ahead. She calmly said, "You're a coward."

He ignored her.

"Not another step! I promise, I'll hurt her!"

Karin's rage swept the chill away.

The leader cocked his head sideways.

"Jugend, will you show her face again, bitte?"

Fearing a trick, the boy flashed the light in Karin's eyes only briefly before returning the beam forward.

"Zara, do you recognize her?" the leader asked.

"I've never seen her before in my life."

Karin twisted against the Jugend's grip.

"Let me go and we both have a better chance. In this dark, we can both get away."

Her suggestion barely registered in his shifting gaze. For the first time, with a sharp tug, he retreated a step.

"Look at her," the girl Zara said. "Not a thing like us. She's blonde, pretty, and most important, submissive. Everything you boys in the Jugend look for."

"Don't talk yourself down, Zara." The leader's tone was playful. "You've been blonde before, haven't you?"

He looked to Ziggy for acknowledgment. The large boy thought for a moment. "I've known her a long time," he began. "I don't remember her as a blonde."

"It's a joke, Ziggy!" The leader shook his head.

"A stupid one," Zara replied. "Like usual."

Karin pushed back against the Jugend.

"What are you waiting for?" she whispered. If only the Jugend eased his grip, she could make a run for it. But the Jugend seemed to sense it. He slipped the hand with the flashlight around her waist and pulled her close. Every muscle and tendon tensed the length of her body. She had to do something.

"Now listen here, Adolf." The leader had turned back to the Jugend, his expression drained of humor. "We can do this one of two ways. You and your little tartchen can wander back in the bushes like you wanted to in the first place and we'll be on our way. Or else Ziggy here can keep coming. Your choice. And make it soon, because we've got an appointment."

The Jugend's light bounced from person to person.

Karin could smell his sour breath and feel his trembling through the grip of his hands and arms. She knew he was frightened, unsure of what to do. The longer he hesitated, the greater the danger.

"Let me go," she pleaded. "I can't help you like this."

The circle continued to close. In the glow of the dancing light, Karin could see them all now more clearly. They were no longer bothered by the beam. Each wore a confident, defiant expression. The leader paused, threw his head back, and tossed the locks of hair away from his face, revealing his other eye. The lid drooped over a deadened orb that looked like a hard-fried egg. It didn't blink or move with the live one.

Slowly, his arm came up and hung in the air like a starter at a track meet. Ziggy and Zara tensed. When his arm swept down, they sprang forward.

Ziggy attacked from the left, Zara from the right. Being quicker, the girl closed the distance first. The Jugend swung Karin around to block her. Karin stumbled, but the sudden movement snapped her instinct awake. She dove to the ground and rolled her body straight toward Zara.

Expecting a kick in the ribs, Karin saw Zara crouch and spring to leap over her instead. But Zara's timing was off, or she lacked strength, and her leading foot caught Karin's hip. As she fell, Karin took a knee in the stomach, knocking the wind out. Beneath Zara now, whose oversized coat felt like a canvas tarp, panic set in. Karin thrashed, fighting against the coat and Zara's limbs and torso, and managed to throw the girl off with surprising ease.

A strange impulse kicked in. Instead of running, Karin scrambled to her knees, coiled and sprang, falling on what now was a lump of woolen coat and red hair. She held Zara to the ground with her own weight, while the girl, like a captured cat, wriggled and snarled. For her stature, Zara was still quite strong, and in the melee, her arm squirmed free. Searing pain sliced across Karin's face in the wake of Zara's swipe, just before a hard blow exploded behind Karin's ear.

Stunned, she felt Zara wriggle out from under her as strong arms pulling her away. They deposited her next to the Jugend, who was face-down in the grass, unconscious.

Ziggy stepped back and waved his knife back and forth. "Let me cut this Nazi dog!" he snarled.

"No." The leader's voice was sharp. "Let's get out of here before more of his goons show up."

"You afraid of a little blood, Frei?" Ziggy asked. "You said you want them to pay. Here's your chance."

"I've told you who I'm after. Not this hundchen."

The leader took a step forward and bent down where Karin lay. His breath, stinking of tobacco and schnapps, streamed over her. He was so close the long strands of hair from the side of his face brushed her cheek. The dead eye, sagging in the mangled socket, no longer bothered her. She was past being afraid. The spark was gone from his good eye. The lid was heavy. His expression carried an unspoken sadness. This one they called Frei—*Free*—did not look free.

"You picked a fine boyfriend," he said.

He stood up and tossed his head sideways.

They were gone in an instant.

Not long after, the Jugend awoke. He rolled to one side and pushed up on an elbow. The right end of his upper lip was a shiny crater of black blood whose flow had mingled with that from his nostrils. He wiped at it with an open palm and drew back.

At least Ziggy hadn't used the knife.

"Are you hurt?" he groaned, trying to sit up.

She dabbed at the growing knot behind her ear. "No."

"Which way did they go?"

She pointed north in the vague direction of the arc of the park.

He rose to one knee, unsteady, and winced. Karin took his arm.

"Surely you're in no shape to follow them," she said.

"We must report this at once. Perhaps a nearby patrol can intercept them. They cannot get away with this. They don't know who they are dealing with."

She helped him to his feet.

He stared after them into the darkness, but only the jagged line of the city skyline could be seen against the stars above.

"Who are they?" she asked.

"They call themselves the Freedom Gang. Their leader, the one in the center, is surely the one called Frei. A twist of Friedrich no doubt. As you saw, they are nothing but rebellious terrorists. They refuse to attend school or join the Hitler Youth. They only steal and vandalize. They terrorize children, women, and fight the Hitler Youth on the streets. They are no better than the Jews—vermin to be exterminated."

"Do you believe me now that I'm not one of them?"

He turned back and looked her up and down.

"Yes, I suppose not." He seemed hardly to care. He was kicking through the grass, looking for something. The flashlight perhaps.

"You should see a doctor," Karin said. "Your nose looks broken."

"Not until they are caught," he replied. "Let's go."

Seeing him face down in the grass, she had felt a twinge of compassion for him. It was gone now.

"Can I please just go home?" she asked.

His expression was that of a hunter asked to let the fox go.

"You're coming with me. Curfew is not optional."

CHAPTER THREE

The Jugend kept a firm grip on Karin's arm as they started off. Pulling her, they moved north through a line of trees, and then beyond, the open park stretched into the darkness. Karin was convinced they would never catch up.

They crossed another gravel path and descended gently across a narrow strip of dew-covered lawn. The Jugend's gait began to change. The rhythm grew irregular, and he paused frequently, pretending to study the horizon. They were losing precious time and not because he didn't know the way. With every step, she could feel his grip tighten and his body tense at the pain. Among the unmoving silhouettes of benches, lampposts, and trees against the star-studded sky, the Freedom Gang had vanished. Yet Karin's companion seemed all the more determined. She was not surprised—his type was common among the boys at school and more so since the rise of the Nazis. Physical weakness compensated by blind devotion and foolish resolve—exemplified by the Führer himself, if one was to believe the whispers—was exactly what they wanted.

At the wide but empty Aachener Strasse, they scraped across the warm pavement. Beyond the far curb, the park continued its wide arc around the northwest shoulder of the city. By the time they were across, the Jugend's grip had weakened. She found herself supporting him now and had to lift him over the curb and onto the concrete sidewalk. Whatever his injuries, they were sapping him of strength. It occurred to her again that she might be able to break free. She was a strong runner, faster than many boys her age, and it would be easy to outrun this one now. Even so, her papers were in his pocket. She could run, but escape would not be permanent. He could easily find her later, and that would bring even more trouble. He knew her name. He knew her father. He had connections to the Gestapo. Papers or not, he would find her.

"Keep going!" he groaned.

The Jugend took a single step forward and cried out in pain. His weight nearly pulled her over. Karin, nearly spent from the effort, was growing irritated.

"We need help. I can't carry you."

To her surprise, he didn't argue. Instead, he unclipped the flashlight from his belt and turned it on. The beam cut through the mist as he swept it back toward the city.

The light reflected off a pane of glass and then settled at a shelter at the bus stop, and attached to it, a phone booth.

"Take me there!"

Karin dragged the Jugend to the booth, and he hobbled inside. Propping himself against the glass, which had been reinforced with crisscrossed wooden slats on account of the war, he lifted the receiver and tapped hard at the switch.

"This is Rudi Kohl, District 13 Commandant of the Hitler Jugend. I must speak to the police at once!" He was instantly irritated. "Hurry up, you idiot!"

He pounded a fist on the telephone's metal box. "What do you mean, the circuits are busy? It's after midnight, you fool!"

Unsatisfied at the response, the one she now knew as Rudi Kohl rattled the glass with his yelling. "This is an emergency! Get this call through or I'll have your head, do you understand?"

He had just paused to take a breath when the sound of a siren started up nearby. The wail rose quickly, drowning out anything he might have said into the phone. A giant beam shot to the sky in the park near to where they had just crossed the street. Karin spun around. In the span of a few seconds the horizon was sliced by a hundred searchlights come to life. Her throat seized. There had been air raid drills all across the city for two years. They drilled at school, diving under their desks at the sound of their teachers' whistles, huddling like fools, she had thought, under their flimsy wooden roofs. At home, she had visited the nearby shelter during one drill, bearing the stale air and cramped quarters with dutiful neighbors. Opa refused to go.

"I'd rather disappear without knowing than to suffocate with my neighbors," he had complained.

The drills were always during the day. The war was two years old, and yet the British had managed only small raids, a few planes testing the defenses around Berlin. This one registered in Karin's mind with a different nature, both in time and scope. The city was aglow with searchlights and alive with sirens.

Rudi Kohl was still shouting into the phone.

"I don't care about a stupid drill! This is real, this gang must be apprehended at once! You don't know who you are ignoring!"

Karin could hardly take her eyes off the larger scene beyond the phone booth, but she saw Kohl's neck taut with rage. He held the receiver in both hands as he shouted, as if choking it. The sirens overwhelmed him, sending him to an even higher level of frustration. After a few seconds, he slammed the phone down.

"I'll see to it myself. I'll have her head, I swear it. Come on!"

Rejuvenated by the rage, Kohl jerked Karin by the arm just as another searchlight went live in the park nearby. The beam stretched toward the west and began to search. Karin was transfixed.

"Let's go, fraulein!" Kohl repeated. But she could not move. Kohl followed her gaze into the sky. In the distance, the searchlights were slivers against the darkness. It seemed as though a section of stars in a narrow band were moving. Then, as they passed through the beams, Karin could make out the slightest outlines of wings. An instant later it was clear—a mass of bombers, too numerous to count, was headed straight for them.

She spun back to Kohl. Surely, he would share her fear—they should find shelter at once. In the glow of the nearby searchlight, she could, at last, see him fully. He had a strong-featured face, with the high cheekbones and prominent jaw that no doubt served him well as the leader of a Hitler Youth unit. Except for the black hair, he was the picture of an Aryan prototype. In the flash of light, Karin could imagine him jutting his chin and barking orders just like her father.

The sirens cried out from all around, their wails in a chorus of despair. Then, beyond the nearby searchlight in the park, bright flashes and sharp booms pierced her eardrums. Karin slapped her hands over her ears and shrunk down. Hidden in camouflaged netting was an anti-aircraft gun, shaking the ground as it fired into the sky.

Karin leaned toward Kohl and shouted, "There's a shelter not far!"

"I will not let them get away!"

"But Herr Kohl—look at the sky! We must seek shelter at once!"

The nearby gun opened up again, vibrating the glass of the phone booth with each round. The sounds, sharp and painful, left Karin's ears to whistle.

Kohl seemed angry, as if the air raid was some cruel interruption.

People all at once appeared on the streets, many of them running, all of them in various states of undress from a raid that had interrupted their Saturday night's sleep. One older couple floated along the sidewalk in white nightshirts, linked arm in arm like a pair of ghosts.

Opa! Before Karin could react, a third and far more menacing sound rose over both sirens and guns—the drone of the bombers themselves. The noise over the park and the city like a tsunami. When she looked up at the sky again, the sight evoked such fear that she dove to the ground. A panic seized her, and she began to claw across the ground on all fours, desperate for the least bit of cover. She found it under a park bench, whose iron frame and wooden slats provided nothing more than the idea of a roof over her head.

The view from the feeble shelter encompassed the western horizon. The bombers could be seen now in greater detail—oblong bodies bouncing on the drafts, wings stretched and straining under the weight of circular engine housings. The dark, wraith-like hulks, on the strength of powerful yet almost-invisible propellers, chewed ever eastward through the air.

Light beams searched frantically. Flak bursts from the anti-aircraft batteries popped all around. But the beams seemed unable to find the planes, and the bursts of flak seemed always behind where the bomber had been. Tiny black puffs littered the sky like harmless black cotton balls.

Karin couldn't look away from the strange scene in the sky until dull thuds sounded in the distance. *Bombs!*

The explosions thumped, then boomed, and barked as they grew louder, more frequent, and nearer. Soon, their thunder shook earth and sky, catching Karin like a sudden storm. She fell to the sidewalk and curled up like an infant under the bench, clamping her eyes shut tightly. Panicked that the world would collapse on her, she tried to cover her head, but an arm caught against the slats of the park bench. She twisted frantically, afraid that in the next instant, she would be vaporized.

Hot air swept over her, choked with concrete dust and an oily scent that reminded her of Opa's shotgun, but more intense. The smell seared her nostrils into the back of her throat.

The raid lasted only minutes or went on for hours—Karin did not know. Earth and sky and everything in them had merged in a singular cataclysm that seemed to absorb time itself.

When it was over, the earth beneath her came to rest, but Karin's body did not. She could not stop shaking. Though the danger had passed, she clutched at the iron foot of the park bench with all her strength. Then, she became aware of the pain from the sustained effort and let go. Her hands broke away like a melted chunk of ice, but the pain remained.

She became aware of her racing heart and tried to steady her breath. One eye cracked open and then the other. Searchlights cast a faint light over the pavement, still scanning the sky but less frantically. Then, one by one, the sirens relaxed. The black clouds from flak bursts drifted and scattered on the breeze.

Eventually, the blanket of stars reappeared, having never been moved.

Karin crawled out from beneath the bench. The nearby flak battery had ceased firing, and the park seemed like before, dark and open. She was drained and dirty, completely bathed in sweat, but unhurt. A wave of gratitude swept over her. She had survived.

From her knees, Karin looked out on the horizon. Beyond the park, the suburbs west of Cologne were shrouded in darkness. For a moment, she felt hopeful that the anti-aircraft guns had protected the city. But then she realized her mistake. The city lay behind her. She turned and wished she hadn't. Cologne was in flames.

CHAPTER FOUR

Countless fires lit the eastern horizon, columns of smoke rising and merging into a singular blanket that spread over the city, obscuring the once star-speckled sky. Strange smells swept in with a hot wind, sharp odors of things not normally burned—oil, tar, and rubber. The spire of the great Kölner Dom stood in silhouette against the haunting orange glow from below. The destruction stretched as far as Karin could see.

A skeleton of red and white metal was all that remained of the nearby phone booth, its wood slats having been useless in protecting the windows. Karin crunched over shards of glass and splintered wood. The Hitler Youth leader Kohl was nowhere in sight, and Karin's stomach seized at the realization that he might have been blown to bits trying to flee.

She staggered on through a field of debris. Boulders of brick-and-mortar chunks, many as large as automobiles, had been cast into the street. Something about the scene did not fit her memory. The proportions were all wrong. She recalled that the phone booth had been right next to the corner of an apartment building, but it seemed so far away now. For an instant, Karin wondered if she remembered incorrectly or had somehow been blasted deeper into the park. But then the explanation became clear. The building hadn't moved; half of it had been ripped away.

"Is this 1400 Neumarkt?" asked a barefooted woman wrapped in a blanket. She was staring at a house-high pile of steaming rubble where the building once stood.

Karin ignored the question and passed the woman by. Then others appeared, some half-dressed like the woman, some in full suits and dresses, carrying suitcases like they were travelling.

Just past the destroyed building, people began to stream out from an almost invisible opening below the street level. These were the lucky ones—they had managed to reach the shelter in time. Karin remembered boys at school telling scary stories.

"I'd rather the bomb hit me, because I'll never know it," one of them had boasted. "But if you're in a shelter and it hits nearby, the blast sucks all the air out. You suffocate like rats in a chimney."

At the time, the story evoked squeals and giggles. Not now. The survivors emerged grateful, dusting themselves off, dumbstruck at the scope of the destruction.

The sight of an old man and his wife snapped Karin to her senses.

Opa!

She pictured him in the flimsy shed behind their house asleep in his chair. He had made a habit of ignoring the test sirens during the day and couldn't help but sleep through them at night. He was a stubborn old man, and Karin had always thought it a waste of her energy to argue with him. The thought of him alone—*or dead*—seized her by the throat. She began to run.

The landscape was almost impossible to navigate. The pavement was torn, blistered, and in some cases burning. Intact buildings indicated streets, but destroyed ones often blocked the way forward. Some of the craters spanned the entire width of the street. She knew Baumstrasse was somewhere to the right, but soon it was impossible to tell north from south, east from west. One block looked as though nothing had happened at all, and the next was an indistinguishable mass of stone, broken brick, splintered wood and glass, and twisted iron. Wrecked cars parked beside untouched ones, while others had been tossed into the craters or swept through the front window of a shop. People wandered aimlessly, clutching loved ones, staring into the sky, rubbing their faces. Everyone was as lost as she.

The path ahead was blocked by a giant crater wider than the street itself and almost as deep. The blast had not only gouged out the enormous hole but blown away the entire front of a three-story building.

Karin looked up in shock. Half of the structure had been torn away and strewn across the crater and street below. What remained of jagged brick, twisted pipes, and splintered beams was exposed from top to bottom like a bizarre, life-size doll house.

A crowd had assembled at the edge of the crater. Everyone seemed to share in the sense of disbelief. Why bomb a street full of shops, apartments, and innocent people?

A few flashlights began to flicker against the exposed structure. Like the doll house, each floor seemed undisturbed. A light came upon a table where a glass vase still stood, its flower standing unaware of the devastation only a meter away.

Next to her, a man studied the third level with slow sweeps of his flashlight. The faint circle of light passed over something moving in the darkness and stopped. Karin sucked in a breath—the beam, faint as it was, had settled on a child.

Excited by his discovery, he returned the beam to his target and urged others nearby to do the same. Soon the details were clear—a boy, about three or four years old, in his night clothes. He held a small blanket in one arm and a yellow stuffed giraffe in the other. Flooded by the sudden collection of lights, the boy raised an arm to shield himself and, in the process, lost hold of the stuffed giraffe. It sailed out into the open space and plunged into the crater, eliciting a wave of shrieks. A woman along the edge of the crowd fainted and nearly fell into the crater. The quick reaction of her neighbors saved her.

The boy staggered forward in his confusion, coming only centimeters from the edge of the floor. The crowd sucked in a collective breath. The boy mouthed something inaudible above the stirring voices below.

The man beside Karin waved his arms for everyone to be silent.

The faint voice echoed. "Mama? Mama?"

Subsequent words were lost in the crescendo of shrieks. The crowd surged in all directions at the terror of what they all expected to happen next.

"Take the lights away!" Karin yelled. "Turn them off!" She pulled the man's arm down. A few lights moved off the boy, then others.

"Take your hands off me! I'm in charge here, fraulein! Kindly step back and let me decide what to do."

Only a few people heard Karin and moved their lights away. The boy raised his arms against those that remained and began to swat at the light beams swarming around him. Eyes blinking, head twisting, his entire body began to spin only centimeters from the precipice. Transfixed, the people refused to realize what they were doing.

"Stop it! Turn them off! You'll pull him right over the edge!" Karin's voice was lost in the swirling commotion. She tugged at the man's arm again. "Look at him! He's confused. He doesn't understand why there is no more floor. You're going to kill him. Do something!"

Incensed, the man turned to Karin in a slow, deliberate motion. He bent down, drawing his blood-red eyes level with hers.

"You're just making it worse," he steamed. "I have this under control. So, for the last time, beat it!"

Before Karin could react, the man raised his suitcase like a shield and gave her a hard shove.

She fell back into the people beside her. One woman, fixated like everyone else, took advantage of the space in the front row created by Karin's fall. In an instant, Karin found herself on the rubble among the legs and torsos of squirming gawkers, her hands and knees grinding painfully against the broken debris.

The agony awoke an anger inside. The boy was only centimeters from the edge of the opening, and she refused to join those who would witness the horror, then wag their heads that something more should have been done.

She clawed beyond the edge of the crowd and scrambled to her feet. Forgetting the fools at the edge of the crater, she moved sideways, away from the throng.

On the far side of the half-destroyed building lay an alley. Except for a layer of grit and broken glass, it seemed undamaged. Racing along the narrow canyon she came to an entryway. The door had been blown out, the only evidence that it had been there was what remained of the twisted metal hinges. Through the doorway she could see the expanse of the crater, and the swollen multitude along its edge, still scanning, still swooning.

The stairs were gone, and how the remainder of the building, just a thin slice, stood upright was beyond her comprehension.

Further along the wall was her only hope—an iron ladder bolted to the side of the building—the fire escape. Karin ran to it and looked up. The bottom rung was beyond reach, but the only way up.

She scanned the alley and her eyes found a row of trash bins. There was no thinking.

She pulled the lid from the nearest one and, ignoring the stench, emptied it onto the alley. She dragged the bin, ignoring the pain from it, banging against her ankles and feet. Within seconds, she was back at the ladder and had turned it upside down. Metal had rusted and crumbled away in spots, but there was no time to look for a replacement.

The bin rocked on its bent lip and the uneven alley pavement. The bottom rim was sharp against her palms, but she steadied it the best she could, and brought first one knee up onto the bottom, then carefully the other. The bin teetered, the rim dug into her hands, but it held.

Quivering with concentration, Karin began the process of standing up by sliding a knee forward and wedging her shoe along the rim. With as much of her weight on her hands, she fought the pain and slid forward the second leg. The bin miraculously held. Now the hard part—letting go and standing up. The lowest rung of the ladder was right above, within reach, if only she could keep her balance.

She strained to rise slowly, her thigh muscles quivering. The bin teetered but held. Her hands swept up past her shoulders, stretched above her head, and slipped above the first rung. Her fingers closed over the cold metal, and she stretched for the second rung. Thin flakes of paint and rust rained down into her face and eyes. In reaction, she snapped her head back, which shifted her weight. The bin toppled sideways and clanged on the pavement. But she had made it. She jammed a knee over the lowest rung and levered herself higher.

A voice called out from the street below.

"Look! On the fire escape!"

Light flickered on the wall in front of her, splashing her shadow across the bricks.

"Come down from there!" a man called. "Wait for the rescuers."

"Or the Hitler Youth!" someone else said. Within moments a small crowd had gathered at the bottom of the ladder.

Ignoring them, she climbed higher. Her body protested, but Karin progressed quickly. At the third floor, she crawled onto the platform below the window. A sliver of light flickered through a crack in the blackout curtain.

Karin pushed in on the frame. It was locked.

She leaned closer. Through the space in the curtain, she could see the boy's crib and the painting of a clown on the wall above it. Her judgment had been correct. This was his nursery.

She wiggled the window frame again as panic returned. It would hardly budge and wouldn't come free.

Then there came a small rumbling sound, and the entire building rocked. Everyone screamed. Karin nearly lost her footing on the platform. Only a single bar of iron, catching her rib, prevented her from a ten-meter fall.

"Hurry!" shouted someone from below. "The building is going to come down!"

Without another thought, Karin removed her remaining shoe and grasped it by the toe. She swung hard, bringing the heel against the glass. With a loud bang the pane cracked but did not break. The impact reverberated through her fingers and loosened her grip. It disappeared into the darkness below.

There was no time to lament the loss. She took off her sweater and wound it around her fist. A few punches later, the hole was big enough for her to reach in. The latch came free, and the window swung open.

Inside, the floor was a mess of broken glass and plaster and a massive open space where the wall had been ripped away. The boy stood where she had last seen him, still confused, still swatting at the light, his back turned to her.

Worried that she might startle him, Karin took a careful step forward. The glass crunched and she winced, her thin stockings no match for the broken shards.

The boy turned around, alarmed.

Karin forced a smile. The boy stared at her for a moment, and then his face relaxed. He tilted his head as if to ask, "What are you doing here?"

Karin steadied her breath and motioned for him to come. The boy swallowed and sucked in a deep breath, hesitating. She smiled once more, hoping for the brightest and most hopeful face she could imagine, and ushered him again. He blinked but did not move.

Then the building shook a second time. The boy staggered—Karin's heart stopped—the crowd swooned. Then, as she was sure he would disappear over the edge, he plopped straight down on his bottom and began to cry. Karin felt it in her throat—*we're out of time.*

She strode forward, thinking she would snatch him away from the edge, crying or not. Near the edge herself, her third stride came down on a thin rug. The rug, covering a gap in the floor, sank down like thin ice on a spring pond. Karin fell through with a yelp, flinging her arms wide in hopes of catching something, anything. Her ribcage slammed against a floor joist, and her spread elbows saved her from certain death. The throng let out another reaction, this one louder than the ones before.

Through it all, Karin never lost sight of the boy, though her legs now dangled in the open space touching nothing but air. Exhaustion had taken its toll. She was on the brink of despair.

I've been a fool climbing up here.

The boy's eyes brightened. Covering his mouth, he giggled, and then mumbled something Karin couldn't hear.

"What?" she asked.

He pulled his hands down. "Do it again!"

Karin smiled at the notion that he thought she was playing a game. His delight was the boost she needed, though climbing out would not be easy. It had been a night beyond her worst nightmare, and her strength was at its end. The boy's smile was the frayed thread between life and death. She had to act now to save him.

"Watch this!"

Like a gymnast on parallel bars, she swung on her elbows. Her legs came up and a foot found purchase at the edge of the floor, but then she stopped. She couldn't move. Her arms had gone to rubber. The crater beckoned from below.

"Again! Again!" The boy bounced in delight. His voice was the only bond that held her in place. Silently, she begged for strength and tried once more. Somehow, she pulled herself up. She let her face rest on splinters of glass, panting.

A poking at her side stirred her back to awareness.

"Again! Again!"

Karin looked up. The boy had crawled away from the edge and was pounding on her back. His dusty blonde curls were matted to his head from sweat. His blue pajamas were dirty and dark in the front. He had wet himself and smelled of urine. Yet still he wanted to play.

The stench provided the final impetus. Karin scrambled to her knees and snatched him in her arms. The move startled him, and he started crying again, but she didn't care. She had him and wouldn't let go.

An easy jump and she was back at the window. The crowd below let out a cheer.

Karin clutched the boy tight with one arm and hugged the ladder with the other. The journey down was as dangerous as anything else she had done, but the boy in her arm gave her new strength. Step by careful step she descended, trying not to think about being crushed under tons of rubble if the building let go.

Two-thirds of the way down the ladder, they were met by a pair of firemen ascending toward them. The first one climbed up behind Karin and peeled the boy away, and he started howling. The fireman passed the boy down to the second fireman and then turned back to her. A strong arm around her waist helped her descend. She was lowered and placed onto a stretcher. The crowd, quite substantial now, erupted in joyous applause.

Karin felt the first wave of relief. She was glad to be alive and grateful for the boy. Yet now his home was gone, and he was surely now an orphan.

A circle of faces hovered over her in the dance of flashlights. One of them looked familiar. The Jugend Kohl? He was speaking to the others, but she could only make out the word "hero."

He leaned down. His voice was just a whisper in her ear.

"I've misjudged you, Fraulein Blik. You are quite capable. Quite capable indeed. We can use girls like you. You will be most helpful. Congratulations."

The words sent a tremor through Karin's already spent frame. She rolled away from him and tried to raise up to get away. A nurse pushed her back down onto the stretcher. Karin was too weak to resist. A moment later, they were sliding her into the back of an ambulance. The last thing she saw beyond the swirl of faces and smoke was a splash of stars.

CHAPTER FIVE

The next morning, Karin dreamed of coffee. She was walking in the Old City with her grandmother when they were met with the smell of freshly-ground beans. Up ahead, surrounded by a flock of umbrella-covered tables, the Café Reichard came into view, where white-aproned waiters served not only the finest roasts, but the most delicious cakes and tortes in the entire city.

As they approached, Karin heard a peculiar sound that didn't fit with the scene, the *sush* of metal in short, stabbing strokes. The sounds echoed a few at a time in sequence, followed by a short pause, and then repeated. Then she was inside the café, where the coffee beans were unexplainably piled in a large mound in the center of the lobby. A nervous barista was scooping the beans into a sack, pausing to wipe his brow, and then continuing. The pile was endless, and he seemed to make no real progress. Someone offered her a cup from beyond the mound, but she couldn't reach it.

The sights of the dream faded quickly with a mix of confusion and disappointment. As she became aware of her real surroundings—the warmth of her bed, the softness of the down pillow, the feel of the stitches of her quilt on her fingertips—she detected a trace of sadness too. Coffee, imported from countries now allied against Germany, had long disappeared from the shops. The memory, however, was all too real. And while the scene faded from her mind, the sounds continued. Listening on, she tried to hold on to the dream, and in her imagination, she took a swallow, hoping to taste the hot brew. Her throat, raw from the previous night's air and oily smoke, punished her with the painful truth, and her eyes shot open.

They had intended to send her to the hospital, but she had refused. She was exhausted, not injured, and her stretcher bearers quickly realized their efforts would be better spent on the countless wounded. The cup of terrible ersatz coffee they offered her must have spawned the dream. She had staggered home and found Opa safe.

When she sat up from bed, every muscle from head to toe felt like it had been ripped from its moorings. Swinging her legs over the side of the bed, standing up, and putting on her robe required supreme effort. Only the sounds, which now she could tell emanated from somewhere behind the house, drew her on.

Tender steps carried her to the window. Even raising her arm to slide the curtain aside was too much, so she pushed a slice open between the panels and peered through. There was Opa, beside his shed, chopping at the sandy soil with his shovel. The sun was high above the garden—it was past noon already. He was covered in dirt and his head glistened from sweat, but he looked determined, possibly even—to her surprise—*happy*.

He scraped a few strokes, scooped it on the blade, and tossed it away, just as she had heard. The hole had grown to almost two meters wide and half that deep. The mound he had piled against the fence rose almost to his waist.

What on earth?

The stairs reminded her of the agony on the ladder the night before. On the table in the kitchen, the newspaper *Kölner Zeitung* left open on Opa's favorite page, the obituaries, which he always checked for notices of old friends, but lately for the death notices from the front. She watched through the back door window undetected. The part of Opa's face that wasn't covered with dirt was red and drenched in sweat. A lock of his snowy white hair had fallen down the center of his forehead giving him the appearance of a younger man.

She pushed open the door. Seeing her, his eyes lit up, and the expression surprised her. He dropped his shovel, clambered over the pile of earth, and met her on the back porch steps. He opened his arms wide.

She flinched. *Was he happy to see me?*

He held his arms in midair for a moment before letting them fall at his side. An awkward silence passed between them, Karin wondering what had come over him. Something was different with him. Could he really be *concerned*? It was more incredible than her dream.

Karin reached up, despite the pain, and squeezed him around the neck. Then she did something she hadn't done since she was a little girl and gave him a kiss on the cheek. Now it was his turn to flinch. When she let go, he had tears in his eyes. Her gaze lingered for a moment, frozen by the realization of how far apart they had become and how easy it had become not to hug or kiss him like she had when she was a girl. Death, war, Opa's grief, her own anger; whatever the reasons, she regretted it now.

"Are you all right, Opa?"

He smiled with a kind of wistful expression, and chuckled softly, something she couldn't recall. "I should ask you this question. You're the one in pain."

"A little stiff," she said. "But it is good to breathe the fresh air."

He retreated to the shed where he took a folding chair from a peg. "You must sit now. Here, it's a good strong chair."

Sitting down brought little relief. Everything hurt. She settled as best she could and asked him about the previous night, since she remembered nothing of coming home.

"You'll find this hard to believe," he said with a wink, "but I slept right through the raid. Lucky for me those Brits have lousy aim. The shed stood strong through it all."

Karin shuddered. A bomb like the one that hit the apartment building would have left nothing but a crater and a few splinters.

"Next thing I knew, about four-thirty or so this morning, there's a fierce pounding on my shed door. One of your school friends, a pretty little girl. Says they sent her to let me know you were all right. 'All right?' I said. I got up from my chair and came out here. It was still dark, but I could see the shape of the house. Just like it is now. Not a scratch. So, what does she mean, you're all right? Then it comes to me. You're not here. You've slipped out again."

For an instant, she saw the old Opa return. Furrowed brow, sour, downturned mouth. Then he paused, took a breath, and rubbed his forehead. He spoke slowly. "I don't understand. I thought with Willem gone you'd not risk that anymore."

Karin felt tears well up. His confusion was her fault. During previous drills, she would hear the alarms and, because of his bad hearing and heavy sleeping, wake him. He went to the shelter only once and then declared he'd rather die in his sleep than suffocate in a dark cave. Still, when she heard them, she'd at least wake him. With drills, it seemed harmless enough. How wrong she was. The raid was infinitely real beyond her most terrifying imagination. Breaking curfew left him alone and vulnerable. She could see it in his eyes now.

"I'm sorry, Opa."

"You could have been killed, child." He never called her anything but her name. And his tone was never so tender.

The tears spilled down her face, her apology almost pointless.

"Your friend—Marie, I think it was—told me what you did. At first, I couldn't believe what she was saying."

"Marie?" Karin hadn't known a soul at the site. How could she know?

"Yes, I think that was her name. A lovely young girl, at least for a Nazi."

"Opa! She's one of the nice ones," Karin said. By it, she meant that Marie, a member of the BDM, was an exception to the typical profile. While boys of the Hitler Youth were egotistical, aggressive, scheming snitches, their female counterparts in the BDM were often the same but with pigtails. Many a nice girl had lost her kindness if not her virtue because of the BDM, but somehow Marie had survived with both.

"They sent her to tell me. You were at an aide station set up in the Park. They would have taken you to the hospital but there were no rooms. You were scratched up and exhausted but otherwise unhurt." His voice began to quiver. "We brought you home."

Karin was astounded at the transformation she was witnessing.

"They say you're a hero," he continued. "The news spread fast. I've already gotten a call from the Zeitung."

"What happened to little Hans? Is he all right? Did you see him?"

Opa shook his head. "They didn't say. I was so worried."

Karin felt a sting in her eyes. Before her stood a grandfather she could hardly recognize and scarcely believe.

Opa brought her some ersatz coffee from the kitchen and a slice of cheese. It was nowhere near to the dream of real coffee she had smelled and tasted only moments before. But it was hot. The warmth helped her relax and ease the tension in her muscles. She didn't want to talk about the raid any longer.

"What are you digging, Opa? Buried treasure?"

"I wish! After last night, I decided I'm not taking any more chances. We were lucky. But who knows how long that luck will last. I'm going to build a bomb shelter."

The playfulness drained from her face.

"I've been a fool to believe the propaganda reports," he continued, as Karin felt a twinge of the old Opa returning. "The anti-aircraft defenses were supposed to protect us. The Luftwaffe would intercept them and drop them over the North Sea."

He took the shovel and started up again.

"The propaganda says up to a thousand British bombers got through last night. Where was the Luftwaffe? That barrel of lard Göring sits on his arse in Berlin and calls that protection. If that's his idea of protection, then I'll build my own shelter, thank you very much."

Karin was stunned. Opa, she knew, had never been a fan of the Nazis, and especially after her father had been killed. But he knew better than to speak so critically in the open. Not that he circulated with many people. Still, neighbors would turn on each other and call the Gestapo. Children informed on their teachers and sometimes even their parents. He needed to be careful.

"Do you even know how to do it?"

"Hermann Fossbender has a set of plans. It won't be the Ritz, but I can make it big enough for the two of us. You know that public shelter up the street is too far. The next raid will be over before I can get there on these old legs. And if it's hit, who wants to suffocate together with a bunch of strangers? I've been collecting old bricks and some stone here and there. And I've got enough scrap iron around here for reinforcing. The hardest part will be scrounging the concrete. But Hermann knows a man north of the city who works at a cement plant. He may be able to supply us with a little, shall we say, 'leftover' lime and such."

She stood up and looked down into the hole. It was almost two meters wide and half that deep. Enough that they could both crouch down below ground level.

"How much more will you dig? I was thinking of planting some vegetables."

Opa looked at her quizzically. Karin knew what he was thinking. Oma, the master gardener, kept the garden as clean as her kitchen, in season and out. She died before the final harvest and autumn cleanup, and so the plot was a ruin of withered stalks among the fresh spring weeds. With nationwide rationing, they'd need what the garden could supply. But Karin had been more observer to Oma than participant.

"Wait here," Opa said. "I have something that might help."

He went into the house and returned a few minutes later with a kind of book under his arm. He handed it to Karin. She smoothed her hand across the binding—leather with a raised floral design.

"Your Oma's journal. I never read it; she wouldn't let me get near it, but I know she took meticulous notes. Kept it with her out here always. She thought of herself as a kind of gardener-poet, if there is such a thing. She said gardening was a spiritual activity. Seems like nothing more than a lot of hard work if you ask me, but it meant far more to her. I never understood that side of her, but maybe there are some notes or drawings in there to help."

Listening to Opa brought a stab of tears to Karin's eyes. He had surprised her again.

"Thank you, Opa. Thank you."

"She would have wanted you to have it, I'm sure," he said.

They stood there for a moment—Karin wearing a grateful smile while Opa's grin tremored with awkwardness. In an instant, Karin closed the space between them and flung her arms around him.

"This is becoming a habit," he said in mock protest.

"Good," she said.

Later that afternoon, Karin returned to the garden, this time with the seeds she had bought days earlier. She had packets for lettuce, tomatoes, cucumbers, beans, carrots, and peas. The man at the store had laughed when she asked for potato seeds.

"Just quarter as many of your own as you want for plants. Set them upside down in a shallow pan of water until the eyes sprout. Those are your potato seeds."

Karin pictured the finely manicured rows that Oma had cared for, but the reality outside was far different. Except for the hole that Opa had started for his bomb shelter, the plot hadn't been touched since Oma last worked it the summer before. Sometime in August, she fell ill and could no longer tend the plants. Weeds took over and choked everything, just like Oma's illness. The plot was a painful reminder, and all of it—weeds and dead vegetable alike—would have to come out. Planting seeds would have to wait.

She scratched and dug and pulled, most of the time on her knees, until the sun had slipped below the horizon. The work brought a sense of purpose as she pictured baskets of fresh vegetables supplementing their sparse rations. She finished in the dark and rolled back onto the same warm dirt that had covered her arms and legs, smudged across her wet face and forehead, and caked under her fingernails. The stars above winked their approval. Body and soul surged with the kind of pleasant exhaustion that accompanied a job well done.

That night, Karin opened the blackout curtains just enough for the nighttime breeze to cool her room, where she read the journal by the light of a candle positioned so that the flame could not be seen from the window.

The pages, wrinkled from age and exposure to the outdoors, crackled as she turned them.

Half garden plans and half diary, every page was a treasure. The garden plans included drawings of the beds, lists of vegetables, herbs, their varieties, and a calendar for planting. The diary, consisting of short, dated entries, was as interesting as the plans, and stretched back as far as the Great War of 1914-1918. There were prayers and poems too:

Bulbs and buds push through Winter
Flowers tell of Spring
Berries and beans, Summer's Joy

Make way for Autumn's harvest
Bread and blossoms side by side
Bounty that the earth provides
Heaven smiles and opens wide
Beauty in our heart abides

Karin closed the journal and held it against her breast. Tears rose with the memory of Oma's voice in the words.

I miss you, too.

The next day, Monday, the announcement came over the radio that school was cancelled for cleanup. Like all students her age, Karin should have volunteered to help. Opa insisted, however, that she stay home to rest, especially after she had worked so hard the day before. As a compromise, Karin agreed to stay home, but not to stay in bed. She spent the day clearing the plot of weeds and dead vegetable stalks and then remembered that every Spring, Oma started with breaking up the soil with the spade. But Oma did everything with deliberation and thoroughness. Karin had more of Opa's temperament—brooding and impatient. The packets of seeds on the bench seemed to be shouting at her: *Hurry, plant me! Plant me first!*

Opa's growing gouge didn't thwart Karin's enthusiasm. There would be plenty of room for everything. She took the spade and began to dig a row. It seemed straight enough to her own eye. Driving the posts and running the string as Oma had always done seemed unnecessary.

Karin opened the packet and peered inside at the seeds. The tomatoes would grow tall. She poured them into her hand and began to sprinkle them along the ditch she had scraped, a few centimeters deep and that much apart.

The seeds ran out about a third of the length of the row. No matter. She would fill the rest with lettuce. Or carrots.

Smoothing the soil over the trench brought a wave of satisfaction. For the first time in memory, Karin had done something without being told, without being corrected, without the threat of punishment. The feeling was exhilarating.

I understand why Oma loved this so much.

In the middle of the afternoon, Opa joined her in the backyard. He brought with him a crumpled piece of paper which he studied as he worked. He would pace the edge of the hole, consult his paper, dig, pace, scribble, and repeat.

She would be happy if he left her alone, each lost to their own private worlds.

The green beans came next. The seeds were large and easy to handle. Karin remembered helping Oma with them. She had poked a hole with her finger, dropped in the seed, and covered it over. Karin started a new row.

"What all are you planting?"

Karin answered without looking up. "This row is beans. Over there, I planted tomatoes."

"Tomatoes? I don't see them. Where?"

She pointed to the first row.

"Where are your seedlings? You can't just throw them in the dirt, you know."

Karin didn't want a lecture, but she didn't understand what he meant.

Opa stepped closer, bent over, and began to shake his head.

"That's not how it's done. Things have their season, their schedule. Just like the trains. Some start early, some come later. If you plant too early or too late, things don't grow properly or come up leaving you no time to plant anything else. Tomatoes need a head start. Did you read her journal? Where did you get your seeds?"

She was instantly defensive and wanted him to leave her alone. She explained that she had bought them at Meissner's. She had just skimmed the plans in Oma's journal.

"Your grandmother would buy starts from the nursery out in Königsdorf. She tried starting her own from seed once or twice but never liked them as well as the ones she could get from Herr Weiskopf."

She noticed something different in his tone. It was less disgusted, less disappointed.

"Your grandmother was very particular about things. Wouldn't let me touch anything except the shovel. I became her plow horse. But I knew this one thing about tomatoes. The best tomatoes come from Herr Weiskopf."

Karin fanned the seed packets in her hands and surveyed them with despair. How quickly had her confidence vanished! She clomped back to the start of the tomato seed row and hesitated. Then, stowing the packets in her pockets, fell to her knees in the soft earth and began to claw at the new row. The tomato seeds were nowhere to be found. She dug for a while, trying to guess where the row was. In the end, she fell back, frustrated, having uncovered no more than a single seed in twenty.

That evening, Karin studied the journal again. Opa's advice was confirmed—she should have bought tomato starts from Weiskopf. Carrots needed soil mixed with sand. Cucumbers needed lots of room and mounds. She resolved to follow Oma's advice as best she could, though she could never hope to absorb all the volume's wisdom in a few nights' reading.

Another verse stood out:
Weeds and lies sprout
and grow quickly without
Truth and good soil
Care and long toil

CHAPTER SIX

When school resumed the next day, Karin found herself in a familiar place, squirming at her desk in the second to last class of the day. History had never held her interest, and the tenth-year version was no different. Names, places, dates—all to be memorized—were as dead as the stalks in the backyard garden. And since Karin had grown up mostly outside of Germany, she had not been subject to the intense Nazification of every subject until moving to Cologne. The process of twisting already boring facts and adding whatever new ones were necessary to spin an epic narrative of the rise of the German Reich and the triumph of National Socialism under the Führer Adolf Hitler would have been comical if it wasn't so deadly serious. Like so many days before, Karin was in no mood for it. Outside, the searing blue sky and its cotton ball clouds beckoned escape. But she had to be careful. Herr Putz, the newly installed history teacher, watched like a midnight owl. The previous teacher, Herr Wurstner, would lose himself in a lecture on Teutonic heroes or the strategy of Bismarck, which afforded Karin long stretches to daydream. Herr Putz, however, could smell boredom, it seemed. As a true believer, a committed Nazi, he was more propagandist than professor. According to the rumors, he replaced poor Herr

Wurstner, a kind man but generally forgettable teacher, because the latter had told the wrong kind of joke during one of his lectures. It went like this:

A soldier lays mortally wounded in Russia. Before he dies, he asks, "I want to see who I'm dying for."

His comrade brings forth a picture of Hitler and Goebbels and touches it first on the soldier's left shoulder, and then on his right.

"Oh good," says the wounded soldier, "Now I'm dying like Jesus—in between two criminals."

Karin only knew the joke because she overheard two girls retelling the story on Herr Putz's first day. When they realized she had been listening, they were terrified and begged her not to report them.

"I don't find it funny," she had said at the time. "But I could care less."

The Gestapo cared. After Herr Wurstner told the joke, a student repeated it at home, and then an outraged parent reported him. Agents visited his house soon after and then whisked him away. What happened in the basement of the EL-DE Haus on Appelhofplatz, Gestapo headquarters, was never disclosed, only feared. At first, it was explained that he was reassigned to the East. No one ever said exactly where, and no one dared to ask. East could mean prison in Berlin, occupied Poland, or the Ukraine. Or perhaps an unmarked grave. One learned to avoid questions, rumors, and jokes. He was never seen again.

From his first day, Herr Putz established a habit of marching in front of the columns of desks like a general in front of his tanks. So attuned to detail was he that he demanded each desk be aligned in precise rows and columns, down to the millimeter. If one was out of place, even as the result of a student bumping it accidentally, he would explode with rage about the laziness of German youth.

Karin was tracing the wispy tail of a cloud when he stopped at the head of her aisle with a stomp.

"Fraulein Blik!"

Karin bolted back to reality.

"Would you explain for the class three ways in which the Versailles Treaty of 1918 sought to humiliate Germany but failed to do so?"

Terror clamped Karin's heart and threatened to stop it from beating. She had not read the assigned chapter. Fear of his wrath was usually enough to motivate her, but lately, Karin spent every free minute in the garden and had neglected the required reading. Such behavior was risky, but irresistible. In the days after the raid, she had found refreshment working in the garden, and the weather had cooperated. She had escaped his selection so far, but now she would pay.

As required, Karin slid out from her desk and stood at attention in the aisle. She moved slowly, pausing to brush the front of her blouse and skirt, her eyes darting from side to side, scrambling to stir up thoughts.

"Fraulein!" he bellowed. "Today, if you please!"

"The Versailles Treaty of 1918," she began with a deep exhale. "Imposed by the Western Powers after the Great War."

"Yes, fraulein, we know that much. Three humiliations! Just three is all I require!"

His condescending tone burned on her face and jumbled her brain. Still, it reminded her of Opa, and he loved to argue with Father on this very subject. She tried to remember.

"For one, they didn't allow Germany to have an army." Her voice was not confident.

"Not just an army, but neither a navy nor air corps! What did Clemenceau, Chamberlain, and Wilson expect? Germany to be weak and defenseless?"

Karin didn't respond. She hoped Herr Putz would answer his own question and launch into a diatribe that would allow her to escape.

He stopped and stretched his neck out toward her. "Well?"

The stares of the whole class upon her brought searing heat up from her neck to her face.

"Did Germany suffer such a humiliation?" It was a strange lifeline in distress.

"No! Not at all!" she replied, cooled by a wave of momentary relief. "Germany rebuilt its army."

"And navy! And mighty Luftwaffe!"

She dared hope he was satisfied, until he crossed his arms.

"Fraulein Blik, did you read the assigned chapter?"

Karin found the edge of her lip and bit down hard. Every part of her was tense and her throat was desert dry.

"Well, fraulein?"

Karin debated whether to tell the truth. She wondered which would be worse, admitting she hadn't or pretending she had. A lie would require an excuse for why she had retained almost none of the content.

"Fraulein, do your ears work? I asked you a simple question—did you read the assigned chapter? Yes, or no?"

She swallowed what seemed like a mouthful of dust.

"Yes, Herr Putz, I did."

His eyes grew large.

"Then you should have no problem answering the question. Two more—and don't delay!"

"I don't remember," she said.

He moved closer. His teeth were stained from years of smoking and neglect.

He parted his lips to speak when the crackle of the loudspeaker, a box on the front wall, interrupted him, saving her.

"Attention, please! Your attention, please! All classes report immediately to the auditorium for Youth Assembly. Classes should now dismiss for Youth Assembly in the auditorium."

The loudspeaker fell silent. The bell rang, the signal that everyone in Herr Putz's room did not hesitate for. Everyone jumped up, as eager as Karin to leave.

Karin let out a breath. She snatched her satchel and books and didn't care to pack them away. Anything to get out of there.

"Fraulein Blik."

She stopped. *No!*

"Come forward."

The class evaporated even faster, and Karin, suddenly alone, felt the strength slipping from her legs as she turned and moved up the aisle. The books and satchel, clutched tightly to her chest, held back the growing tremors. She stepped carefully to the front of the column and stopped.

Herr Putz waited for the last student to clear the room and for the hallway outside to fall silent. Seconds, perhaps minutes passed, Karin could not tell, because the entire time he stood frozen in front of her, his eyes locked onto hers. Her stomach was a tempest that reverberated throughout her entire body. Having thought the bell had saved her, the snare was all the more terrifying. As the moments stretched on, she began to wonder if passing out would be better than consciousness.

Just as she wavered, he swallowed deliberately, dropped his chin, and spoke in a low but measured voice. Later, she concluded that he knew exactly what he was doing.

"Don't pretend for a moment I don't know what you're up to, Fraulein Blik. I'm not that weakling Herr Wurstner, do you understand?"

He didn't wait for an answer.

"Reading the assigned material is not a suggestion, fraulein. Times do not afford us the luxury of laziness." He launched into a lecture on the cruciality of knowing history in order to avoid repeating its mistakes, a tirade against lazy German youth and their ingratitude for the sacrifices of others. It was the same speech she had heard a hundred times before in some form or another, only this time, she was his private audience. As he snarled on, she hardened. If this was the extent of her punishment, she thought, she could endure it.

But it wasn't.

He stepped closer. Now she could smell tobacco and his fourth-day-in-a-row clothes. He spoke just above a whisper.

"A girl like you should know better. A girl like you has no room for mistakes."

A girl like you? What was that supposed to mean?

He leaned even closer, and she sensed him pressing in was a kind of a test to see if she would step back.

"Do you think you can hide behind those blue eyes and pink cheeks forever? You are a blossoming rose. You think you won't stand out among the rest of those common daisies?"

The words came as a challenge but almost sounded like a warning. Something inside rose up to meet it. She remained fixed where she stood.

"Everyone must play their part, fraulein. However big, however small. I am just a simple history professor." He paused to draw in a slow breath. "My charge is to mold you, strengthen you."

His right arm came up, not to strike; but slowly, the palm opened toward her face. It stopped, cupped at the curve of her cheek, chilling her skin to ice.

It hung by her face for a moment as she clenched her jaw in defiance. Something quivered in his expression. He blinked a few times, closed his hand, and then awkwardly formed the fingers into a point. He leaned back and cleared his throat.

"As for you, the story has not yet been written," he said, now wagging that same finger. "But I'll tell you, it promises to be a bold and epic chapter."

How could he say such things?

"You are not like the others. Your friends will meet infantrymen home on leave, who'll snatch up the first woman that winks at them. They'll make fine dutiful wives and mothers. Oh yes, especially mothers. They'll do their duty and give the Fatherland their sons by the dozens. But they are common, ordinary. You are neither of those. You are special. You're expected to act like it."

Karin was red with rage.

"Pardon me, Herr Putz, but I'm barely sixteen! Special?"

Suddenly she realized she had actually spoken the words. Her rage turned to embarrassment, and then back to fear.

Herr Putz watched the near instant transformation of her face and smiled. "I want a written essay on the subject on my desk tomorrow."

"Yes, Herr Putz."

He held her eyes with his stare until the sour heat rose from her stomach into her neck and then spread across her face. Then, apparently satisfied, he flicked his glance at the door. She didn't hesitate.

CHAPTER SEVEN

Karin was one of the last to enter the auditorium. The flat, rectangular room featured a high ceiling with open iron rafters, louvered windows along its long walls, and a polished wood floor. With a short stage at one end and metal cages protecting the large, globed light fixtures among the beams, it served as both an assembly hall and gymnasium. Today it was configured with blood-red banners that hung from the rafters, each one emblazoned with the white circle and black swastika. The podium stationed at the center of the stage overlooked perfect rows of folding wooden chairs accommodating the school's nearly four hundred students. The most eager among them had filled the front rows and those indifferent the back. What few seats remained were found in the middle, so after a quick glance at the field of faces among whom Karin could not find her friend Marie, she sat down among strangers. Just as well, she thought. She could find Marie afterwards. Knowing what was coming, Karin was content to remain as she was, anonymous and alone.

The headmaster, Herr Brandt, was a short, bald, wire-spectacled man in a wrinkled black suit. The handful of steps onto the stage required enough effort that he was panting by the time he crossed to the podium. There, he mounted a short wooden box to improve his stature. Everything was always staged, Karin knew.

He moved slowly and deliberately, retrieving a sheaf of paper from his suit pocket, placing it on the lectern, unfolding it, and smoothing the center crease with his plump fingers. Peering out over his low-slung spectacles, he scanned the sea of students and then rapped the microphone with his stubby knuckle, as painful as it was deliberate. To make it worse, he leaned forward on strained toes and blew into it with short puffs. The blasts, like those of a steam train's brakes, caused everyone to wince.

"Students of the West Cologne Hochschule," he boomed. "As you know, the spring term is coming to a close." The foolish beginning evoked a cascade of cheers.

"Silence!" The headmaster seemed genuinely surprised by the reaction and had to enlist the teachers stationed along the walls to restore order. Karin sat with her eyes closed, quietly sharing in their enthusiasm with her own vision of working in the garden.

His speech was the same as the year before—recruiting boys to join the Hitler Jugend and girls to the BDM. He would drone on, jabbing his finger in the air at different moments in the speech, moments that seemed to Karin more random than dramatic. Like Herr Putz, he covered much of the same ground, reminding students of the great injustices done to Germany after the First War and of the triumphant rise of the Reich. Unlike Herr Putz, who looked for any reason to rail against lazy students, Herr Brandt took a softer tone.

"We conclude this school year, a historic one in the history of our nation, with a call to duty! As our armies march to victory, we, here on the home front, do our part, too. You, the Youth of the German Reich, are the future hope of our great Fatherland

and beloved Führer! For a young boy or girl there is no greater act of service than to join the youth organizations that build character."

When the speech finally ended, boys and girls were dismissed to separate rooms where the recruiting effort would intensify. Her anxiety growing, Karin lingered in the auditorium, looking for Marie. She found her in the front half of the assembly among a group of acquaintances. Karin knifed sideways through the outgoing stream of students and touched Marie's arm.

"Oh, Karin, I was wondering about you!" her friend said through a broad smile. Marie's large brown eyes lit up her entire face, a welcome boost for Karin.

Marie slipped her arm inside Karin's and pulled her close. They squeezed through the narrow doorway into the hallway outside and joined the flow of girls heading to the cafeteria.

"I looked for you earlier. What happened?"

Karin rolled her eyes. "Herr Putz happened."

"One of his moods?"

"Something like that."

Marie patted Karin on the arm.

"Oh dear. Escaping the wolf only to meet the bear. Don't worry, I'll be with you."

Karin wasn't surprised at Marie's attitude; in fact, she had counted on it. Marie was the kind of girl whose loyalty came naturally, unlike Karin. The one-sided nature of their friendship—Marie always encouraging, always available, always giving—gave rise to a growing sense of guilt, because Karin could not reciprocate. She had only the vaguest understanding of why. Trusting Marie, or anyone really, seemed somehow to be giving into something else, something larger, that Karin avoided, even feared. But reproach would have to wait. Karin needed Marie.

They filed into the cafeteria and sat down at the long tables. Current BDM members, mixed with non-members and carefully selected individuals, shared stories of their enjoyable and rewarding experiences in the group. Leaders knew that orchestrated pressure from peers was far more effective than patriotic speeches. The sessions would conclude with new recruits sealing their commitment in an anticlimactic but typical German fashion—filling out a form. Although the technique assured that a high percentage of eligible students would sign up each year, it was never complete. Cologne, known for its independent culture, harbored more than its share of less-than-enthusiastic supporters of the Nazi regime.

A girl about Karin's age, thin and wiry with a bookish face, was the leader of her table where six other girls had gathered. She introduced herself with an airy voice as Fraulein Ermintrude. She directed the girls to introduce themselves. Elfreda, Zilke, and Marie spoke first. Karin knew them already from their shared classes. They were already members of the BDM. The remaining three were younger, and their names were lost to Karin the moment after they had spoken.

Just as they had finished with introductions, Frau Hingis arrived and took the empty seat beside Karin. She was a substantial woman, tall and of classic German looks—broad-faced and broad-shouldered, her once blonde hair now gray, pulled tight behind in a braid. Her features were sharp despite her age, which Karin judged to be near sixty. She regarded the girls with a quick glance until she came to Karin. She smiled purposefully.

Karin managed a nervous smile back.

"Well, Fraulein Ermintrude, do you have the questions?"

"Yes, Frau Hingis."

"Then proceed at once. Don't let my presence bother you. I'm just interested to listen in." She kept looking at Karin. Her intentions were not very subtle.

Ermintrude cleared her throat and asked the first question.

"What will be your favorite activity this year in the BDM?"

A hand shot up to Karin's left. Elfreda, whom Karin knew more by volume than friendship, always tried to be the first to speak, in class or out. She could be heard from anywhere in a room, and it didn't matter who was listening or whether her answer was accurate. Everything out of her mouth seemed designed to promote or draw attention to herself.

"I'm going to write letters to the soldiers in the East," she said, even before Ermintrude acknowledged her. "I'm going to write a hundred of them. Some of them will write me back. One of them will marry me."

The girls laughed.

Seeing Elfreda and Frau Hingis so close together gave Karin the odd sensation that they were the young and old version of the same person. Despite Elfreda's wild, frenetic energy, they shared the same braids, the same thick frame, the same exaggerated air of importance, and the same devotion.

Ermintrude squirmed, unsure of how to respond.

"What if he has a girl already?" The question came from Zilke, who was situated between two of the new girls at the far end of the table.

"He'll forget her and choose me!" Elfreda answered, lifting her nose in the air. The girls laughed again. Karin couldn't help but smile at Elfreda's boldness.

Frau Hingis cleared her throat and lifted an eyebrow at Ermintrude.

"Yes, thank you Elfreda," Ermintrude said, her voice wavering a bit. "Who else would like to respond?"

Zilke straightened in her seat and turned to Frau Hingis. "I like singing." Her response was almost monotone, parrot-like.

There was a pause. Like the others, Karin expected Zilke to elaborate but when she smiled, folded her hands together, and sat back in her chair, everyone realized that was it.

Ermintrude seemed pleased enough. "Yes, thank you, Zilke. And next?"

Marie, sitting next to Karin, stirred nervously and then raised her hand to speak. She grinned sheepishly, her shoulders bunching together, and looked at Ermintrude out of the corners of her eyes, as if to avoid too direct a look. In that moment, observing Marie's quiet demeanor, soft features, Karin thought, *She's the prettiest girl here.*

"Yes, Marie, please."

"I like storytelling," she said in a soft voice. "I love to read and hear stories around the campfire."

"Just like your sister," Elfreda said.

Everyone went still for an instant, staring first at Elfreda, and then at Marie. Karin didn't understand what everyone else seemed to know.

Marie let her eyes fall and shrank back into her seat.

"Elfreda, that is quite enough," Frau Hingis said. "Marie, thank you for speaking up. That is a wonderful part of the BDM."

The silence was heavy for a moment. *Marie's sister?* Karin didn't know that Marie had a sister.

"What about you, Fraulein Blik? What do you look forward to doing in the BDM?"

Karin heard Frau Hingis, but the question didn't quite register. Elfreda was a terrible actress, and her look of innocence fooled no one. *What had she meant?*

"Fraulein?"

Karin gathered herself. "I'm not joining this year," she said.

Elfreda's eyes popped. The other girls squirmed in their seats. Karin smoothed the folds in her skirt and tried her best to seem casual.

"How old are you, child?" Frau Hingis took over.

"Sixteen," Karin replied.

"You were eligible at age twelve. You should have joined then. Surely you know this."

"Yes, Frau Hingis, but I've lived away from Germany and—"

"I understand," Frau Hingis cut her off, "but your father's status cannot protect you—I should say—*excuse* you forever."

"Yes, Frau Hingis, I know. Father's death was almost three years ago now. But it's not him. That's not the reason."

"Then what?"

"My grandfather. He's alone now. My grandmother died last November, and I'm the only one left to take care of him."

Frau Hingis maintained a steady gaze and firm expression.

"Yes, fraulein, your situation is well-known to us all. I'm very sorry that your grandfather is grieving, but thank goodness, he still has you. But a grandparent's death is not considered a valid exception."

While Karin considered her response, Elfreda butted in, feigning innocence again.

"So, Karin, what's your answer? What's your favorite BDM activity?"

Her cruelty came naturally, it seemed. Karin seethed with anger. She looked at Elfreda, but the words were for everyone.

"I'm not joining."

"Well, there it is. She doesn't support the Fatherland," Elfreda said and folded her arms.

"Be quiet!" Frau Hingis barked. "That's a strong accusation. Karin's family has suffered a great deal for the Fatherland. Her father gave his life for our country. He died a hero."

"And Karin saved that boy in the air raid." Marie, bless her.

"Too bad Karin doesn't share that opinion, Frau Hingis," Elfreda said, unfazed.

"Elfreda!"

"Ask her!"

Frau Hingis stood up. "You'll hold your tongue!"

"You don't think your father is a hero, do you, Karin? Go on, admit it!"

Karin shot to her feet. Had Elfreda been closer, she might have gotten a slap. Or worse.

"I'm not joining. Not this year." She turned to leave.

"Sit down, Fraulein Blik."

"She has no right, Frau Hingis. I'm leaving."

Karin walked away.

"Fraulein Blik, I warn you! This will be reported. This will not go unnoticed."

Karin paid no attention. She didn't stop until she was outside and across the yard behind the school. A line of oak trees marked the border of the school grounds. It was as far from the building as she could go without leaving the property. At the base of a large tree, she plopped down on the grass and leaned back against the trunk. Above, the young leaves stirred in the warm breeze and flickered in the bright afternoon sunshine. She closed her eyes and tried to let the warmth envelop her, but her pulse was racing.

"Karin?" The voice was Marie's. She was standing an awkward distance from the tree. "Are you all right?"

When Karin looked back, students were streaming out of the doors. She hadn't even heard the dismissal bell. "You shouldn't be seen with me. You'll get reported too."

"Elfreda is a beast."

"I should have known better."

"You're not alone. She does that to everyone. Finds a weakness and pounces. She thinks it impresses Frau Hingis."

"Did she send you?"

"Frau Hingis? Heavens, no. I came on my own. I'm concerned for you."

"You think I should join?"

"Don't hate me, Karin, but it's not as bad as you think. It's not like the Hitler Youth—we don't march. We take long walks sometimes and learn new recipes with the rationing and all. We might actually have some fun—together, I mean. I could use a friend like you there with me."

Karin smiled and patted the grass beside her, beckoning Marie to sit down. She seemed eager to comply. Karin wondered with a tinge of regret why she hadn't been a better friend to Marie sooner.

"What did Elfreda mean about your sister liking campfires?" Karin asked.

Marie's eyes fell. "It's a long story," she said. "Long and boring. I thought everyone knew."

"I'm not exactly in on things around here. But it's all right. You don't have to tell me."

Marie got up. "I have to go."

Marie hadn't been sitting for more than a few seconds. Just long enough for Karin to make a mess of things. Here was Marie, reaching out, only to be embarrassed.

"Will you reconsider?" she asked.

Karin looked at her with new appreciation. The kind of girl whose countenance was at once delicate, almost elegant, but somehow strong underneath. Marie seemed unaware of it.

"I'll think about it," Karin said with a grudging smile. "I could sure use some help in the kitchen."

CHAPTER EIGHT

That night, after a simple supper of plain bread and boiled potatoes, Karin cleaned away the dishes while Opa retired to the living room. He switched on the radio, like he always did, teeth-rattling loud, and sank down in his padded chair. The news would hold his interest only briefly before he either fell asleep where he sat or retired to his projects in the shed, only to fall asleep there. Either way, Karin had not known him to sleep in his room since Oma died.

From the kitchen, Karin had no trouble hearing the German State News Agency's report on Saturday night's raid.

"Nearly one thousand British aircraft attacked an area focused on the Altstadt and the industrial zone of Nippes. But thanks to the adept anti-aircraft crews and quick response of the Hitler Youth organizations, the population remained safe, and the damage to life and property minimal."

Something else Opa always did was argue with the newsreader.

"Minimal? Tell that to the people on Aachener Strasse!"

"Hospitals and medical aid workers responded heroically, treating nearly five thousand minor injuries, such as cuts from broken glass and ankles twisted during transport to air raid shelters. About three thousand homes were damaged in the raids."

Karin pictured little Hans and wondered what had become of him.

"That means at least a thousand deaths!" Opa bellowed. He took pride in discerning the truth behind the propaganda and had hardened his tone, Karin judged, since Oma's death. But she also felt he was too free with his doubts about the regime. It was one matter to voice them inside their own walls, but she worried he would say the wrong thing to a neighbor or the grocer. Karin often worried that one day, like Herr Wurstner, Opa would slip up.

The broadcast continued according to the standard form: state a simplified fact and then swamp it with propaganda. The arrogant British attacked civilians, the heroic Germans shot down hundreds of their planes, served heroically, and stood defiant. The Führer vowed to repay.

Knowing his blood would rise, Karin left the plate she was washing in the basin, walked into the room, and switched off the radio.

Opa didn't protest. He pushed up from his chair.

"A thousand British bombers," he clucked. "Just imagine when the Americans start up!"

Just then, the door buzzer sounded, giving them both a jump. She looked at him. *Had whoever was there been standing there long? Would they have heard Opa?*

"Are you expecting anyone?" he asked. Karin shook her head. The buzzer sounded again.

When she opened the door, she could not contain her shock. On the porch stood Rudi Kohl, the Hitler Youth leader, and a pair of figures behind him. Kohl's hair was neatly combed and greased, and gone were any traces of the fear and distress from their previous encounter.

"Fraulein, the light!"

In her surprise, Karin had forgotten to turn off the light in the foyer, a clear violation of the blackout orders. Light splashed beyond the porch and revealed a black Mercedes at the curb.

"*Entschuldigen Sie, bitte!* My apologies! Please come in."

Karin switched off the light, and they entered quickly. When Karin had closed the door and turned the light back on, she saw plainly now, Rudi Kohl, in his black uniform, and with him, two men. Even without their military uniforms, the men were immediately recognizable to Karin by their trench coats and wide-brimmed Fedoras. Gestapo. The one in back was a thick-necked nobody, the muscle. The one in front sported a brown leather coat buffed to a bright shine. The important one.

The trio moved—without invitation—to the living room where Karin's grandfather stood frozen beside his chair, eyes wide.

"Allow me to introduce myself. I am Rudi Kohl, Central District leader of the Cologne Hitler Youth."

For a boy no more than seventeen, he was entirely in command. He turned confidently to the two Gestapo men.

"And this is Herr Erich Gossen, head of the Secret State Police, and his assistant Herr Kruger."

Herr Gossen, Karin observed, was nothing like the Gestapo men she saw with her father in Luxembourg. Handsome but not tall, Gossen wore a confident smile and bright eyes. He seemed groomed and polished—the politician to Kruger's thug. He shook Opa's hand and looked straight into his eyes, a genuine greeting absent the intimidation Karin expected. Then he turned to Karin and took her hand in his.

"You are of course the hero Fraulein Blik," he said, also taking her eyes with his. He bowed, still holding her hand. The charm seemed real and confused her.

He refused Opa's offer for tea and had them sit down.

"My profound apologies for the unannounced visit," he said. "We won't be a minute."

The Gestapo never announced their visits, Karin knew, but still the apology seemed somehow genuine.

He looked at Karin with a broad smile. "It seems, my dear, that you have caused quite a stir in the city. I don't normally concern myself with matters more suited to Reichsminister Goebbels, but since I knew your father, I offered to help. And I imagine that if you are anything like him, your act of service the night of the air raid is not something you wish to draw attention to. This restraint makes your actions all the more admirable and endearing—not only to me, but to the city, and yes, even the nation. You'll be pleased to know, fraulein, that reports of your heroism have reached the ears of the Führer himself. He is impressed, although not surprised. He expects nothing less from a good German girl."

Karin was not so taken by the mention of the Führer as the mention of her father. Gossen had known him? Had he known what he was planning for Luxembourg? How had he died?

"Which brings me to the point." Gossen's smile had faded only a little.

"There will be some attention brought to you, fraulein, which cannot be avoided. The German people need inspiration, and heroes like you, especially young and pretty, can help in times of adversity such as was suffered last weekend. Surely you can appreciate that, fraulein?"

"What kind of attention?" Karin asked.

"There will be a ceremony in the coming weeks. It will coincide with the annual induction of new BDM members and feature a visit from a representative of the Führer himself. He will honor you personally."

"Please, don't make me give a speech."

Gossen laughed. "Of course not, my dear. We suffer no lack of speechmakers. All that's required is you attend and receive the medal that will be awarded to you."

To Karin's disbelief, Opa had transformed. His countenance had changed from suspicion to pride, and he was sitting tall in his chair. For Karin's part, she was filled with dread. But as Gossen continued, describing the magnitude of the honor, Karin began to consider that perhaps such an event could be endured for a night and be done with. Perhaps it would keep Frau Hingis at bay. And drive Elfreda wild with jealousy.

Yes, it would be worth the attention just to see the look on Elfreda's face!

Gossen stood up to leave. To Karin's astonishment, Opa stuck out his hand. Gossen shook it, and Opa began to work it like a pump handle, thanking him profusely for his visit. The group moved to the foyer, and Karin put her hand to the light switch, eager for them to return to the darkness.

Gossen raised his hand to the switch. The touch of his hand on hers sent a bolt up her arm.

"There's just a couple of other items," he said, taking her hand a second time. "I understand you are not a member of the BDM."

The blood left Karin's face.

Gossen smiled and moved a step closer. "It's understandable, up until now, given the remarkable circumstances, of course. First your father, and his heroic sacrifice, and then recently, suffering the loss of your grandmother." He acknowledged Opa with a look of compassion.

Then, turning back to Karin, he added. "But it's time. It's important for us, and it's important for you, yes?"

Karin couldn't look away. He had set the perfect trap, and it was impossible for her to escape. A quick glance at Opa, who seemed thoroughly hypnotized, and she knew she could not resist.

"Yes, Herr Gossen."

"Very well, then. I knew you'd see it that way." He smiled and withdrew his hand.

Rudi Kohl made to cough. "Excuse me, Herr Gossen. May I?"

"Oh yes, I almost forgot the other thing. Leader Kohl has a request as well."

Sweat beads had gathered on Kohl's face, and he was working his tongue over his lips like he had just finished a journey across the desert.

"Some among the ranks may grumble at the sudden—shall we say—transformation of a girl who has not been part of the BDM until the ceremony. I thought—we thought—it would be helpful for everyone if you could accelerate your service prior to the ceremony."

"Accelerate?" Karin asked.

"Yes. And we have the perfect fit. You see, we have a recent opening, and it would be my—our—honor if you would volunteer in the Hitler Youth office. Three afternoons per week—after school of course. Light work, organizing, a bit of filing."

Karin was completely unprepared for both turns of events. The ceremony was one thing, enduring Nazi pomp and circumstance for a few hours for a chance to humiliate Elfreda. The memories would fade and hopefully the jealousies, too. She could have her summer unbothered in the garden. But working for Kohl, the boy who had been willing to turn her in for violating curfew, was another challenge altogether. But how could she refuse?

"You seem to have found the perfect solution," she said, completely void of enthusiasm.

"Then good night, fraulein. Good night, sir." Gossen clicked his heels and left.

Kohl handed Karin a small card.

"My card. See you tomorrow at three," he said.

Gossen gestured for Kohl and his assistant to leave first. When they had gone, he turned back to Karin and smiled. He extended his hand and gave Karin a photograph.

The scene showed four happy figures in swimming clothes, arm in arm, posing during an afternoon in the sun. Karin immediately recognized her mother in the center, every bit the Hollywood starlet at the pinnacle of her youthful vibrance and beauty. She was flanked by Schlinge—a young, decent-looking, and yet unscarred version—and on the other arm, the handsome Gossen. To Karin's surprise, her father, Max, was on the end next to Schlinge.

"Yes, fraulein, we all knew each other back then. Happier days, without the cares of the world to weigh us down. Of course, only your mother hasn't changed."

"Then you know that one," Karin said, pointing at Schlinge so as not to have to say his name.

Gossen's smile flattened. "Yes, of course. Heinrich and I know one another quite well. We were rivals for a time," he added with a chuckle. "For your mother's affection, that is. Max outsmarted us both. And you are a wonderful reminder of him."

"I hate him," Karin said, still pointing at Schlinge, and then regretted it.

Gossen displayed no shock. "Yes, I heard about the engagement. I understand your perspective, fraulein, I do. But Herr Schlinge is a very powerful man, and so you must keep that emotion to yourself."

Expecting a harsh response, Karin was surprised at his sensible tone. She let out a slow breath. "Can I ask you something, Herr Gossen?"

"Of course, fraulein. If I can be any help to you…"

"Do you know what happened in Luxembourg? Do you know how my father died?"

Gossen lifted an eyebrow slightly and then nodded. "I assumed you would have been told. She hesitated, and then said, "I don't believe them."

"My dear Karin, I don't intend to upset you, but the event was thoroughly investigated. The Luxembourg authorities gave us the pistol possessed by the Luxembourg boy, Hansi Broussard. The boy was the only one who could have done it."

She let out a slow breath.

Gossen tilted his head slightly as the idea registered. "You knew this boy, didn't you? Perhaps you had *feelings* for him that might cloud your judgment?"

"He didn't do it," Karin said calmly.

"Think of your father, dear. He loved you. Surely any infatuation with that boy isn't stronger than a daughter's love for her father, is it?"

"I'll stake my love for my father on it."

"I see," Gossen said. "You're absolutely convinced?"

Karin nodded.

"What do you think happened?"

"I don't know," she replied. "But I find it awfully convenient that *he* escaped." She stabbed her finger at Schlinge's image again. Then, like a sudden air raid siren, her contempt for Schlinge was swallowed by fear. Gossen's calm and understanding demeanor had elicited openness from Karin, and she perceived it now as a kind of trick.

"I'm sorry, Herr Gossen," she stammered.

Gossen smiled again, lowered his eyes, and slowly raised a hand for her to stop.

"Max was honest and passionate in his service to the Fatherland, and I can see you are your father's daughter. Think nothing more of it."

He rotated his hand down, extending it to Karin, and clicked his heels.

"Herr Blik, Karin, I thank you for your time and bid you good night."

Karin stood at the door while the roar of the car faded away, unable to move.

CHAPTER NINE

When on the next day Karin arrived at the address listed on Rudi Kohl's card, the structure was nothing like she imagined for a Hitler Youth office. Rather than an imposing stone fortress she envisioned, 140 Blumenstrasse was a simple, unthreatening, two-story storefront with tall windows on the lower level. Drawn blackout curtains, a few chain links hanging from a bracket above the door, and a hasty coat of dull gray paint removed any trace of what kind of shop the place had been. A realization quickly followed. This was another of the countless properties confiscated from Jews, Karin had no doubt, an occurrence so common it had become easy to forget.

She rang the bell and braced herself. In the corner of her eye, she detected movement in one of the curtains. *Had he been watching?* The lock turned, and the door swung open. The sunlight hit his face. He was paler than she remembered.

"Well, well," he said, the smile switched on. "You have passed the first test—finding the place."

She shuddered at his attempt at humor, if that was indeed his intent.

He held the door open and stood with his back against the wall. She ascended the handful of doorsteps and hesitated. The entry was very narrow to start with, and with him pressed against the wall, even more so. She slid past him awkwardly, feeling his eyes on her as she moved by.

Are we alone here?

The room, lit by a single bulb on the ceiling, was a kind of canyon, with tall but empty shelves lining the back wall, a narrow passage for the shopkeeper, and a waist-high counter that split the room in two. The shelves, walls, and counters were of the same dull finish as the exterior of the building. Only the parquet floor, dark along the counter but still yellow along the perimeter, gave evidence to its history. If not for the piles of paper that covered the counter and the black beast of a typewriter nearly buried under them, Karin might have imagined a pharmacy or hardware store.

"Welcome to District Nine, Fraulein Blik. Headquarters of the Hitler Youth. Here we will serve the Fatherland—togeth-er." His official smile had never left. The words, had they been printed on paper, seemed harmless enough. Still, Kohl's tone and rhythm—the pause before the word *together*—seemed calibrated just to the edge of sinister, even for someone not much older than Karin. She forced herself to breathe normally.

"Are you all right, my dear?" he asked.

Was she so terrible at hiding her reaction? Or was he more perceptive than she imagined? True to his name, Kohl—the wolf—she had the feeling he was stalking her, watching for weakness, waiting for her to stumble. The method of attack was not clear to her, but something about him brought a constant sense of—*pressure*.

"Yes, Herr Kohl, I'm fine." She turned away, trying to buy time, pretending to look around and take interest in the new surroundings. The room was suddenly hot, and she felt lightheaded. The conclusion was inescapable—they were indeed alone.

"Fraulein, when we are together, I insist that you call me 'Rudi.' Is that understood?"

Karin's expression froze. It was understood but not to be believed.

"When it is just us here, working together," he continued, "there's no concern for rank or formality. So please, try it now. Say, 'yes, Rudi.' Try it now."

"Yes—Rudi."

"See, that's much better. They say that when trying to learn something new, you should repeat it three times. Then it becomes natural, don't you agree, fraulein?"

He led her with the lift of his eyebrow.

"Yes, Rudi."

"Excellent! Now may I call you 'Karin' in return?"

"Uh, well, I suppose that's only fair," she stammered, and then quickly added, "Rudi."

"Very good, Karin. Very good indeed. This will be our private secret. In public, we will keep things formal, mind you. But very good indeed. Thank you, Karin. You see? A moment ago, you were feeling uncomfortable. Now you look so much better."

She was not feeling better. He had outmaneuvered her again. She had tried to flee, but the wolf had run to block her escape. He was circling. She was dizzy. It was only a matter of time that he would move in and make the kill. For now, he was chasing, pursuing. Relentless, he would exhaust her before the final moment.

She was not quite ready to surrender. The break gave her mind a moment to try to recover, to fight back, to consider another way out. Her mind was a blur. Somewhere on the edge of her consciousness, an idea tried to break through.

"Rudi, I'm afraid I'll disappoint you." The words came as a surprise. She let them hang in the air. She was like prey playing dead.

Kohl let the words sink in and then began to laugh. He slapped the counter, sending papers flying, and threw his head back in a growing surge. Like everything else about him, it seemed manufactured.

"Disappoint me? From the moment I first saw you, Karin, I knew there was nothing that could disappoint me." His laughter trailed off and, in its place, emerged a faint smile. Wistful at first, the corner of his mouth turned up with a slight twitch, his eyes narrowed, and all at once, his expression was menacing. He took another step forward. Karin retreated a final step. Her back was against the windows.

"You see, Rudi," she responded, "I cannot type. In fact, I know very little about clerical and secretarial duties. And from the look of things here, I am concerned. I don't wish to disappoint you."

The brilliant start of her answer was ruined by its finish, the criticism of the office. She knew it the moment it left her lips.

Rudi, having quickly resurveyed the chaos, took no offense. "My answer stands. I have no doubt you will far exceed my expectations." He snapped his heels together. "There's much to be done. Let's get started."

He turned away to present the room with a sweep of his arm. "This is the main office where you will work. This counter will serve as your desk." He returned to the window and opened one of the heavy blackout curtains. "Light, much better, don't you think? And you will make an excellent impression on anyone who passes by."

Innuendo, like the cabinets that lined the wall, seemed to be a built-in feature of Kohl's operation.

"The hallway there," he continued, indicating a passageway at the back right corner of the room, "leads to the back door and a courtyard. The back door shall remain locked at all times. To the right at the end of the passage is the toilet. The door on the left is my office. I work behind a closed door, frequently involved in conversations of a sensitive nature that require utmost privacy. Should you need me, you will knock first and wait for my reply before entering."

So much detail, such procedure, so official. What could be so private for a Hitler Youth leader? These were boys, after all, and though they were being groomed for future service in the Wehrmacht or SS, the Hitler Youth had no official role in the Nazi apparatus. And except for political indoctrination, which everyone in Germany was subject to, the Hitler Youth boys Karin knew were like Boy Scouts—occupied with marching, hiking, camping, all kinds of sports and outdoor adventures. Hardly the kind of work that justified the air of superiority Rudi created for himself.

He turned back to the front of the room, glancing briefly out the window before crossing to the stairway tucked up beside the front door. It was narrow, steep, and at the landing, curved sharply up with triangular steps.

"The second floor is strictly off-limits, as is the cellar, whose door will remain locked at all times. Is that understood?" In a flash, he was the stern authoritarian whose question was not rhetorical. Karin nodded.

"Very well. Now, your duties. We will begin with some simple collating."

He gathered a stack of papers from the end of the counter. They were bent and twisted in all directions. Making no attempt to straighten them, he simply thrust them at Karin.

"These are attendance reports from the local Hitler Youth chapters. Each week the local leader fills out a form, tallying the number of members present, the number of new members, and the numbers for various kinds of activities—political instruction, calisthenics, camping, marching, and so on. You will collate the results from these separate reports onto a single page. Attendance and activities represent the columns across the top; results from each local chapter form the rows. Transfer the information from the individual chapter reports onto this master report and sum the totals for each activity."

He thrust the sheet forward. "This is merely a guide. Use the typewriter."

Rudi handed over the rest of the stack.

"These are the reports since January. You will create three monthly reports. I expect them to be finished before you leave tonight. Any questions?"

Karin considered reminding him of her typing deficit but decided against upsetting him further. At least he had moved beyond the innuendo. He needed real help with the reports. She would find a way to muddle through.

"Herr Kohl—excuse me, Rudi—the BDM meeting is at seven tonight. Frau Hingis will be very upset if I am late. Tonight, we are making care bundles for the soldiers in the East."

"Then you'd better get started," he said, punctuating his reply with a click of his heels. Then he turned and left, withdrawing down the back hallway.

At the sound of his office door closing, Karin leaned against the countertop and let out a long breath. She had survived the interaction. Now to the task.

A survey of a few pages picked randomly among the mess yielded few clues as to how to organize things, so Karin started by simply straightening every sheet into neater piles. Consistent among each piece was a date, so she divided the stacks by month. The earliest reports were from January—Kohl was five months behind! Not the kind of impression he would want to make on his superiors.

Beginning with January, she sifted through the reports and tallied the activities on a blank sheet of paper. She created columns for everything she thought would be important to Rudi—attendance at meetings, kilometers marched, training activities, and the like. To her shock, curfew patrol was prominent among the reports, and many included narratives of encounters like the one she had experienced the night of the raid:

Distrikt 7 – Aktion Bericht – 20 Januar 1942

4 Jugends led by OberstammFührer Klingman confronted a gang of 9 curfew violators near Industriestrasse and the North Rhine freight terminal attempting to break into a tool shed. They resisted apprehension forcefully with self-made weapons of chain, clubs, and knives. We surrounded them and attacked with swift and decisive action. Hitlerjunge Meier suffered a sprained ankle in the scuffle and the gang fled, retreating among the docks north of our district. We reported this activity immediately to both the police and Distrikt 6 Headquarters whose jurisdiction applied.

Reading between the lines, Karin suspected that the opposite was more likely true. The Jugends stumbled across the gang, were attacked, and forced to flee. The Jugend Meijer probably twisted his ankle trying to escape. Despite the propagandistic tone, it was easy to get lost in the descriptions. She tallied eighteen similar reports for the month. Suddenly, it was six o'clock. She had lost track of time and only managed to finish a single month's tally.

She feared her prediction would come true after all. Kohl would indeed be disappointed. What would he do to her?

She looked at her report, the stacks on the counter, and then the typewriter. An idea came to her. She had data for the lone month of January. With a little creativity, she could extrapolate figures for the remaining months. How would Kohl know the difference?

There were a few typewriters in the secretarial classrooms at school, but she had never actually used one herself. She knew the basic idea that the paper wrapped around the roller and keys struck an inked ribbon to imprint the letter. But the specific procedure for loading the paper was a mystery, and she couldn't conquer the levers and knobs to make it work. The minutes flew by, and frustration turned to panic. Her plan had failed. It was twenty past six. She had to go. She would knock on Kohl's door and beg for mercy. Hadn't she warned him?

Karin turned away from the typewriter, and her heart jumped. Kohl was standing in the doorway of the back hall, watching her.

"Rudi, I was just coming to see you," she began.

He ignored her and strode forward into the room, blocking her in behind that end of the counter. He stared at her for a moment and then down at the neat piles on the counter.

His eyes narrowed. He found her hand-written report and began to study it.

"I told you I'd disappoint you," she said.

He finished reading and put the paper down.

"I would have typed it, but I don't know how."

"Karin, you underestimate yourself. You've made an excellent beginning. They have typewriters at your school, no?" She nodded. "Then see to it you learn how to use one. You may go."

The street was in the shadows when Karin left the office. She could make it to the BDM meeting on time, but just barely. She quickened her step beneath the orange sky with a new sense of strength. She had survived. Without question, Kohl was not to be trusted. In fact, she considered him quite dangerous. He had power, and if she wasn't careful, opportunity. But she was not without her own power, she thought, as she blended into the stream of commuters on the city streets. Her first day had yielded a crucial insight. Kohl was not simply disorganized; he was disappointing his superiors. The knowledge invigorated her as she walked. He needed her.

CHAPTER TEN

K arin didn't need a clock to tell her she was late for the BDM meeting. Tramline Eighteen, midway on its outbound route from the Altstadt to the western suburbs, came to an unexpected halt due to a police roadblock. Several officers had set up a hasty barrier with their cars, stopping traffic in all directions. Twenty minutes passed without explanation. Karin was not alone among the confused and then frustrated passengers. Finally, the tram driver spoke with an officer and reported back that a gas line was being repaired in a nearby building, the result of the bombs. As soon as she heard the news, she disembarked to finish the journey on foot. The slim margin for being on time had been lost. Frau Hingis would not be understanding.

About forty girls had already gathered when Karin slipped through the doors of the sports hall. They were in the second stanza of the opening song, the ubiquitous Horst Wessel Lied, whose tune and lyrics had so over-saturated Karin's mind that her lips moved automatically.

Die straße frei, den braunen Battallionen
Die straße frei, dem Sturmabteilungsmann
The streets free for the brown battalions,
The streets free for the Stormtroopers...

The word "free" carried Karin back to a memory she thought forgotten—that night in the park, Kohl and the Freedom Gang, and their leader named Frei. *Free.* She saw again that stare, those black eyes down into her while she lay on the ground. He did not seem free.

It would have been an excellent time to arrive, Karin thought, except for the all-seeing eyes of Frau Hingis up front. She sang a shrill soprano over the scratchy gramophone while her generously padded arms flapped up and down. Her expression turned from rapture to rage in the instant she met eyes with Karin.

The stare lasted only a moment, but the message was delivered—*I see you*. And when Karin shrank back, it was acknowledgement enough. Frau Hingis lifted her chin back to heaven, inhaled enough to expand her already formidable bosom, and let forth again her joyous strains to the Fatherland.

The song ended, and Frau Hingis fell back from the podium. Her plump cheeks, bright red, and the perspiration, bathing her face, were a mix of exhaustion and ecstasy. Elfreda once teased that the Horst Wessel Lied was Frau Hingis' lone exercise each week and dubbed her "Frau *Schweißig*"—"Frau Sweaty." Such teasing was very risky for Elfreda but was one of her many tricks designed to keep herself the center of attention.

The girls were arrayed as always in perfect rows of folding wooden chairs. Frau Hingis reigned from on high behind the dark oak lectern. The music having concluded, Karin knew from having attended these recruitment meetings before, that it was time for the patriotic lecture. She swabbed her face with a yellowed handkerchief and began:

"Less than a year ago, the twenty-second of June 1941, our brave soldiers left their loved ones here in the Fatherland on an historic march east. Facing the Jewish and Bolshevist hordes, they crushed the enemy at every turn, pushing them back nearly fifteen hundred kilometers to the very gates of Moscow! After a rest and refit during the terrible Russian winter, our heroes have rejoined their quest and are on the move again. Their boots are on the Red Army's necks and, this spring, with might and courage, are poised to finish the enemy off in every sector of the front."

Frau Hingis, like every other political speaker, grew more passionate by the minute. Her face, already pink from singing, flushed a deeper hue. The sweat on her forehead began to streak down the sides of her face.

Worse still were the words themselves. The descriptions evoked images from the newsreel films: German soldiers, some riding on the great steel Panzers, others marching; the great army of mechanical locusts stirred up columns of dust that darkened the sky. As the old woman thundered, Karin pictured Willem, his fair cheeks caked with dirt-turned-to-mud from his own sweat. In her mind's eye, he was marching—endless hours of marching against the backdrop of burning villages in the vast Ukrainian plain. Images Karin had stolen from newsreels and the booklet Herr Putz made them read: *Vorwarts, Immer Vorwarts! —Onward, Ever Onward!* The articles made a lasting impression, bringing to life the endless space, dusty kilometers chasing the enemy, and the hordes of swarming, biting flies.

Was he hungry? Had he fired his rifle yet? Was he still alive?

Frau Hingis poured it on just like the news on the radio, films at the theater, and other lectures. The themes were always the same: the Red Army, as the Soviet forces were called, was a ruthless horde of barbarians who both tortured and killed civilians, even women and children. The beasts would rather shoot prisoners than feed them. Karin knew that propaganda colored everything, but the images in her mind were terrifying all the same. What made the situation worse was that Willem had promised to write. After all these weeks, she had still not heard from him.

For several minutes, Frau Hingis stayed with the war, saying much but saying nothing. The German heroes, unspeakable hardships, the will to victory.... The speakers were different but the speeches the same. And Karin was disappointed in herself that she hadn't grown more used to the pattern by now. The shouting, the cheers—the effect was always the same: be afraid and obey. Frau Hingis performed to perfection.

"We all play a part in our nation's struggle. We of the BDM are at the front of the parade, the head of the column. And tonight, we will fulfill our duty to our brothers in arms. Tonight, we who enjoy peace will have the opportunity to contribute to the aid of the soldiers in the field. Tonight, we will stand with them, ready to sacrifice as they press on to victory!"

She pointed to the wall behind the girls where a row of tables had been assembled. This was not the norm for their meetings. Along the tops of the tables, a variety of crates and boxes had been distributed along their length.

"Our chapter has volunteered to assemble what shall be called 'care boxes' for our soldiers in the field. You will fill the boxes with practical items to encourage them in their glorious service. Tonight, our goal is one thousand boxes! One thousand boxes—one for each year of the Reich! One thousand boxes will supply an entire division with a taste of home. An accomplishment to remember! And something, I might add, that does not go unnoticed—this effort will help us in our quest to gain the audience of the Führer himself, who rewards the sacrifice of the local chapters. Let the girls of the Mettendorf BDM be the ones the Führer favors!"

The girls seemed to know that the climax had been reached. They rose in unison, Karin too, and thundered their approval. Karin, surprised by her own reaction, joined in with genuine enthusiasm, a feeling driven in part by the fact that talk of the fighting was over, yet even more by the idea of helping the soldiers. Her imagination returned to the picture of Willem. He was in his uniform just as she had seen him at the Bahnhof, a sheepish grin on his face. He would receive the box like a Christmas present.

Frau Hingis gave instructions. Lists were posted on the back wall. The girls were dismissed, and the crowd formed around the lists as they searched. Their names were arranged in alphabetical order followed by a number. Karin, seventh on the list, was assigned to Group Seven. The name below her started the sequence over at One. She scanned the names as other girls pressed in to look. Her heart fell as Marie was assigned to Group Two.

Karin eased back, disappointed, knowing there would be no point asking for a change. A bark from Frau Hingis warned them to quit talking and get moving. Karin shuffled through the girls, managing only exchanged frowns from a distance with Marie. At the last table, Karin's disappointment was doubled. Leaning over the table, milling through the boxes, was Elfreda. When Karin drew near, she seemed to sense her presence and spun around.

"Well, well, you can't stay away from me, can you, Karin?" she said, eyebrow lifted sarcastically.

"I could have if I had made the lists myself," Karin answered.

"Very funny. Now listen here. Frau Hingis said the girl who works the hardest will get to shake the Führer's hand when he visits. So, keep your pretty face out of sight and let me do my job."

"Don't worry, Elfreda. You're welcome to him."

Elfreda's eyes popped. "What's that supposed to mean? Don't you know I could report you for a remark like that?"

In a dramatic gesture, Karin pursed her lips and tapped on them with an upright index finger, looking away in mock thought. "Hmmm. The word of a tattletale against the daughter of a war hero. Yes, that would be interesting."

Before Elfreda could respond, they were joined by four others. The tallest one among them, a thin girl whose silver-rimmed glasses stood out against her rust-colored hair, spoke first.

"Gather 'round, girls." She paused for a moment and made a quick count. "Good. We're all here. We six make up Group Seven. I'm Ingrid, our leader for tonight."

Ingrid's eyes darted nervously behind the magnifying lenses. And despite near constant adjustment, she could not manage to keep her glasses on her nose. Her movements were like a hummingbird—she flitted from the girls to the table, the boxes, and back again.

"As you can see, each group puts something in the boxes—tins of coffee, cooked beef and smoked fish at Group One; hard sausages and cheese at Group Two; cakes, peppermints, cigarettes, sugar, and so on." She zipped back to the table, retrieved an item from each of two larger boxes, and held them high. "Our group finishes things off with a heavy pair of wool socks and a rolled white handkerchief."

The task seemed easy enough to Karin, and the others in the group seemed eager to get started, especially since the first groups had already begun, and boxes were working their way down the line. Ingrid seemed unconcerned.

"Everything has been planned precisely. Space in each box is at a premium, so listen carefully." She held up the socks. "Roll each pair from the toe to the ankle. Be sure to roll it as tight as you can. That way it takes up less space when we pack it in the box."

She zoomed back to the table and snatched a large white cloth from a bundle. It was about a meter square, and Ingrid displayed it to the girls like a magician about to make something disappear.

"The kerchiefs are to be folded this way: take it by the two corners and fold it in half. Then fold it in half again so that all four corners remain together." She spoke to them like they were children. "Then lay it on the table and smooth out the wrinkles. Fold it in thirds and roll tightly by the short end. Any questions?"

Across from Karin, a round-faced girl asked why it was so much larger than a normal-sized man's handkerchief.

Ingrid looked back at her like she had been insulted, but before she could say anything, Elfreda seized the moment.

"Haven't you heard? The Russians never bathe. They are so covered in vermin and lice that our soldiers will be sneezing their heads off. The large handkerchief will come in handy!"

The girls exploded with laughter except for Ingrid. She didn't get the joke.

"No! No, girls! This has not been confirmed! And it's not funny!" Her leadership power had disintegrated in the blink of an eye. The girls were focused on Elfreda, who had taken a kerchief, wrapped it around her head like a scarf, and began to mimic an old woman. She bent over, hand on her back, and pantomimed walking with a cane.

"The Bolsheviks say hot water is unpatriotic! If Comrade Stalin doesn't bathe, why should I?"

She lifted her nose, sniffed the air, and then made to cough. The girls howled. Ingrid was white with rage.

"What is going on here?" The voice came from behind the circle. When they spun around to look, it was the one Karin feared most—Frau Hingis.

Elfreda removed the kerchief from her head so fast her hair was left in a snarled mess. The girls snapped to attention where they stood.

Ingrid tried to save face. "We were organizing ourselves for the tasks, Frau Hingis."

"Hardly! It looks more like skit night at summer camp. I must say I expected more from you, Fraulein Flosser." As Ingrid wilted, Frau Hingis turned to Elfreda, who had unsuccessfully tried to jam the kerchief in the rear waistband of her skirt. Frau Hingis reached behind the trembling girl and snatched it away. "And as for you, Elfreda, I'm not surprised. Did my instructions include playacting?"

"No, Frau Hingis."

Frau Hingis ignored Elfreda's contrition. Her face was hot red. "German boys are fighting and dying this very night. And here you stand making jokes. You should be ashamed." She turned to the others in Group Seven. "And all of you for encouraging it. I have half a mind to put you all on report."

Karin shuddered. "On report" meant they were subject to punishment. Hitler Youth boys were routinely punished with severe physical fitness tests such as ten-kilometer runs in the cold rain, endless minutes of pushups, and even beatings if the transgressions were severe enough. The Nazis viewed BDM girls in a different light—weaker and unable to stand the same physical discipline. So, to maintain discipline the BDM relied on another powerful force—humiliation. Being put on report meant that Karin's squad would be called out from the other girls and prohibited from participating in activities until they had paid their proper penance. Frau Hingis had been known to go so far as to mimic the boys' punishment. They were all familiar with the story, passed down from the older to the younger girls, of a squad caught passing cigarettes during a summer camp a few years ago. Frau Hingis made them clean the camp bathrooms with only a single rag that she had cut into small pieces. Each girl was forced to scrub the floor on hands and knees with a square of cloth only a few centimeters square. Some versions added a terrifying postscript to the tale. When upon their return, one of the girls told the whole story to her father, a mid-level Nazi bureaucrat, who was said to have had Frau Hingis suspended. Two weeks later, he was found dead in his office. The police ruled the death a suicide, but the legend exploded from there. Whatever the truth, the story had a powerful effect, with the result that future lapses in discipline were rare. Still, Karin feared the worst until the thought occurred to her that Elfreda stood to lose the most from being put on report—her dream of presenting flowers to the Führer, should he ever visit, was surely dashed. The knowledge showed on Elfreda's face even now in an expression drained of color.

"Please, Frau Hingis, forgive me!" she pleaded. "Truly I was trying to encourage the girls—that our soldiers will be well-cared for by our work. I only meant it for a joke, nothing more."

"That's enough, Elfreda. Explanations and excuses—they're the same to me. But one more outburst, and I'll find you a dirty bathroom to clean somewhere. Is it clear?"

Elfreda's eyes were on the floor. "Yes, Frau Hingis."

The girls were amazed. Such an unexpected pardon was beyond belief.

"Fraulein Blik, a word please." Karin's swallow stuck in mid-throat.

The woman retreated a few steps and waited for Karin to follow. Away from the group's hearing, she spoke, "It is not acceptable to be late."

Karin was staring at the scuffed linoleum floor.

"Yes, Frau Hingis. I was delayed returning from the Hitler Youth office."

"Did you arrive at the expected time?"

"Yes, Frau Hingis, exactly at three in the afternoon, as requested." She dared a glance up.

"And when did you finish?"

Karin wanted to explain about the damaged tram but knew Frau Hingis would not permit her to answer a question she had not asked.

"About six-forty."

"Lord in heaven! What took you so long?"

"The office was a mess," Karin began, her voice breathy enough to carry the hint of exasperation.

"I beg your pardon?"

"Forgive me. Herr Kohl had me organize his reports and summarize them." This line of questioning was going nowhere. Karin looked away. "I don't know how to type. I haven't taken the secretarial courses yet."

Frau Hingis huffed.

"What do they teach diplomats' children when they are out of the country? We'll have a generation of idiots to thank them for!" She wagged her head. "I won't have you embarrassing the BDM. You'll start attending the typing classes at once."

"But I am not scheduled to take them until next year."

"I'll speak to the headmaster. He won't like it, but yours is an important assignment."

Normally, such pressure would have sent Karin into a downward spiral of fear. This time the instinct of survival rose up instead.

"May I offer a suggestion, Frau Hingis?"

Frau Hingis blinked at the directness.

"What is it?"

"I'm happy to oblige and start the typing classes, but in the meantime, might I take Marie with me? She could help—not just with the reports, but with my training."

Karin wondered where the words had come from. Surely Frau Hingis would scoff at the notion.

Instead, she pinched her eyes beneath the heavy folds of skin surrounding them.

"I'll not have a pair of squawking hens giggling away the reputation of the BDM," she said, as if by reflex.

"Marie is an excellent typist," Karin offered. "She can teach me while helping with the projects. We'll finish sooner, and you can be sure Rudi will be happy."

"Rudi? What is going on between the two of you?"

"Nothing! Herr Kohl, I meant to say." Karin felt silly.

"Don't ever let me hear you address him in that manner again. As for your request to have Marie help you, I will consider it. In the meantime, I suggest you find a way to work faster. Now we've wasted enough time already. Back to your group. There's work to be done."

Karin turned to leave.

"Fraulein Blik."

"Yes, Frau Hingis?"

"You will not let us down. Is it clear?"

"Jawohl, Frau Hingis."

Karin rejoined the group, relieved. Frau Hingis might not agree with her suggestion, but the fact that she was considering it brought a surge of confidence to Karin. And a sense of hope.

The girls took no notice of Karin returning to the tables to load the boxes. But a moment later, everyone looked up, as if on command.

Frau Hingis had not left. Even more astonishing, an uncharacteristic smile had replaced the scowl Karin had encountered only seconds earlier.

"I have something special for your group," she announced. She reached into the pocket of her dress and withdrew a small glass object. She held it up for all to see. It was a blossom-shaped crystal perfume bottle with a small rubber squeeze bulb.

"Elfreda, hold out your kerchief."

Reacting as if dazed, Elfreda raised the cloth slowly. Frau Hingis took aim with the perfume and pinched the bulb with a quick squeeze. The girls were enveloped by a sweet cloud of cinnamon and rose petals. The scent lifted Karin's spirit with the memory of her grandmother, who always kept stashed in her sleeve a delicate handkerchief doused in her favorite *l'eau de cologne*.

"This will be our secret. When a soldier opens his box, he will be surprised, not only by the wonderful gifts, but by the sweet aroma. The food and socks will revive his body, but when he takes this kerchief—this kerchief from the girls in Mettendorf—he will think of home, and it will revive his heart."

What surprised Karin in that moment was how easily she was overtaken, not by the perfume, but by the feelings evoked from Frau Hingis's words. The old woman's eyes were glistening, and she was looking away as if to a far-off place or memory—an incredible transformation from the ferocity of moments earlier. Perhaps she had lost a husband in the First War or had a son in the East now—Karin had no way of knowing. Yet, in the woman's eyes, Karin saw for the first time something more than the witch of legend.

"A little goes a long way," she said. "Can I trust you to use it sparingly to cover the thousand kerchiefs?"

Elfreda stepped forward, her back straight and shoulders arched, like a volunteer for a dangerous mission. She held out her hand.

"Yes, Frau Hingis! I'll make sure to spray each one!"

The old woman pursed her lips together and held the perfume close. Elfreda's hand hung in mid-air.

"Thank you, fraulein." She ignored Elfreda's request with a snap of her wrist and a sharp turn to Karin.

"You do it," she said and gave the bottle to Karin.

Then, back to Ingrid. "I expect no further interruption, is that clear?"

"Yes, Frau Hingis, of course." Ingrid seemed resurrected, her eyes back to their furious twitching. "You can be sure Group Seven won't let you down."

Frau Hingis let out a heavy sigh. "You already have," she said. "Now get to work."

The girls looked at each other for a moment while Frau Hingis moved off. Ingrid's entire body had taken to twitching. Elfreda's lower lip was turning out in the beginning of a pout when she met eyes with Karin. Instantly, it thinned to a sneer.

"You better watch your back," she said in a low growl.

Karin stepped into the circle and crossed directly to face her. She raised the bottle between them to break the stare.

"Take it," Karin said.

Elfreda's arm snapped up, and she clutched the bottle in her hand. Then a suspicious look pinched at her eyes, and she froze.

"Is this some kind of a trick?"

"No trick," Karin replied. "I just don't care."

The answer must have satisfied Elfreda because she snatched the bottle away. Their eyes remained locked.

"That pretty face can't hide what everyone knows. You might fool Frau Hingis. But Rudi Kohl will sniff you out. Just wait. And when he does, watch out. You'll never be one of us."

Elfreda turned away. A cloud of perfume enveloped everyone. The taste of it made Karin want to throw up.

CHAPTER ELEVEN

After the debacle with the tomato seeds, Karin took enough time to study Oma's journal to sketch a rough plan. She had enough seeds from Meissner's to begin a modest vegetable garden, but Oma's journal brimmed with notes for all kinds of other crops—spinach, parsley, chamomile, sage, and thyme. Those could wait until after the first planting. For now, she would follow Opa's advice on how the Great Cathedral had been built: *one stone at a time.*

Under wispy clouds on a warm June afternoon, Karin put the first phase into action. With the trowel she broke up a small line in the soil and sprinkled the lettuce seeds. In another row, she poked in peas and more beans. On the other side of the plot, she gathered the cucumber plateaus, sprinkled their seeds, and then formed the potato mounds. The quarters were just beginning to sprout in bowls of water in the kitchen. The afternoon's progress overcame lingering discouragement about the tomatoes.

Only the carrots remained. Oma's notes described digging a trench as deep as the trowel and then filling it with dirt mixed with sand. This would give them plenty of room to stretch out.

Karin scraped off the top layer of soil with the trowel. Below it was compact and hard. Reversing the wooden handle in her hand, she began to stab at the earth with an overhand motion. The chunks were stubborn—clumpy, red, and peppered with stones. In no time, she had drawn a sweat. The exertion felt good, but as she paused to catch her breath, the result in front of her was broad and meandering—more ditch than trench. The second flurry of strokes was no different. In the third wave, the blade clunked something hard, and the handle snapped.

The soil was rocky enough that Karin's first thought was she had hit a larger stone. But something in the sound was not quite right. It was hard like metal but also hollow. She would need Opa's shovel.

When the shovel cut easily into the earth, she regretted not using it from the beginning. The broken trowel blade came out with a scoop and revealed the top of a stone at the center of what was to be her carrot row. It would have to come out. A few shovelfuls only uncovered what apparently was a much larger stone than she had expected. As she dug more, its unique shape and presence among no others of its kind made her wonder: *Did someone put this here?*

With the hole as wide as her shoulders, she finally uncovered an edge, then a corner of what was roughly a rectangular shape. Curiosity equaled concern for the carrots. The blade nosed under the edge, and she levered back on the handle. The stone rose up.

Karin's eyes widened.

Beneath the stone lay a black metal box covered in a fine layer of dirt.

The thrill of discovery set her hands to quick work. The soil was compact around the box, but the shovel proved valuable. Soon, she had two corners exposed and began to twist and pull on it. Rocking back and forth, slowly the box wriggled free. It was heavy, but she dragged it out of the hole, clumps still clinging to it.

The box had a small latch on the front with a lock. She pulled on the lid. Her spirit began to sag.

Her thoughts turned to Opa. Surely this was his box. It was just the kind of orphaned scrap she would expect to see in his shed. He saved everything. But what was this? What deserved special protection of a box, and hiding it in a hole in the ground?

Karin wondered if it was money. She had heard stories of Jews and others withdrawing their money from the bank and fleeing the country before the war. Why hide money in a hole? It didn't make sense.

The key had to be somewhere. Opa would know.

She jumped up, turned to the shed, and then froze.

He had hidden the box for a reason. He would not be too happy that she dug it up. But if he didn't want her to find it, why didn't he say something before she started digging the garden? Had he forgotten about it?

She thought about the money. It would do them good. Ration cards limited almost everything—meat, butter, oil, bread. With money, there were ways to find everything. Opa hadn't had real coffee in months.

The idea struck in a brilliant bolt.

I'll surprise him for Christmas.

Karin cleaned the clumps from the box and carried it to the narrow workbench under the overhang of the shed. Among the half-empty flowerpots, glass jars, and empty seed packets, Karin searched for something to pry the latch free. A wooden stick, one of the leftover row markers, snapped easily. Next, a rusty nail bent as she pried and hurt her fingers. Something bigger, stronger was needed. The broken hand trowel?

She wriggled the broken stub of blade under the latch and pressed down. The edge slipped and nearly sliced her fingers.

She changed her approach. Holding the box between her knees, she levered down with both hands on the blade. The latch held at first, but she had not applied all her strength. She squeezed with her knees, clenched her teeth, and strained with all her might. The latch popped with a sharp snap. The sudden release caused the handle to fly, the box to fall, and Karin to tumble backward on the ground. But she was elated. Scrambling up, she found the box on its back, its lid propped open.

At first glance, her elation was short-lived—no coins, bills, gold, or jewels spilled out. Instead, the box was filled with old rags, the same oily, smelly things littering Opa's shed. Was this some kind of prank? She peeled away the top layers and found something more—an odd shape wrapped tightly in another layer of rags and bound by string.

Karin lifted it from the box. It was heavy to her hands.

The string came off, and the cloth fell away.

Her breath stopped.

A pistol.

"Gott im Himmel!"

Karin jumped at Opa's voice. She looked up, frozen in the stare of being caught red-handed.

Opa nearly tripped trying to reach it. He snatched it from her, an easy enough feat because from the moment Karin realized what it was, she had been cradling it in her hands like it was a live snake.

He stepped back a few steps, his face creased with anguish. As he began to examine the pistol, turning it over in his hands, Karin knew the one cause of his expression—private guns had been confiscated in Germany for as long as she had known. The very presence of it in the box, in the hole, in his hand now, was illegal, and discovery of this would land him instantly in jail. This explained, of course, why he had hidden it in a box and buried it in the backyard. But it didn't explain why he had kept it in the first place.

Opa's expression revealed something else. Not so much fear of discovery—but something behind those twitching eyes. Had he forgotten it was here?

"What is this, Opa?"

The question was like trying to wake a heavy sleeper.

"Nothing!" he snorted. The pistol was like a time bomb in his hands now. He was looking for somewhere to put it, and the longer he waited, the more dangerous it was to him.

He had wrapped it again with the cloth and was staggering wildly for the box when a sharp knock on the side gate startled them both.

Opa slammed the lid of the box and slid it among some flowerpots on the shelf under the shed. The knock came again.

"Who is it?" Opa called. Now he had found the shovel and held it across his torso with two hands like a weapon.

"Postal service," came the voice from the other side. "I have a telegram for the fraulein."

Karin ran to the gate and let in a spindly old man in gray uniform.

"How long have you been standing there?" Opa asked.

The man flared his nostrils like he smelled something foul and began to shake his head. He was confused. "I tried your front door, but there was no answer. Then I heard noise back here and came around."

Opa pulled his shoulders back and crossed the plot, throwing up chunks of earth as he strode.

"What did you hear?"

The man took a step back, still confused.

"I'm not sure I follow you."

Opa swept past Karin with the shovel raised.

"Nothing?"

"Whoa, old man, calm down. I'm just delivering a telegram. If you'll sign here, I'll be on my way."

The phrase "old man" seemed curious given the delivery man's own advanced age, but more concerning was Opa's sudden militancy.

"Please, Opa," Karin said, worried that he was raising, not quelling the suspicion. "He's just making a delivery."

She stepped between them and took the telegram. With a quick scratch on his pad, she led him back toward the gate and out. The battle was averted, but Opa was pale and shaking.

"It's all right now. He's gone."

"No more talk. You never know who's around." Opa turned toward the shed.

Karin's attention was on the telegram, marked from Berlin. She opened it and read:

Thrilled re: BDM. Sad to miss ceremony. Planning big event. Will call after. Love, Mother

Typical Mother, Karin thought. Not only were her plans always more important than Karin's, but she would also rather spend the money on a telegram than a real phone call. As the deliveryman had demonstrated, telegrams brought the drama of a surprise delivery, the sharpness of the economic, abbreviated phrases. Best of all, from Mother's point of view, they were impersonal. She could have cared less about the actual news and how Karin felt about joining the organization they both knew Karin had avoided for as long as possible. But sending a telegram was so official, so important. She could brag about it at her next party, one of the countless gatherings of ambitious Nazi bureaucrats at the center of power. Her mother, Ursula, charmed important, influential, rich Nazis, married or not. Karin could hear her now, *"As soon as I heard the news, I sent a telegram congratulating her!"*

Karin crushed the paper and tossed it to the ground.

"I don't want her here anyway. I don't want to go myself."

Then she realized Opa hadn't asked. He had disappeared into his shed.

CHAPTER TWELVE

At school one morning, two men's appearance at the door brought immediate silence to the room.

Karin, wondering who had played the role of informer this time, kept her gaze ahead except for an occasional glance at the men.

The one in front, slightly shorter than average, with a gray face and salted hair, was speaking to Karin's nervous mathematics teacher. The one trailing him was taller and when Karin saw him, her heart dropped. He had accompanied Gossen that night he and Rudi Kohl first visited. Her teacher gave Karin an anxious look, the men's gazes followed, and then he pointed. The one in front snapped a finger.

"Fraulein Blik," he said, and her stomach fell to the floor. Every eye turned to her; their shock mixed with relief. Karin opened her mouth to speak, but only an airy word leaked out.

"Come here," the leader commanded. Karin stood up, one hand firmly on her desk, and took a deep breath. Then a step.

"Gather your things," the man added, evenly, unconcerned at the terror such words could induce. Nervous, she kicked the leg of the desk, sending an echo through the classroom that made the students jump. Books spilled from her desk and the chair fell over. Silent sneers and imagined judgments weakened her.

Marie jumped down to help.

"Don't worry, Karin," she whispered, gathering up the books and pencils. She clutched Karin behind her upper arm and helped her to stand. Karin rose unsteadily. Because of Marie, she found strength to turn and stride forward.

The leader indicated Karin to exit the room, and the two men separated to let her pass through. In silence they escorted her down the hall and out the front doors of the school to a car waiting at the curb. Karin tried to reassure herself that she had nothing to fear, but it wasn't the truth. The assistant strode quickly past her and opened the back door of the car. Karin saw polished shoes, knees, and finally the shadowed face of Herr Gossen himself.

"Good heavens, child! Have you seen a ghost?" He closed a brown leather portfolio and extended his hand. She swallowed hard and climbed in. The doors were slammed shut behind her and in the next instant, the car roared off.

"I suppose certain people react in fear when they see our men," he began with his characteristically disarming smile, "but that's what I want—from guilty people, that is. You have nothing to fear from me, Karin, I assure you."

His words were anything but reassuring. But as they drove, and his attitude remained cheerful, she came down from the peak of fear. They bounded through the streets of the central city for a few minutes until Gossen eventually tapped the portfolio that had sat across his lap.

"I'm sorry to startle you, fraulein, but as you can imagine, I'm quite busy. You'll soon learn and be able to relax around me, I have no doubt. I have two purposes for our visit today. We are on our way to the *Kölner Zeitung* office. Some important—excuse me, some *very important* people—are interested in your story. Soon you will be more famous than you can imagine, and you deserve it, of course. Your heroism will inspire people all across the Reich, and that's just the beginning. If things go as I expect, you will attract some very important attention from our comrades in Berlin. Forgive me, I'm understating things again. By 'very important' I really mean *the most important* attention. Do you understand what I'm saying?"

"The Führer?" Karin asked, almost in a whisper.

"Let's not get ahead of ourselves, but yes. Such things take careful and delicate planning—there's the calendar, security, war progress, et cetera—but let's just say for now, it's more than a possibility."

He seemed almost giddy, Karin judged, until his expression changed.

"On the second matter, not unpleasant, but not nearly as exciting, I thought I would speak to you about our previous conversation the other night in your home."

The topic of Schlinge could be nothing but unpleasant.

"Your passion is admirable and understandable," he said, "both your feeling about your father's unfortunate death and Herr Schlinge. So, I decided to take a look, although you didn't ask me to. I hope that was all right with you." Karin couldn't believe her ears.

"Yes, of course," she managed.

"Some background is necessary. In the autumn of 1939, Luxembourg was a sovereign state. When the war began, Grand Duchess Charlotte claimed the Grand Duchy's neutrality in her public statements, but in truth she was closely allied with Britain and America. I believe she is in the United States or Canada right now, as a point of fact. And so perhaps you know that your father was sent to Luxembourg to address this alliance and seek better relations with Germany."

"So, he was a member of the Gestapo?"

"Yes, technically, but on loan from the Abwehr, the arm of the Reich that deals in foreign intelligence."

She wanted to say "a spy" but thought better of it.

"What's important to understand is that, because of our common Volk, Germany was going to bring Luxembourg back into the Greater Reich one way or another."

Karin also dared not challenge Gossen's conception of Luxembourg's commonality with Germany and rejection of German influence.

"All this to say that your father and Heinrich—that is, Herr Schlinge—operated under the authority of the Cologne district, which includes the Moselle region. I was but a junior rank at the time, but the operation in which your father was killed was commanded from our headquarters here. Therefore, the post-operation debrief was conducted here and the report created here as well, before sending it on to overall headquarters in Berlin."

"Is that the report? May I see it?"

Gossen tilted his head slightly.

"No, and no. Such things are kept extremely secret and never leave the archives. As much as I like you or would like to share it with you, I must uphold my oath. Sadly, I have not seen the original report, as it was sent to Berlin."

Her heart sank.

"However, some investigative notes and artifacts were left behind, as well as some early summary drafts that contributed to the final report. In this portfolio I have written my own notes and summary of some facts I trust you'll find helpful, if not reassuring."

Karin regretted having said anything the night they first met. Her dream of the hidden truth was more appealing than the real truth, especially if the real truth went against what she imagined. Her reality was crumbling like a bomb-weakened apartment building.

"Do you want to know what I learned?" The question seemed genuine, it seemed to her, and he also seemed to understand the weight of it. She squeezed the armrest of the car door and pressed herself against the leather seat back.

"Yes," she said.

Gossen, seeming to sense her anxiety, paused, still wearing that disarming expression.

"The truth will set you free, didn't I read somewhere?" He opened the portfolio on his lap, revealing a lined pad covered with ink-written notes.

"I cannot tell you the precise nature of the operation," he began.

"I know they meant to kill the Grand Duchess," she said, hoping to cut through the preamble.

"That was not the objective. The purpose was to persuade her to seek help from her historic protector, Germany."

"By blowing up the Grand Ducal Palace. I saw the truck parked by the entrance of the Casemate tunnels. The one from Trier. It was used to carry the explosives stolen from the mines."

Gossen's expression changed in an instant. "Who told you this? Unauthorized disclosure of such information is a serious breach of protocol. Did Herr Schlinge?"

Karin caught the tone of his suggestion. Was he tempting her to use this information to undermine Schlinge?

"Your friend from Luxembourg, Hansi Broussard," he answered himself. She decided that was a good enough answer. Gossen's expression changed again with the advent of new avenues of thoughts and calculations.

"What did Herr Schlinge tell you?"

She paused, thinking carefully. "I saw him that evening, at about half past seven. I had been told to pack my things quickly—to fit everything I wanted in a single suitcase."

"Schlinge told you?"

"No, Fritz."

"The butler."

"Yes, and our driver."

Karin hadn't thought much of Fritz in the years since her father's death. Fritz had been kind to her. Kind to Hansi. Fritz protected them both when others were too busy.

"I kept asking where my father was," Karin continued, "what happened to him, and why the rush to leave. And where was my mother? Why had everyone disappeared suddenly? Fritz broke the news about my father. I asked him how he died, but Fritz would only shake his head."

Long-forgotten memories rose like garden mists. Fritz had been very upset but seemed to have held something back. At the time, Karin thought it was just his emotions—he was used to faithfully serving invisibly, and the situation was testing him beyond his ability. Fritz had loved Max, Karin knew, but back then, only her own questions and grief mattered.

"Yes, your man Fritz was interviewed after the fact. Not surprisingly, he had little to contribute at the time. His driver's log shows the last trip was the morning of the operation. A regular trip to the mechanic for oil, gasoline, and a tire check. Otherwise, a quiet and routine day. That is until later, and your encounter."

"Who told Fritz the news?" Karin asked.

"Heinrich," Gossen said. "He took charge of the household after—"

"Where was Schlinge when Father was killed?" Karin interrupted.

"He was at a scheduled meeting in the city with the Luxembourg gendarmes."

"During an important operation?" Karin asked. "Seems an odd excuse, don't you think?"

Gossen pinched his mouth and narrowed his brow. "The report says that Heinrich's role that particular day was indirect. He was to maintain a normal schedule in order to not arouse any suspicion. Your father's role was direct, on the other hand, to conduct the mission while Schlinge maintained appearances, as it were. Had everything gone according to plan, Max would have been at your house at the deployment moment, with Heinrich at his meeting. Events would not be directly traceable to either of them."

"Awfully convenient for Heinrich," she said derisively, regretting it as soon as she said it.

"Despite your feelings, fraulein, I urge you to show more respect." Gossen folded his portfolio and exhaled heavily. "I'm sorry to say, Karin, I truly am, but I see no evidence that Heinrich—Herr Schlinge—had anything to do with your father's death. There is another explanation, despite what you might wish to be true."

"You're on his side, then," she said, defeated, and well past her normal boundaries for speaking to adults, let alone the Chief of Gestapo.

"I'm on the side of truth," he answered. "And I'm not afraid if that truth were different than I understand, or if it's threatening to Herr Schlinge."

"Even if Herr Schlinge is your friend?"

"*Especially* if he is my friend. There is the law, as well as the bond of friendship. The latter demands a higher standard, because it involves trust. If what you might wish to be true, that Schlinge had something to do with your father's death, whether through negligence or malice, and he hid this from investigators, then Herr Schlinge—despite being my friend—is the worst kind of man. Not just a lawbreaker, but a betrayer. A traitor to his friend and his Führer."

Gossen swept invisible dust from the cover of the portfolio. "Schlinge, as you know, is a powerful man. More powerful than me. But not above the truth. Not above the Fatherland nor the values we swore to uphold with our lives. But I cannot act on mere feelings and suspicions, nor hopes. I sympathize, I do, and I am sorry you have been robbed of your father. But without evidence, there's nothing I can do except to offer you friendship and support. It's the least I can do for an old friend like Max."

Karin collapsed inwardly, knowing he was right. She had no evidence, not a shred. Like he said, her suspicions were built on the vapor of emotions. The only evidence was the truth in her heart and Schlinge's presence in Berlin with her mother.

"Herr Gossen, may I ask you something?"

He nodded.

"Did the report mention Hansi Broussard?"

"Only indirectly. You see, Karin, after the operation failed, the Luxembourg government expelled all German diplomats. You, your mother, and Herr Schlinge left that evening. The house staff were given forty-eight hours to vacate." That night was the last time she had seen Fritz.

"The investigation conducted afterwards was prior to the annexation of Luxembourg in May 1940, and so interviews of locals or those left behind were not conducted. In other words, Hansi was not interviewed."

He hesitated. "We only have the words of Herr Schlinge on the matter."

Karin frowned. "He blames Hansi."

"Hear me carefully, Karin, for I'm going to tell you the truth, as I promised, but it carries a warning. Herr Schlinge reported that he had captured Hansi and locked him in the cellar of your house the afternoon of the operation, before he left for his appointment. He believes that Hansi managed to escape, went to the tunnels, and shot your father."

"But Schlinge wasn't there, you said it yourself."

"Exactly," Gossen said, "and we are all policemen first, anything else is built on top of that. So, we know that what Herr Schlinge is saying regarding Hansi's role is simply what we'd call interpretation. It's not evidentiary, not facts."

"Conjecture," she said.

"And fortunately, or unfortunately, depending on one's perspective, your friend from Luxembourg is not alive to dispute or confirm any of this."

Karin said nothing.

"I don't intend to be insensitive about your friend, Karin, believe me. But hear my warning. Everyone knows that these statements are what they are. They don't carry the weight of evidence. But no one was on trial. They are not disputed, because we don't need to."

"But they make an impression," she said.

Gossen smiled. "If girls were permitted to join the Gestapo, you'd be my first candidate," he said. "Which is to say, you must be very, very careful with what you do with your keen insight. Let me remind you again that Herr Schlinge is in a very powerful position above both of us. We must be careful to respect that, no matter what we feel, and even, dare I say, new facts were to be uncovered. To that end, should you remember anything, please come to me first. You see, under the new annexation order, which I know to be coming very soon, Luxembourg will officially take its place as part of the Mosel Gaul region of the Reich and fall under my jurisdiction. Any new facts must come to me. It's for your protection. Do I make myself clear?"

Karin nodded. She wondered if he was intentionally being ambiguous. Was he subtly pushing her to look further? But how, where? Was he afraid of Schlinge? It seemed so. But also, if she was true to her instincts, intrigued.

They rode the rest of the way to the Zeitung's office in silence. When the car stopped at the curb in front of a three-story stone building on Breit Strasse, a reporter and cameraman were waiting, looking bored until the moment they recognized the car. Gossen's assistant seemed to exit before the car had fully stopped and opened the door for Karin.

"Another word of advice, Karin. Let these men do their jobs. Follow their direction and answer their questions if they have any, simply, directly. No talk of fear. That helps no one. You simply did your duty, thinking of the Fatherland, the Führer, that sort of thing. You'll inspire us all, I have no doubt."

The car pulled away without another word.

The men greeted her without enthusiasm, and she was led around the corner to a section of the block damaged by the raid. The photographer positioned her in front of a pile of broken stone and brick and told her to stand tall. Lift her chin. Look off into the distance. Hands on hips. Completely unnatural, but the two men seemed pleased. The camera clicked and bulbs flashed, searing her eyes with white spots. They had her climb partway up the pile and do it again. They were even more pleased.

The photography finished, the reporter flipped his pad open and studied the page.

"Maximillian Blik was your father, yes?"

She nodded.

He made a mark in the pad, then flipped it shut before stowing it in his coat pocket. Then he gave her some coins.

"Danke, fraulein. Treat yourself to a cone of roasted nuts down at the corner for your trouble. We'll take it from here."

"That's it?" she asked.

He nodded. "Don't worry, we already know the story."

"They're always the same, fraulein," the photographer said. "Just different names."

"Only the faces are different," the reporter said. "And you've got a pretty one. You're going to be famous."

CHAPTER THIRTEEN

Karin pondered Gossen's words for many days. Was he hinting that there was evidence to be found? But where? She reviewed the conversation over and over, trying to discover any hints. It all seemed to lead to nowhere. Dead ends. Or more correctly, tied-up ends.

Then one day Opa was digging at his bomb shelter. To her it seemed he was moving dirt from one pile only to start another, then back again. She brought him a glass of iced elderberry water. He must have noticed her perplexed study of the various diggings along the back fence because he stopped and pointed toward the Great Cathedral.

"One brick at a time, remember?" he answered her unspoken question with a grin.

The mantra gave birth to an idea.

"Do you remember Fritz, Opa?" she asked.

"Your driver, yes. Odd little man, really. When you, Max, and Ursula would visit, he would fuss over that car every second you were here. Your mother flicked a cigarette once and it bounced off the side panel. You'd have thought she'd kicked it with her spiked heel. As soon as they were out of sight, he bent over, studying it like an archaeologist. He'd brush and then breathe on it, buff it with his handkerchief, change angles, and do it all over again."

"I don't remember him that way," Karin said. "He was very kind to me."

"Oh, I didn't say unkind, just energetic, nervous. If he treated you well, I'm glad."

Opa wiped the beads of perspiration from his forehead and smiled. "Your mother would have surely tested him."

Karin smiled at the joke. "How would I find him?"

"He's still living?"

"I hope so, but I have no idea, really."

"What happened to him after Luxembourg?"

"I don't know," Karin answered, "but I've been thinking about him lately. I'd like to visit him if I could."

"Speaking of your mother, you could try asking her," Opa offered.

To ask Mother would risk alerting Schlinge. If Fritz was a source of evidence incriminating Schlinge, the latter would take note of Karin's inquiry and try to stop her, she felt sure.

"Good idea," she said instead.

CHAPTER FOURTEEN

The familiar hum, deep and sonorous from beyond the curve, was the sad signal that the tram was approaching. Karin had waited after school as long as she could, while flocks of girls, sparkling in their white blouses, dark wool skirts, and bouncing braids, giggled onto three successive trams. They were destined for leisurely strolls near the Cathedral and along the Rhine, no doubt, while she would be confined to the Hitler Youth office. For once, she envied them.

Frau Hingis had had almost a week to consider Karin's appeal, and both she and Marie had heard nothing of it. Joining typing class so close to the end of the term hadn't helped much. The other girls were well beyond the basics, hammering out full pages without watching the keys, while Karin was still learning where to put her fingers. At the office, she had managed only the simplest lists. Rudi hadn't seemed to mind, and so Karin watched the tram shudder to a stop with the sinking realization that her plan had failed.

Karin let the others board first and then followed, step by labored step. She slipped past the chattering pack without so much as a glance and fell onto a bench in the rear.

The driver had just rung the bell and closed the doors when Karin heard someone pounding on the glass. The doors came open again and she looked up. There, at the front of the tram, stood the flush-faced Marie, beaming. Karin could hardly believe her eyes.

When they arrived at the Hitler Youth office, Rudi was holding court in the front office, where about a dozen boys in the Hitler Youth uniform of white shirt, brown shorts, angled belt and swastika-emblazoned field cap were gathered.

Marie, seeming impressed, smiled. "Sometimes they're rather handsome in their uniforms, don't you think so, Karin?"

She shrugged. "I suppose. But the Hitler Youth—they're not exactly real soldiers."

"True enough. But your Willem is a proper soldier. I bet he looks handsome in his uniform."

The picture of Willem at the train station flashed in Karin's mind, making her chuckle.

"What's so funny?"

"I'm just remembering when he left. I went to the Bahnhof with his family. Willem wore his dress uniform, and at the time, I thought he looked kind of silly—like a boy in a man's uniform. Now that I see these boys with Rudi..." she hesitated, then finished in a whisper. "Willem was braver than I can ever imagine."

"Have you still heard nothing?"

Karin nodded. "It seems I'm writing to the wind. There's nothing much left to tell."

"Have you told him you're a hero?"

The door opened and the boys poured out, leaving Rudi alone at the entrance.

Karin introduced Marie and explained that she had asked Frau Hingis for help.

"Marie is an excellent typist. We'll have the reports prepared in no time."

"Even the mighty Frau Hingis yields to your charms," Rudi said, pivoting to Marie. He snatched her hand and held it until her cheeks reddened.

Inside, the papers strewn on the counter at Karin's last visit had been transformed into stacked columns.

"I took it upon myself to attempt some organization, but alas, I have created only the illusion of order."

He took a page from a small stack and held it up.

"This is an example of a handwritten report from a local Hitler Youth commander. It describes local chapter activities from week to week, on a variety of subjects— marching, knot tying, political instruction, and so forth."

With a clap of his hands he crumpled the page, startling the girls. "These are meaningless. But these..." He waved one in the air from a different stack.

"These are Aktion Reports. I've only made a start, but these are critical. Find them and compile a summary—the total number of actions, the district with the most of them, and the numbers of criminals they encountered. Is that clear?"

"Yes, Rudi," Karin answered. She had Marie by the hand and tugged. Marie nodded in agreement.

"I'm briefing Herr Gossen on our gang fighting activity across the city, so I need this to be finished well in advance of the ceremony next week. Nothing impresses the Gestapo like a thorough report, after all. Well, I can think of a few other things, but they're not to be discussed in polite company. Do I need to request additional time from Frau Hingis for you to work?"

"That won't be necessary, Rudi," Karin assured. "We'll have it for you."

"Excellent. Then I'll leave you to it." He turned and disappeared down the back hallway.

"The good news," Karin said after a few minutes of sorting, "is that just because it seems so difficult to him, Rudi thinks the task is actually difficult. Just skip these with lists and find the reports with paragraphs. Like this one."

"The language here is quite unusual, don't you think?" Marie finally said. "And the meeting times are strange—very precise and always after curfew. What is an 'anti-criminal special operation'?"

Karin answered just above a whisper. "Bureaucrats talk that way. A 'criminal' or 'communist' is anyone out of uniform. 'Responded in kind' means the Hitler Youth attacked first."

"Why do they talk this way?" Marie asked. "So sterile, it sounds even more frightening."

"It makes the violence seem routine and helps them keep their distance from what they are really doing."

"You're already an expert. How did you get so smart?"

Karin felt the weight of her past return in a flash, and the air all at once hard to take in.

"My father," she said. "I realize now he was just like them."

"I thought he was a hero. The medal, the honor."

"Don't you realize, Marie? You can't believe everything you hear. Even the little that's true these days gets twisted. The truth becomes unrecognizable. My father was a good Nazi—no, a great one—according to them. He worked tirelessly and spoke like these reports: numbers, facts, figures, everything so cold and scientific all the time. But there was a look in his eye, the tone of his voice. Something I realize now that didn't quite align with the language.

"When I was a little girl, we moved almost every year. He was called a diplomat, and though he would work at the embassy or consulate offices, he would be in his office from early in the morning to late at night. I was always free to enter. As a young girl, I remember how special it felt to slip inside my father's office while he was working or on the telephone. I would wait, just inside the door, until he saw me there. He would wink—that was my signal, and I would tiptoe across the thick carpet and climb into his lap. He wouldn't stop what he was doing, but I was safe.

"One day, during his last assignment in Luxembourg, I walked in on a conversation I wasn't supposed to hear. I was older then, fourteen. My father didn't wink. The look I got was worse than if he had aimed a pistol at me. After that, the office was locked. I didn't feel much like sneaking in anyway…"

Karin's voice trailed off. The memories, buried for so long, had surfaced quickly and powerfully. She was both surprised and alarmed at herself. Marie had asked about something completely different, hadn't she?

"What happened to him? How did he die?"

Karin hesitated. She had trusted Marie a great deal already, and perhaps it would be good to let out more. But Karin was afraid that bringing these memories to light and giving them a place in the present would undo the fragile footing she had found at school, in the Hitler Youth office, and on the threshold of joining the BDM.

"We'd better keep going," Karin replied.

Karin scanned the counter for a pad of paper and pencils for them to record their statistics and began opening drawers and opening cabinets along the wall.

Her eyes stopped at a dark volume among a collection of magazines and catalogs left behind, she supposed, by the office's previous occupants. The spine read: *Köln Adressbuch.*

She pulled it free, cleared a space between the stacks, and paged quickly to H. Helms, Helwig, Heminger... *Hengel.* The Luxembourgish name was alone among Hegels and Henschels. Karin jotted the address onto a corner of a report and shoved it into her pocket.

Before she could return the book to the cabinet, Rudi appeared in the hallway.

"Just checking on your progress—" he began, and then his gaze dropped to the open volume. He stepped closer. "Looking for someone in particular?"

Karin shut the book calmly, her heart drumming. Marie went still.

"I'm... embarrassed to say," Karin answered.

Rudi smiled thinly. "We'll have no secrets here. Confession is good for the soul, don't you agree, Fraulein Voss?"

Marie managed a pained nod.

Karin lifted her eyes, contrite. "An old boyfriend," she said with a sheepish grin. "He's not listed. And you're right. I should be finishing the report. Please forgive me." She slid the book back into the cabinet and gathered a stack of reports.

"In the future, please confine such...pursuits...to your own time."

"Yes, Rudi," Karin said. "The report will be finished in time, I promise."

When his door shut, a wave of relief crashed over Karin. She grabbed Marie's hand and pressed it to her own mouth to keep from laughing. Marie did the same. They had survived.

Returning to their work, Karin enjoyed a new sense of closeness with Marie. For the first time since Willem had left, she had an ally.

As Karin collated her results, she noticed a frequent mention of Nippes, the industrial area just north of Central Cologne, one of the areas targeted by the British air raid.

Three reports stood out from the others. The operations were all conducted by District 14, and for whatever reason, District 14 had no other reports. And while the other reports referred generally to "unauthorized gatherings of youth" or "youth gangs," the reports of District 14 mentioned a gang by its name: Freiheit. Freedom. Another difference stuck out—the generic encounters always included a sentence or phrase explaining that the Hitler Youth "struck back swiftly" or "met force with force." But the Freedom Gang was simply pursued, observed, and its activities reported.

"Marie, do you have any reports from District 14?"

She shuffled through the short pile quickly. "Just one," she said, holding it up. "Why?"

"I'm not sure," Karin replied. "It just caught my eye, I guess."

The one Marie found fit Karin's analysis. It was surprisingly free of the propaganda bravado laced in all the others. The pattern was clear. The Freedom Gang was given to vandalism, sometimes severe. In one case, a city bus had been attacked. They had set up a roadblock and pelted the bus with rocks, breaking several windows and injuring several passengers. They didn't steal anyone's purse or wallet; they simply attacked the bus and then retreated, as if only for the sick pleasure of it, according to the reports. In response, District 14 was called upon to investigate the incident and search the area.

Karin couldn't help but connect the Freedom Gang with the strange boy Frei. The connection was too strong to be a coincidence. She wondered what was so different about him and his gang that they were treated specially.

Altogether, they pulled sixty-two special operations reports from the stacks. District 14 had completed the most of any district—eight. Tallying the total number of "criminals" from the reports took longer, but the girls worked together, Marie reading off the numbers and Karin recording them. Then they both added the figures as a check of one another's math. If the reports were to be believed, the Hitler Youth had fought 457 "criminals" in the last three and a half months.

With the collating finished, Marie moved to the typewriter. Karin gathered up the loose pages and returned them to their neat stacks on the counter. Despite the nature of the work, the sense of accomplishment and silent camaraderie had a calming effect on Karin. They were a good team.

"My father wasn't the hero everyone imagines," she said. "He was a spy. I didn't know it at the time, but he worked for the Gestapo."

Marie slowed her typing, staring straight ahead.

"In September 1939, just at the start of the Polish invasion, my father was trying to persuade Luxembourg to join with Germany, like Austria had."

"I thought Luxembourg was always part of Germany," Marie said.

"Not until the war in the west started two years ago. They were an independent country, and proud of it. When Father couldn't convince their Grand Duchess to join Germany peacefully, he organized a plot to kill her."

Marie turned around. The color was gone from her face.

"My father was plotting to blow up their palace. The bombs would have killed the Grand Duchess and thrown the country into chaos. It was all my father's doing."

"What happened, Karin?"

Karin shook her head. "I don't know exactly. All they told me later was that Father was dead. Shot dead. By someone I knew, who now they say is also dead."

Marie's eyes were giant. "And you don't believe them?"

Karin didn't answer.

CHAPTER FIFTEEN

Karin and Marie met at the Neumarkt and took the tram east, crossing the Rhine on the Hindenburg suspension bridge. Through the cage of steel cables, coal barges churned against the muddy current below, loaded with mountains of coal on the edge of sinking. On the far bank, some cranes belched steam and smoke above the jagged rooftops of brick warehouses; others lay dead, their steel arms mangled among the heaps of black rubble. Fritz and his sister Susanne lived somewhere beyond in the flat, dull sprawl of Deutz.

Only the twin towers of St. Heribert's Church stood out above the landscape of three-story flats that seemed indistinguishable from one another. When they got off the tram, Karin was doubly grateful for Marie's presence. Among the drab and grimy coveralls and aprons, their red, navy, and white BDM uniforms drew notice. And Marie's hand-drawn map was a sure guide in the narrow, shadowy streets.

Still, when they had reached their destination, Karin wondered if they had made a mistake starting the journey at all. The hallway of the brick tenement was dark and smelled like stale cigarettes and sour wine, and the stairs creaked. A dog barked from behind a closed door, causing both girls to jump.

"We've come this far," Marie encouraged, pulling Karin on.

At apartment three, Karin took a deep breath and knocked on the door. The door scraped open to reveal a woman in her seventies, whose sharp eyes shone with suspicion at the sight of their uniforms.

"The Hitler Youth sends girls now? To this neighborhood? I already gave this month, and I don't have enough as it is." She began to close the door.

"Please," Karin said. "We're not collecting for the support fund, Frau Hengel."

The woman seemed startled at the mention of her name.

"Are you Fritz's sister?" Karin asked.

"Go away," she said, and began to close the door.

"Please, Frau Hengel. My name is Karin Blik. Fritz was my driver for many years. I remembered that his birthday is soon, and I want to wish him well in person. Do you know where he is?"

"Blik, you say?" Frau Hengel frowned. After a moment, she pulled back on the door and had them come in. Though simply adorned, the flat was neat, clean, and smelled like a pine forest. Nothing like the outside. She had them sit down on the narrow sofa and offered them some acorn tea.

"When's the last time you saw him?" she asked.

"Almost three years ago," Karin replied.

"He's sleeping right now."

Karin brightened. "We have time, don't we, Marie?"

Frau Hengel pushed a lock of silver hair into her scarf. Her face was heavy with worry. "He sleeps strange hours. He's not well."

Karin's heart dropped. She remembered Fritz as energetic, even in his advanced years.

"Is he dying?" she asked.

"It's not his body," Frau Hengel answered. "Something has happened to him. He's not right. My brother was always so bright, quick. We didn't see one another very often, but when we did, he always had lively stories to tell me about the rich folk."

She was suddenly embarrassed.

"It's all right," Karin said. "I remember him that way too."

"Now, he mostly sleeps, and it's a strange blessing. Because when he's awake..."

She got up, went to the window, and lifted a small box of groceries up to the table. "Listen to me, I've said too much, and to strangers in uniform!" She started unpacking the vegetables and groceries. "He really can't be left alone. A nice boy downstairs brings me these from time to time, but I'm worried. All the young people are in uniform now, him too. If someone reports my dear brother's condition..."

"Don't worry," Marie said. "We won't tell anyone."

Karin looked at Marie with confusion. *What did they mean?*

A moan rose from behind a door and grew louder like an air raid siren.

"You must go now," Frau Hengel urged.

"Please," Karin begged, standing. "Let me see him."

Marie tugged at her sleeve and motioned to leave.

Frau Hengel rushed toward the rising cries. "Go, before the neighbors start banging on the ceiling. I can't have them calling the police."

Karin followed her. "Please, just let me wish him happy birthday."

Frau Hengel pushed the door open.

"Who's there?" came a scratchy voice. "Who is it?"

The voice, though weak and gravelly, was clearly Fritz's.

The smell exploded over Karin, but it was nothing like the shock of seeing her old companion standing by the bedside, trembling in his soiled nightshirt. Fritz had never been a large man, but now he was positively a skeleton. Karin stopped.

"Fraulein Karin," came the gravelly voice softly. "Karin?"

Karin started to cry as she eased her way forward.

"It is you," he said, eyes brightening. He raised his arms to her, still trembling. She closed the distance and embraced him, though the foul smell was nearly unbearable.

He held her weakly for only a moment before letting go, the effort seeming to have spent his energy.

"I'm sorry, dear girl," he said, his own tears streaming. "Don't look at me." He turned away and lost his balance until Frau Hengel and Karin caught him.

"You've caught him in a better moment," the woman said. "Go and sit back down while I get him cleaned up."

"Let us help. Can we get the bath going? Anything?"

Frau Hengel looked away for an instant and then agreed. "There are clean clothes hanging in the bathroom. If you would be kind enough to put the kettle on the stove for the bath, I'll get him undressed."

Karin and Marie heated the water for the tub and retrieved Fritz's clean clothes. They returned to the front room while Frau Hengel moved him into the tub. Marie suggested they strip the bed. They removed the soiled sheets and cleaned the oilcloth cover. The work kept Karin's sadness and confusion at bay.

The moans and cries started up again. Frau Hengel tried to calm her brother, but his distress only seemed to escalate.

"Fritz, it's me," Karin said from the door. "Can you hear me?"

Fritz quieted for a moment. "Who is it?" he called, fear in his voice.

"It's me, Karin."

"I don't know anyone by that name. Who let you in here? Is it the Gestapo? Don't let them see me in here! Don't let them take me. Don't let them!"

"No one's going to take you," his sister said, but her assurances were only met with thrashing in the water and louder cries.

"Stop it!" he cried. "Don't make me eat that! Please! Not that! Suze, I beg you!"

After a few seconds of splashing and muffled protest, the bathroom fell silent. A few minutes later, Frau Hengel led a glassy-eyed, but calm, clean, and freshly dressed Fritz back to the bed the girls had changed. She opened the bedroom window and swatted at the smell. The outdoor air of the Kalk factories was hardly better, but she lit a candle to try to help.

Fritz rested, letting his head tilt toward the dancing flame.

Standing at the bedside, Marie slipped her hand in Karin's.

"Say a prayer for our dear Fritz," Frau Hengel said.

Karin and Marie left, both in tears. What Fritz knew or not about Schlinge no longer mattered.

CHAPTER SIXTEEN

After their visit, the girls resolved that even if Fritz could not help Karin, they would help him and Susanne. Each week after, they saved a little food and rode the tram to Deutz, where they looked in on Fritz and helped Susanne with cleaning and conversation.

On one journey, the tram was barely halfway across the bridge when the stop bell rang, surprising everyone. The bell rang a second time, and then a third, and then repeatedly. A group of three boys and two girls about Karin's age had gathered up front, some working the cord, others poking and teasing the tram operator. Their attire was strange for summer or any other season—heavy overcoats, upturned collars, pale makeup on the girls, long, unkempt, and unbraided hair obscuring their faces. The attack was timed perfectly during the longest stretch without a stop, leaving the operator no choice but to press on to Deutz.

A man near the front stood up to confront them, a mistake. One of the girls met him mid-stride and struck him sharply in the center of his chest with the heel of her hand.

"Sit down, old man," she said, sneering.

The man wobbled and fell back into his seat. One of her comrades grabbed her wrist and thrust it high in the air, tugging the cord again to ring in the new champion. The others laughed while the passengers stared in horror. Karin realized this was the girl she had seen that night at the park, and the boy with her was the one called Ziggy.

She stood up.

"Karin, no!" Marie hissed.

"I see you Mädel back there!" the boy shouted. "You'll keep to your seats unless you want those pretty faces messed up."

Karin glared at him. Marie tugged at her arm. In the end, Karin plopped back down.

Finally, the tram screeched to a stop. The doors opened and one of the pack said, "Let's skedaddle!" in English. They poured onto the sidewalk and disappeared down one of the narrow streets, but only after tussling the tram operator's hair and stealing his cap.

The next day, when Gossen's car appeared at the curb after school, Karin was nervous, but less so than the first time.

He handed her a newspaper. "Today's edition. It's official: You're a hero."

Karin looked at the headline and caption: "Daughter of a Hero a Hero Herself – The Madel Saved a Boy, a City, and the Nation."

"That's a gift. I'm very proud of you."

The front page featured a photo of Karin standing on the pile of rubble, almost expressionless, inset with a smaller photo of a boy she had never seen before. He wore brown shorts, a white shirt and a too-big field cap that tilted endearingly to one side. The copy was generic except for one sentence: *Fraulein Blik, age*

16, inspired by her father Maximillian's sacrifice for Führer and Fatherland, braved the crumbling building to save young Hans, a future soldier and leader.

"The photographer said you have a gift for it," Gossen said.

A gift for feeling nothing, Karin thought.

"I understand you found your old friend," Gossen continued. "That's keen detective work. Well done. Have you learned anything new?"

She tensed.

"Be at ease, fraulein, we keep an eye on you. It's for your protection." He tapped the newspaper and smiled. "Now that you're famous."

"Fritz is in poor health," Karin answered. "He lives with his sister who tends him like a nurse. He barely remembered me."

"And so, you and your friend—Marie, I believe—have been visiting him and his sister with extra food. Very kind, admirable. I'm sorry to hear he is unwell, for both your sakes. A bit of advice: next time, let me help you. If you have interest in a subject or someone, something comes to mind, just ask. That way, there's no suspicion between us. Understood?"

Karin swallowed hard and nodded, eager to escape the confines of the backseat of the Mercedes.

"One last thing. Tell me what happened on the tram."

Pulling weeds in the garden later that afternoon, Karin began to doubt Herr Gossen's explanation for watching her. She resembled any of a thousand girls that could have shown up on the front page of the Zeitung. Why waste the manpower following her?

The questions about the tram incident churned in her mind. Her answers were simple and true, mostly.

Did the gang hurt anyone? No, they were just a nuisance.
Had you ever seen them before? No.

Certainly, he knew she had met the gang the night Rudi caught her breaking curfew. But to admit she recognized Ziggy and the girl on the tram seemed unwise, although Karin couldn't explain to herself why. Did he suspect a closer association? She dismissed the notion and turned back to Fritz.

Did he think she was going to learn something from Fritz? Beneath the broken shell, did Fritz really know the truth?

The next day, Karin decided to test Gossen's goodwill. He had given her his secretary's telephone number at Gestapo head-quarters. When she connected them, he sounded surprised. "Fraulein, to what do I owe this pleasure?"

"I do have a question, if you don't mind," she said.

"Excellent. I'm so pleased you made the call."

"The report we discussed about Father's death—when was it prepared?"

"One moment. Let me find it. Why do you ask?"

"I'd like to know if it was completed before or after my friend Hansi's death."

"As we already discussed, your friend was not interviewed for the report."

"I remember," Karin said. "It's not important I suppose, but I'd like to know if the report was completed before or after he died."

"Very well. The report was completed in February 1940, about two and a half months after the events which included Max's death. But leafing through the notes again, I see an addendum, dated 31 May 1940. It escaped my notice before. It states that Hansi Broussard was temporarily held in custody before attempting to escape, and—*oh my*—he drowned in the attempt. I'm sorry, Fraulein."

Karin fought to keep her voice steady. "Does it say exactly how he died and what was done with his remains?"

"No, Fraulein, I'm afraid not."

"Would he have been returned to his family?"

Gossen sucked in a breath. "Being technically wartime, I'm sorry to say there's no military obligation to do so."

"Then they left him by the riverbank?"

"It doesn't say. Now Karin, please—"

"You know who was chasing him, don't you?"

"Heinrich is a professional police officer first and foremost, and he knows the boy was your friend. I see what you are suggesting. It's out of the question."

"Schlinge could be lying. Excuse me, *Herr* Schlinge. He could have invented this story simply to shut me up."

"Fraulein, I must stop you. This is not acceptable. You cannot accuse an officer of the Reich in such a manner, especially without detailed proof. I have been quite understanding, helpful, sympathetic even—to this point. And despite your desire for something to be awry, it is simply not. I think it's time for you to turn to more worthy pursuits for the present and future. Let the past live in the past."

When she didn't answer, he pressed. "Don't you agree, Fraulein? You have great promise and purpose to fulfill. I hate to see it ruined chasing the wind."

Karin felt a gurgling rage in her guts but knew what the situation demanded.

"I'm sorry, Herr Gossen. I'm grateful for your help."

"Good girl. Let's turn the page."

CHAPTER SEVENTEEN

The next Thursday when Karin and Marie arrived at Fritz's house, he was dressed and sitting at the table, where a cup of something hot steamed. Susanne had met them at the door, holding the medicine bottle.

"I'm trying a smaller amount, and it seems to help," she said, "but he will either get sleepy or—well, let's just hope he won't be like last time."

Susanne turned to her brother. "Fritz, your friends are here. Remember I told you about them coming today?"

The girls sat down. Fritz studied them, squinting, blinking. Karin, directly across from him, extended her hands to him. He placed a bony hand on hers. The skin was rubbery and cold.

"Dear Fritz, it's me, Karin. It's your birthday soon," she said. "I brought you a gift."

"Seventy-one," he said.

"Congratulations," Karin smiled, and slid a jar across the table.

"Your favorite," she added. "Blackberry jam. Remember how you loved it in Luxembourg?"

His eyes twitched with alarm. Karin, Susanne, and Marie exchanged worried glances.

"And you have a gift for Karin, remember?" Susanne said urgently.

She guided Fritz's hands to a box wrapped in plain paper, bound with string and a loop of white ribbon she had brought up from beneath the table. His eyes brightened.

"Oh—for you, dear Karin," he said, and slid it toward her.

"So generous, Fritz," she said, and with a glance to his sister, "What a lovely ribbon."

"Open it now and open it later," he said.

"You want her to open it now?" Susanne clarified.

He nodded.

Karin carefully removed the ribbon and then the wrapper. The cardboard box, much taller than wide, might have held a small bottle of perfume, she guessed, for inside was a felt bag with a golden drawstring. She loosened the gather and discovered, instead, a miniature bronze statue on a felt base. The obelisk featured a golden angel at the top and two bronze figures at the base: one a fallen soldier, the other his companion. She recognized it at once.

"Ice cream," Fritz said, smiling.

"Yes, I remember. I loved the ice cream."

Karin explained. "The statue is in Luxembourg City near the Pont Adolphe overlooking the valley. It's called the Gëlle Fra—the Golden Lady. Fritz would take me there from time to time after school. We'd walk, looking over the casemate walls, and have ice cream."

"Take good care, Karin," Fritz said. His face turned to worry.

"I—I will, my dear Fritz, I will. Thank you for the lovely gift. I'll treasure it always."

Karin got up and gave Fritz a kiss on his cheek. Tears formed and he began to tremble.

"Open it later," he said.

The other three looked confusedly at him and then at each other. "I'll keep it on my windowsill," Karin said. "Just the place for it. Every morning I'll see it and think of you and our fond memories."

"Not all," he murmured.

"Yes, I know," she replied.

Karin wondered if the door she thought had been locked with Fritz had suddenly opened. She glanced at Marie, who seemed to have read her mind. Marie's expression was strained, in warning.

"Fritz," Karin asked, "do you know how Father died?"

Alarm flashed on Susanne's face.

"Shh, they'll hear you," Fritz snapped. "They'll come for us."

"Who, Fritz?"

"Him. You know, the black hats. They know you're here and are on their way even now. You'd better go. Quickly!"

"No one's here but us," Karin reassured him.

"He knows I know. He knows! Don't let him take me, Karin. Don't let him!"

"Don't worry, Fritz."

"Go! Take it and go. Open it later. Just go!" His voice and gestures had gained surprising strength.

Susanne twisted the lid off the medicine bottle.

"No! Not that!" he yelled.

"Please, Fritz," Karin said. "You're safe. I promise I won't let anything happen to you. But tell me—did Schlinge have anything to do with Father's death?"

"Ow!" Fritz howled. "Go! Hurry! No!"

Susanne threw her arms around her brother and held him. "Help me," she pleaded to the girls.

"What, Fritz? What did he do?"

"Karin!" Marie said. "Stop it!"

"Please, Fritz, I must know. I can help you."

Fritz thrashed. Susanne had him, but just barely. Marie took the medicine dropper and wedged it between Fritz's teeth. He crunched down, broke the glass, and spat blood and glittering shards. They held on for a few more anxious seconds until the medicine took effect.

"*Go*," Susanne demanded.

"I'm sorry," Karin said.

"Just go! Leave us!"

Marie pulled at Karin. "Please."

Karin gave Fritz one last kiss. His lips moved in silence. "Open it later," he whispered.

On the way home, Marie hardly looked at Karin until she finally confronted her. "How could you?"

"He knows something," Karin answered.

"But he's suffering. Don't you care?"

"Maybe he'd feel better if he could tell me."

"Do you hear yourself? Has it crossed your mind that our encounters with Fritz and his sister have nothing to do with what happened to your father in Luxembourg? And therefore, nothing to do with you and what *you* want from him? Has it occurred to you that in your quest for the truth, you are crushing someone you claim to care for?"

Karin remained defiant. She was convinced Fritz knew something and was trying to tell her, even in the unusual gift.

The Gëlle Fra statue in Luxembourg City was a gift from France to Luxembourg for helping them fight the Germans in the Great War. Fritz was not a fervent Nazi, but he was a loyal servant of the Fatherland. Such a gift seemed entirely out of character. What was he trying to say?

They rode the rest of the way in silence. By the time they parted ways, Karin knew Marie was right.

"I owe you an apology, Marie. I was too hard on him. If you knew the old Fritz, you knew he could take it and give it twice back."

"But he's not the old Fritz," Marie answered. "I know this is important to you, but it's not the way. Don't let yourself—" She stopped.

"What?" Karin asked. "Say it."

"Don't let yourself become like them."

CHAPTER EIGHTEEN

As instructed by Frau Hingis, the girls met at an old dance hall near the Neumarkt in the shadow of the great Cathedral a full hour before the event started. Karin, the new member, would be escorted by experienced BDM members Marie, Zilke, and Elfreda. Nothing was left to chance. Frau Hingis would have them looking perfect for the ceremony. In a small room behind the main hall, three of them buzzed about with nervous excitement, alighting repeatedly in front of a tiny mirror someone had brought and propped hastily on a shelf. Elfreda and Zilke jockeyed the hardest for a view, though Elfreda's elbows and size dominated. Karin stood apart, trying to ignore their chatter, anxious for the whole thing to be over. She slid her hand into her pocket and touched the token she had hidden for courage—the Gëlle Fra statue—and remembered Fritz's strange words: *open it later.* Perhaps this was somehow what he meant.

Marie, interested but uncompetitive, eventually found a good-enough reflection in the glass that protected a portrait of Adolf Hitler on the opposite wall. Watching her turn her head slowly from side to side, Karin observed how pretty she was. There was something innocent in her that Karin both admired and envied.

Zilke and Elfreda eventually calmed down, settling on an arrangement that, as usual, favored Elfreda. She stood in front, closest to the mirror, while Zilke looked over her shoulder. Thus settled, they primped and preened, smoothing hair, pursing lips, batting eyelashes.

Karin approached Marie and caught a glimpse of herself in the glass of the portrait.

Her blonde hair was, like the others, braided into two pigtails and highlighted by curled white ribbons. Frau Hingis would have nothing to complain about. She was the picture of Aryan beauty, though she refused to acknowledge it. She didn't care.

"Look who's staring into the eyes of the Führer," Elfreda teased, her voice bathed in sarcasm. "How sweet. Perhaps one day you might be the one to finally bear him a child."

Karin refused to be dragged into battle with Elfreda. She left the portrait and moved back to a table.

"Don't get me wrong, Karin," Elfreda kept on, still facing the mirror. "You do have the looks. Blonde hair, blue eyes, rosy cheeks, a perfect figure—just what every Aryan wants. But I think you're more Rudi Kohl's type. You'd definitely improve his offspring."

Zilke giggled.

Karin, pretending not to hear, smoothed her woolen skirt and studied the shine of her black leather shoes.

Elfreda wasn't finished. "Yes, I know, you're not listening. You never do. Always on your own. And that's frowned upon these days, you know. The boys want someone nice and compliant, don't they, girls? Someone to cook for them, clean up after them, take care of their babies, and grow them into soldiers. I'm ready to do my duty. In fact, I'd like to start as soon as possible, if you know what I mean."

Zilke's eyes grew wide.

"I bet you know what I mean too, don't you, Marie?"

Marie said nothing.

"Don't you?" Elfreda repeated.

"You're not making sense," Marie finally said.

"I mean that your family has had plenty of experience."

Marie began to tremble.

Karin got up and elbowed Zilke out of the way.

"You're a witch," Karin said. "You'd better watch yourself."

Elfreda spun around. Her eyes were large, and her nostrils flared above the sneering smile.

"Well, well. The golden princess wants to pick a fight. This should be fun."

Karin, who made it her practice avoiding confrontation, felt a tremor of doubt from within. Elfreda seemed to love it. Sensing Karin's hesitation, she stepped closer.

Karin sucked in her lower lip and bit down—her only defense against the inner quakes. A fistfight here, before the ceremony, or anywhere for that matter, would land them both in detention, jail, or even exile. Would Elfreda risk it?

"So, what are you going to do about it?" Her voice was just above a growl.

"Perhaps I might have a conversation," Karin answered. The words just came to her.

"A conversation? Are you joking? Conversation is for the weak! I don't *discuss* things with my enemies—I smash them!"

"I didn't mean a conversation with you," Karin said, her voice steadier than her insides. "I think Rudi—or better yet,

Herr Gossen—might be interested in your little joke about the Führer."

Elfreda snapped back like she smelled something bad. "I didn't joke about the Führer. I was joking about you."

"That's not the way I heard it," Karin said. "It sounded to me like you were doubting the Führer's ability to have children." Karin's maneuver hinted at another well-circulated but very dangerous rumor that the unmarried Adolf Hitler was incapable of fathering a child.

"That's not what I said."

"Really? Your meaning was obvious. Didn't you think so, Marie?"

Marie turned up a slight smile.

Elfreda flashed her glare back and forth between them.

"You wouldn't. No one would believe you. And Zilke heard me," she pleaded, turning to her. "Didn't you? It would be two against two."

"Yes, that's right. The word of two loyal secretaries to the District Kommandant of the Hitler Jugend Rudi Kohl, against a nobody and her friend. I like our chances."

The girls stood eye to eye for a tense moment. The air was dead still. Karin realized all at once what she had threatened—and her confidence disappeared with the speed of a burst balloon. She found no strength in her legs.

But then came a knock at the door. Frau Hingis.

"It's time now, girls."

Elfreda snapped away from Karin's stare with a defiant toss of her chin.

"We'll see," she huffed. "You're not fooling anyone with that phony loyalty, least of all Rudi."

She brushed past Karin close. She wore her rage like perfume.

Karin staggered a step back and found strength from a nearby chair. Elfreda's blow was sharper and more powerful than any threat against Marie. She seemed to know the one thing Karin wanted most to keep secret. Her heart wasn't true. At least not true to the Nazis.

Outside in the hall, Frau Hingis's face crinkled in the usual frown. With a flick of her arm, the girls knew to fall in line behind her. She clicked her heels, spun around, and led them away. They marched to one of the double doors at the end of the great hall, where she stomped to a halt.

"This is a solemn occasion," she said. "There is to be not a hint of a snigger, giggle, or smirk. You are women of the Reich now."

The door opened. One by one, they entered a dark passageway, a makeshift waiting area of black muslin suspended from a wooden frame where the air was heavy and smelled of old canvas. A faint murmur of voices could be heard beyond the veil. They paused.

A drum sounded in the distance, low and hollow. *Pumm, pumm, pa-pumm.*

Others joined the first. The tempo quickened, and the chorus of drums created rolling thunder in the hall. A shiver ran down the back of Karin's neck. Marie, directly in front of her, turned and clutched Karin's arm.

"This is so exciting!" she whispered.

"Silence, girls!" the old woman hissed. "Maintain your line. Backs straight, shoulders back, arms at your side. Face forward!"

The pounding roar rose to a furious climax and then abruptly stopped. The last beat echoed over the silence.

The curtain parted. The structure that once hosted raucous dances and joyous wedding banquets was now a dark and sacred National Socialist cathedral. Its congregation, a sea of brown and black, the Hitler Youth, stood at rapt attention. A mass parted down the center by a wide aisle. At the front, the flock of white was the BDM girls in their own section. Like religious tapestries, long red banners, emblazoned with the black swastika on a circle of white, hung from the rafters. On the stage, a choir of Hitler Youth manned massive timpani drums, and at its center, atop a bunting-draped platform, rose a polished lectern, the pulpit.

The drums began again. This time, the rhythm was slow and steady, a march. Frau Hingis stepped aside. The moment had come. Like brides to be married, they would walk the aisle. They would become Maidens of the German Bund.

Elfreda, at the head of the line, twitched like a racehorse in its gate, waiting for the signal from Frau Hingis.

A light flickered near the stage. A Hitler Youth on one side of the aisle had lit a torch and lifted it high above his head. He bent his arm forward and touched the unlit torch of a Jugend on the other side of the aisle. They began to alternate, back and forth. One by one, the torches sputtered to life, their yellow-white flames streaming black fumes upward that filled the hall with a sharp oily scent. The shape formed by the raised torches crept toward them like a fiery dragon and gave Karin a shudder. This was all too much. She had been to rallies before—no German could avoid the parades and pageantry of National Socialism—and she had thought she could get through this. But she had underestimated the regime's skill and power. The use of color—black and red; light—darkness and fire; and primal sounds overwhelmed the senses with a tsunami of power and fear.

The last torch lit. As Frau Hingis had explained earlier, that was the signal: *the drums will start again, and you will march to the stage, at their tempo.* Yet no one moved. Something was wrong. Elfreda should have started.

Karin dared not move first. The pounding of her heart was indistinguishable from the drums. She had been told to keep eyes on the back of the girl in front of her—Marie—and wait for her to march.

There was a commotion at the front of the line. Over Marie's shoulder, Karin saw black figures moving near the front of the line. Then, startling Karin, Marie jumped sideways to make way.

A figure appeared at the front of their line, a shadow against the backdrop of flames. *Rudi?*

He came to Karin at the end of the line and took her arm. Before she could react, he pulled her forward—past Marie, past Zilke. *Past Elfreda.* Elfreda took on the face of a wounded bear, whose cubs had been stolen.

At the head of the line, Rudi paused and tossed a glance back. Frau Hingis had formed the girls back into line, even the reluctant Elfreda.

Satisfied, Rudi clicked his heels together and turned to Karin.

"Now!" he barked and began to march. They fell in rhythm with the drums, step by step, drawn by the hypnotic power of their beat. Everything conspired to overwhelm—from the flickering flames to the smell of burning oil, the swirl of red and black and the raised arms in rigid salute. She the bride, he the proud groom, in a grotesque monster wedding. Her hand squeezed the statue until it hurt. By what strength Karin walked, she didn't know.

CHAPTER NINETEEN

At the front of the hall, Rudi paused and signaled Frau Hingis. She nodded and ushered Elfreda and the others to sit in the front row. Karin turned to follow but was barred by Rudi's arm. Her heart thundered above the pounding drums. She would not be joining them.

He hooked her by the elbow and pulled her forward. They climbed the handful of steps, side by side. If not for Rudi, she might have faltered. The rungs of the fire escape, weeks before, had been far easier.

They took the stage in the wash of the deafening drums. The air was thick and oily from the torches. Rudi moved with purpose, pressing on toward a circle of light at center stage. They pierced the beam, he tugged on her arm, and she spun around in a daze. The light was blinding, but she could feel every eye trained on her.

The drums roared to a climax and stopped. The last echo faded, leaving the room breathless and still. Rudi was at her side, but she was utterly alone.

Click, click, click, click. Sharp footsteps from the left side of the stage broke the silence. Karin turned to look. From the darkness, Herr Gossen emerged, leading a column of followers to a row of chairs behind the podium. In his crisp, black wool business suit and tie, he stood in dashing contrast to the uniformed mass of Hitler Youth. His close-cropped hair, greased and parted with a precision that matched the distinct cut of his jaw, marked him as a gentleman, more bureaucrat than stormtrooper. Meeting eyes with Karin, he paused and acknowledged her with a warm and confident smile before proceeding on. To her surprise, the gesture had a calming effect.

Behind Gossen followed a young boy, whom Karin judged to be no more than eight or nine years old. Unusual for one so young, he was decked out in a Hitler Youth uniform. Gossen reached the second to last chair and turned to the boy. He guided him with gentle arms to his seat where he sat stiff-backed in wide-eyed wonderment. *Could this be Gossen's son?*

Gossen stayed standing, which obscured Karin's view of others entering the stage. She managed glimpses of a line of ceremonial Hitler Youth honor guards escorting someone who seemed to be taking more time than others. Then, as this slower figure sat down, something in the profile and the way he nearly fell to his seat sent a tremor through her.

Gossen stepped toward the front of the stage, as if on cue, while Karin's gaze didn't move.

The man, free of his escort now, leaned forward and adjusted his position in what seemed a slow and deliberate act. He twisted just enough for his face to penetrate the column of stage light above him. A bolt shot down her spine. She'd have recognized that square forehead and pale eye anywhere. The scars and eye patch were only confirmations. Heinrich Schlinge, of Gestapo headquarters in Berlin, was a surprise guest, and not just unwelcome, but terrifying.

Karin was about to look away when his eye found her. She froze, unable to break away from his sharp, cold stare. Despite the diminished appearance, he was still able to project that unforgettable sinister presence.

Herr Gossen came to the lectern. Mercifully, the spotlight left her and Rudi and shifted to Gossen, affording Karin a view of an eerie haze that floated above the sea of faces. Gossen took a deep breath and then thrust his right arm high.

"Sieg Heil!" he shouted.

Three thousand arms shot up in response.

"Sieg Heil!" came the echo.

"Sieg Heil!" he repeated, and they responded again. He started a chant, call and response, executed with precision until the throng was at a frenzy. The raw energy was staggering. Gossen brought the mass to a climax, bouncing on his toes, snapping the salute with all the might of an Olympic shot-putter.

His arm came down to rest at his side.

A wave of cheers rolled forward. Gossen lifted his chin and closed his eyes to let it roll over him. The drums pounded, the cheers building in crescendo, only to crash on stage with applause. Herr Putz and Frau Hingis were but amateurs. Here stood a professional.

"German Youth, I greet you in the name of our beloved Führer Adolf Hitler. He sends you his warmest greetings from Berlin, where he stands tirelessly against the enemies of the German people, both without and within."

Unwilling to settle down, the throng burst in another thunderous ovation that surprised even Herr Gossen. He smiled, let it build, crest, and crash again before he raised his hands in gentle encouragement for everyone to sit down.

"We gather tonight in defiance of our enemies to celebrate the courage of our fellow citizens."

Despite the propaganda, Karin felt drawn to the sound of his voice. It fit his appearance—smooth and self-assured. He spoke without aid of notes, and the words glided over the room without effort. Unlike so many of the minor public figures that sought to upgrade their status by mimicking Hitler, Gossen neither blustered nor thundered. He was naturally gifted, projecting sincere belief and authority, not lost even on Karin.

"Our armies stream ever eastward, by all means and on all fronts. The brave soldiers and airmen are cutting vast swaths in the enemy forces. As a year ago, our new spring offensive has been wildly successful. The gallant German army has the Soviets on their heels and desperate once again. Every one of you knows someone—brother, father, cousin, uncle—marching east. Trapping the enemy in Leningrad, crushing the defenders of Moscow, or pushing them into the Volga at Stalingrad, the Red Army is finished. By the first rains of autumn, it will be over."

As the crowd registered their approval with thunderous applause, Karin thought of Willem. Perhaps her images of him alone in the dark were mistaken.

"In Africa, General Rommel has the Tommies on the edge of disaster. The Brits are barely hanging on, and Cairo is sure to fall within weeks."

More roars. He shook his fist in the air. "The Jews and Bolsheviks have risen against us, but we defy them all! We will crush them in their sleep! The Reich will prevail! The Führer has prevailed! Heil Hitler! Heil Hitler!"

The mob leapt to their feet. The chorus was thunder and then a storm. The sound shook the platform beneath her and threatened to lift the roof off the arena. A terrible chill rippled up Karin's back, snapping her back to reality.

Herr Gossen let them go on again, nodding his approval until just the right moment once more, just the instant before the surge eased off.

"It is my great honor to introduce one of our beloved Führer's closest advisors. He has come on the instruction of the Führer himself to speak with you tonight and to congratulate you for your heroism and faithful service to the Fatherland. He is no stranger to the dangers of war. He has risked his life for the Fatherland not only in the Great War but also in the current struggle. Prior to his appointment as an advisor to the Führer in Berlin, he served the diplomatic mission in Luxembourg. And tonight, he comes from the Führer's side to speak with you. Allow me to introduce my longtime friend and a great servant of our nation, Herr Heinrich Schlinge!"

Herr Gossen lifted his arms heavenward, and the mob responded instantly in another wave of adulation. He stepped back, turned to Schlinge, and ushered him forward.

Schlinge, with the unsteadiness of a much older man, rose. The praise from the crowd seemed to settle him and he shuffled forward to the lectern, where the two men exchanged whispered greetings.

Gossen drifted back with a final gesture, and the crowd cheered again. Then he turned, paused, and looked straight at Karin. His gaze was serious and penetrating and lasted but an instant. And without a word, he had said a great deal.

I know everything.

The words penetrated to her heart as if they had been audible. She didn't doubt them in the least. Whatever Gossen knew about what happened to her father, and whether Hansi had killed him, he would keep to himself if it did not align with the version of truth believed by his "friend" Schlinge. In the turn of a head, her path shrunk from the concrete sidewalk in front of Rudi Kohl's office to a razor's edge.

Schlinge was nothing like Herr Gossen. His voice, raspy and halting, was no doubt caused by his injuries. The monotone was hardly loud enough to carry to the back of the hall despite the microphone. He had to grip both sides of the lectern just to remain standing. Still, his mere presence inspired fear.

"A few short weeks ago, the British Air Force launched a brutal attack on the people of Cologne. The Luftwaffe estimates that one thousand aircraft participated in the raid. Of course, our brave defenders located the bombers quickly with their searchlights and blew them from the sky. Almost four hundred of their aircraft did not return to Britain. And at this rate, by autumn, the British Air Force will have nothing left to fly but paper kites."

He paused, expecting a response from the crowd, but his power and timing were nothing like Gossen's.

"Among the bombers that got through, a few reached the industrial districts of Ehrenfeld and Nippes. However, most of the bombs fell in civilian areas. Such is the ruthlessness of Winston Churchill, forsaking the civilized rules of war for a soulless and brutal form of warfare aimed at innocent women and children."

Opa's rules for propaganda kicked in—a little truth, a load of lies. Schlinge made it sound like a minor attack, but Karin knew firsthand it had been massive, unprecedented in size. Had four hundred planes really been shot down? It was impossible to know for sure. And as for the question of whether the British were targeting civilians, Karin could only rely on what she had seen and heard and smelled. Thick smoke, crumbling buildings, cratered streets. Dazed people and little Hans. Little, soiled, orphaned Hans.

"The English completely underestimated the will and resolve of our Führer and the citizens of Cologne. Within moments of the attack, a heroic response began. In one case, an unexploded bomb hit a factory, landing in an oil tank. The workers, without regard for their own safety, but only thinking of the potential disaster if the bomb were to ignite the tank, worked tirelessly to drain the oil so demolition experts could disarm it. Not only did they save many lives, they saved their factory and the oil as well. The Hitler Youth and BDM girls also did their part, serving heroically alongside other brave civilian service organizations."

He proceeded to tell the story of the ripped open building, and Karin felt her cheeks grow warm. When he told of her rescue of little Hans, she was breathless.

"Before you tonight sits the boy who was saved." He turned back to the young boy, who stood up as if it had been rehearsed. Karin was stunned. *That boy?* Little Hans was no more than four years old, of that she was certain. This boy was at least twice that age. Why would they use a substitute?

"Young Johann's father, a hero of the Polish campaign, serves in the Sixth Army, which is streaming toward the Volga even now. Sadly, due to the despicable ruthlessness of the British, his mother was killed, leaving Hans an orphan now. But thanks to the courage of a team of BDM girls, he has a chance for a healthy life and service to his Führer."

Finally, as if Schlinge had said the secret password, the audience responded. On their feet again, they erupted with applause.

Karin could not believe her eyes. It was a deliberate lie!

From the rapt look on the other girls' faces, they, with everyone else, believed it whole. Karin felt sick. Schlinge continued.

"The heroic action of the brave girls has not gone unnoticed. The story of the boy and the rescue has attracted the Führer's notice. When I discussed it with him just yesterday, he asked, 'What is in the spirit of those Kölners that they would stand up to Churchill in this way?'"

To Karin's ears, the quote sounded manufactured, just like the nine-year-old Johann.

"'I don't know', I replied."

"'Then go and find out,' he said. And so, I have. And it's obvious to me from the moment I stepped on stage that this is an exceptional city and an exceptional group of boys and girls."

In mentioning them directly, Schlinge had finally struck gold. They nearly blew the stage down.

"I am proud to present four young girls, who, like all of you, represent the finest qualities of our Fatherland—virtue, loyalty, industry, and purity. Each one has been selected and approved as true heirs to the Aryan race—strong and courageous, healthy in mind and body, and above all, devoted to the National Socialist cause and our leader, Adolf Hitler."

The chants did not stop. Schlinge had to shout in the microphone. Finally, Herr Gossen rose from his seat and waved his arms. Only then did the crowd settle.

"And among these four heroes, one has distinguished herself with special bravery. Fraulein Blik, please step forward."

Karin was terrified. Every eye, wider than before, was fixed on her. They adored her as one of their own. If they only knew how she despised it all.

She crept forward and met Schlinge at the lectern. He reached into his suit pocket, withdrew a thin case, and opened it. He lifted a medallion on the end of a wide red ribbon.

"It is a special honor for me. Fraulein Blik's father was my superior and my friend. Three years ago, he answered the call of his nation to serve the Führer in a foreign land."

Karin winced.

"Maximillian Blik," he continued, "served the Reich with honor and distinction. Having begun his career here in Cologne, he served in Norway, Paris, and Luxembourg."

They moved to Luxembourg just after her thirteenth birthday, and at first, the city's medieval fortress built into the cliffs was charming, a refreshing change from stuffy, formal Berlin. Germany was at war and her father dead before her next birthday.

"In Luxembourg, I had the privilege to serve with Herr Blik. Through the course of our service, he uncovered a network of Bolshevik terrorists plotting to attack Germany."

Lies. The terrorist network was imaginary. The plots were hatched by her own father who had tried to overthrow the Luxembourg government.

"He gave his life for his people and his Führer. And now his daughter Karin, whom I've known since she was a baby, honors her father's memory well. I present this medal for bravery to her." He held the medal high, waved it from one side of the room to the other, and then presented it to Karin with a proud nod. She thought she might be sick. She wanted to run, but he held her with that single penetrating eye.

"Maximillian Blik honored his oath. An oath of loyalty, even to death. An oath just like the one you are about to witness from the hero's daughter and her companions. I urge each one of you, assembled here tonight, to recommit yourselves to this solemn oath. Germany faces great enemies gathered all around us—Britain and America to the west, the foul beast Russia and her communist hordes to the east. They seek our destruction! But under the magnificent care of our great leader, we will not be defeated; we will triumph no matter what evil threatens us. And those enemies within us, those few who remain, brainwashed as they are by foreign and Jewish propaganda, they will be crushed. You, as loyal followers of our Führer, will stand in the homeland to protect our nation, to support our gallant soldiers in their march to victory!"

For the first time, his voice had risen to a crescendo. He turned to Karin.

"Welcome this, your sister, and her comrades tonight in your glorious ranks!"

He rotated stiffly back to the crowd and let go of the podium with his right hand. Karin wondered if he might stumble, but he shuffled one leg back to steady himself and shot his arm skyward in a crooked but effective salute.

"Sieg Heil! Sieg Heil!" The crowd joined in. She marveled at how it was possible, but the room exploded in another chorus of chants. "Sieg Heil! Sieg Heil! Sieg Heil!"

The cheers continued. Now Schlinge had them in his command, stoking the flames of their passion, which grew and grew into a feverish roar. He kept going until his strength seemed sapped and it did not matter. The boys and girls roared on.

After another moment, Schlinge, suddenly as masterful as Herr Gossen, knew the precise timing for what came next. He raised an arm for silence. The voices finally quieted.

"In this dark hour, when all courage is required, it is time to renew our devotion."

He paused to let the crowd breathe, and then called out, "Repeat after me: In the presence of this flag of blood, I swear an oath:"

He paused, and the mob chanted in unison. Schlinge glanced at Karin, as if checking to see that she was saying the words. Her mouth was open, her lips moved, but there was no power in her voice, and she couldn't tell if any sound was coming out. Schlinge kept going.

"I will render unconditional obedience to Adolf Hitler, the Führer of the German Reich and people..."

Something cold and black filled her heart.

"Fulfill my duties as a boy of the Hitler Youth or maiden of the German Bund..."

"Serve the homeland..."

"Bear children for the Reich..."

"And defend the Fatherland, even with my life, if asked by my Führer..."

"So help me God."

The climax of the oath had only just finished when a loud electric buzz burst from the loudspeakers. The hum rose, piercing the ears.

"Achtung! Achtung!" The voice sounded official. Everyone looked up and around and at each other.

"Achtung, Achtung!" the voice repeated. "We are under attack."

The crowds sucked in a collective breath.

"We are under attack by the Hitler Youth, the BDM, and most of all, the Austrian himself!"

Karin's heart seized. This was neither joke nor misguided prank, but instead, a blasphemy of the highest order. Whoever had spoken would be arrested and sent away. Possibly shot.

Herr Gossen ran to the podium and seized the microphone in his fist. His face was white with rage.

"You will cease at once!" he shouted, but the power had been turned off to his own microphone. He pounded his fist into it to try to rouse it back to life, but it was being controlled from a remote room.

The spotlight that had been directed at the lectern suddenly jerked away. It found a spot on the wall where, over one of the red banners, a white sheet was unfurled. Hand-painted letters echoed the American Revolutionary motto, in English: *Live Free or Die!*

CHAPTER TWENTY

The crowd roiled in confusion, but Karin knew at once. This was the work of the Freedom Gang.

The speaker crackled again.

"Achtung, Achtung. Your freedom is under attack by the National Socialist Party. Seek shelter immediately."

The spotlight raked the audience back and forth. Shouts, raised fists, and calls for revenge punctuated the tumult.

Herr Gossen ran forward, pulled a pistol from his coat, and fired at the spotlight.

A chorus of shrieks brought the crowd to momentary silence. Rudi grabbed Karin and retreated to the row of seats. The fake Hans was on the floor, cowering under his chair. Schlinge, because of his damaged eye, looked like he was staring through an invisible telescope.

Gossen fired again. More screams. The spotlight retaliated, taking direct aim at Gossen. Blinded, he staggered back for only an instant, and then, raising a hand to shield himself, fired a third time. The spotlight exploded in a shower of sparks, leaving the hall in darkness except for the small lamp on the stage lectern. Gossen kept firing, capturing the terrified faces in frozen flashes until the pistol clicked empty.

"Find the lights for heaven's sake!" he barked.

Moments later the lights flickered on. The smoking hull of the spotlight hung limp on its stand on the platform at the rear of the auditorium. Men in plain clothes appeared at the side and rear doorways. Gossen directed them with jabs of his pistol.

He jumped down to the floor and stopped. The hall looked like a field after a windstorm. Boys and girls were sprawled on the floor in every direction, heads down beneath chairs strewn and tossed like stalks of wheat. Only now were they beginning to climb to their feet. In the next instant, every exit was jammed.

Karin scanned the stage. Rudi had disappeared. She gathered the quivering Hans into her arms.

"Don't worry now. You're safe here with me."

He looked up at her anxiously for a moment and then thrust his face into her side, sobs exploding.

Marie and the other girls had disappeared among those pushing for the exits, leaving Karin with Hans and the other stunned guests on the platform. She wanted to leave, but every time she moved to stand, Hans cried out.

Scanning the crowd, she caught sight of Frau Hingis's gray head. Like a hen, she had her arms around Marie, Elfreda, and was plowing through the chaos.

Karin waited another minute or two and then tried again. He squirmed and kicked against her lifting him into her arms.

"Everything is all right," she told him softly as they crossed the stage.

"Who is it?" he asked.

"Just some boys clowning around."

They descended a short flight of stairs on the right and filed into a half-lit hallway, the boy clutching her hand. The group of guests and performers shuffled forward in hushed unease, their footsteps echoing against the plastered walls. Shadows from swinging bulbs flickered on either side, past closed doors. At the far end, the corridor bent left, and a pale glow spilled across the wall.

Voices carried from around the corner. Karin halted, pressing Hans gently behind her to shield him. She edged forward, just enough to glimpse the source without revealing herself.

"You were supposed to have them under control," came a sharp voice. *Schlinge.*

"It will be, I assure you," replied Gossen.

"Your assurances are as slippery as they've always been," Schlinge snapped. "Your charms may have carried you this far, but I will not tolerate such incompetence for long."

Gossen's reply was silk over steel. "Need I remind you, Heinrich, that those charms, as you call them, include the careful curation of certain facts about you? Your so-called heroic past—your edifice of loyalty to Max and the Reich—is built on delicate scaffolding. Reports. Investigations. Ones I myself prepared on your behalf. Without me, it might all come crashing down. So, *my old friend*, let me warn you..."

"Herr Gossen, come quickly! We found something!" a third voice called.

The revelation was sharp against Karin's throat. Gossen knew the truth about Schlinge and yielded it with precision. She realized now he cared nothing for justice, only power. Truth was merely an instrument, and one he had used on her, too. Years of Schlinge's lies should have prepared her, but Gossen was different. Schlinge was a hammer, Gossen a surgeon.

Hans tugged at her sleeve. She realized she had stepped too far forward. One of Schlinge's men glanced back. With a quick breath, Karin pulled Hans with her, retreating into the group behind them. She bent low, murmuring to the boy, and slipped deeper in, praying she hadn't been seen.

Just then Rudi appeared, worming through the people crammed in the hallway.

"You're safe, Karin."

His face was pale, and he was trembling, like someone who had been lost in the woods and suddenly found.

"Are you all right?"

"Yes—of course. I just—"

His eyes darted over her shoulder. She turned and saw Schlinge. Gravity seemed to have ravaged the damaged side of his face even harder in the two years since she had seen him last, but at least the sagging skin had covered the eye socket on his right side.

Schlinge studied her for a moment. His single eye, sharp enough for two, revealed that he wondered if she had overheard him arguing with Gossen. Without thinking, her fingers slipped around the statue in her pocket and gripped it hard.

"What are you doing here?" he snarled at Rudi. "Are you going to take this humiliation cowering in a back room while your comrades find the perpetrators?"

"I was only thinking of the fraulein, Herr Schlinge," Rudi stammered.

"She's safe with me. You embarrass yourself and the Hitler Youth. Be gone!"

Looking like he'd been slapped, Rudi turned and fled.

After a brief silence, Schlinge spoke. Gone was the intense stare.

"Your mother sends her greetings. You know, even with one eye, I can see quite clearly. You've become quite beautiful, just like her."

Karin focused on a crack in the wall.

He continued. "I don't blame you for resenting me, especially now. You've endured more than your share of suffering, Karin. In many ways, it seems like only yesterday we were working together, your father and me. He was special, you know. To lose him, and then your grandmother, I can only imagine for you."

"That's not all," she said.

"The Luxembourg boy was not good for you," he said. "But I don't wish to upset you."

Schlinge's sympathy was no more real than the fake Hans in her lap. The last time she had seen Schlinge, it was only the influence of her mother on him that kept him from throwing Karin in prison, or worse.

"That is the distant past, Karin. I care only about the present. I understand you have a friend that recently left for the front—Willem, I think was his name?"

Karin looked up.

"Gossen told me. He recently left to serve in the Sixth Army, am I right?"

She looked right at him. "I've forgotten about him already. That is the distant past. I care only about the present."

Schlinge's eye twitched.

She returned to stroking the fake Hans's hair.

"Who is this boy?" she asked. "What happened to the real Hans that I rescued?"

"He's being cared for," Schlinge answered without hesitation. "As you saw yourself, the bombing traumatized him severely. The spotlight here would have been too much for him."

"Does it matter that it's not the truth?"

Schlinge coughed on his own saliva. "What matters is that you saved him, and that people know it."

"And that I go along with it."

Schlinge lifted the side of his mouth into a smile. "Your mother's looks, and your father's brains."

He shuffled a step closer and dropped his tone. "A piece of advice, Karin. Despite what you think of me—or of the Fatherland—believe that I have your best interests in mind when I tell you this: beware of the games grown men play. Beware of men in fine suits and smooth smiles. Behind every lint-free lapel and every polished leather glove lies a breastplate of steel and a fist of iron. Herr Gossen is trying to use you. If you serve his purposes well enough, he'll praise you, flatter you. But the moment you fail him, or the moment he no longer has use for you, he will discard you. And if you dare to oppose him—then 'discard' will not be the word. Not at all."

The tiny figures at the base of the statue bit into Karin's palm. "I thought you were old friends," she managed, exasperated with more unsolicited advice.

Schlinge's lips twitched in something between a smirk and a sneer. "Old friends make the fiercest rivals. Never forget it."

CHAPTER TWENTY-ONE

With calm returning to the hall, Schlinge's men escorted him away, leaving Karin, the boy, and the others to find their own way out.

Karin sank to the floor. She gathered the fake Hans in her lap and rocked him gently, stroking his hair. Moments later she realized she was doing it more for her own comfort than his. She stopped and put a hand under his chin. His eyes, chocolate brown, were open and calm.

"What's your real name?" she asked.

He tensed.

"Don't worry, I can keep a secret. I won't tell."

"Matti," he whispered. "Can I go home now?"

"That sounds like a great idea."

They got up and returned to the stage, crossing and descending to another long hallway that led to the exit. Boys were still gathered around the doors, but the atmosphere had changed to something less like panic and more like being let out of school early.

When they came to the room where she and the girls had gotten ready, Karin pushed on the door, but it moved only a little, causing a ripple of shrieks inside.

Frau Hingis's face appeared in the crack.

"Fraulein Blik, thank heavens you're all right! And the child!" She snatched Matti from her and smothered him in her arms.

"Herr Gossen will have my head if anything happens to this boy. In the panic, I brought the girls here."

She leaned close to Karin.

"Please don't say anything about this. I owe you a debt of gratitude, fraulein."

Karin never considered the idea, although it wouldn't hurt to have a measure of credit with her.

"I think it's safe now," she said. "Everyone is leaving."

Frau Hingis hesitated, but some other girls took Karin's word and left. Soon the room was half empty. Elfreda, her face tear-stained and puffy, was being comforted by Zilke, who held her hand. When Marie saw Karin, she jumped up and threw her arms around her friend.

"Let's go," Karin said, pulling Marie forward.

"Don't leave me!" Elfreda squealed, but Karin ignored her.

In the hallway outside, Marie asked, "What was that strange announcement?"

Karin pulled Marie close and spoke in her ear. "I think it's one of the youth gangs we've been reading about in the reports."

"My heavens! The nerve—in front of that man from Berlin!"

"I think that's exactly why they did it."

"What do you mean?"

"I think they wanted to embarrass Rudi. You know how he tries so hard to impress Herr Gossen? Well, here was his big moment, and look what happened. The gang he is supposed to be controlling or arresting—I'm not sure which—they turn up at his big event and make him look like a fool."

No sooner had the words left her mouth than Rudi appeared through a side door. There was no avoiding him in line to leave among the mass of boys and girls jammed at the double-doored exit. He was bathed in sweat and nearly breathless, but looked glad to see them.

"It's safe now," he huffed. "All clear."

Karin tried to hide her disappointment. "Did you catch them?" she asked.

"They'll not get far," he said, still heaving. "My teams are on them. They'll pay dearly for this."

How quickly he had forgotten Schlinge's reprimand, Karin thought.

"Trying to get away without us?" Elfreda's voice echoed up the corridor.

"I'd hoped so," Karin said just to Marie.

Elfreda, still red-faced, let go of Zilke and closed the space quickly. Seeing Rudi, her snarl transformed to a smile.

"Herr Kohl, how nice to see you again." She dipped in a curtsy and extended her hand. Rudi touched it awkwardly and let go.

"I'll escort you home, fraulein," he said, turning back to Karin.

"Thank you, Herr Kohl, but that's not necessary. I'm sure you have more important things to do. We can manage just fine, can't we, Marie?"

Marie hesitated.

Elfreda pushed forward. "Don't listen to her. We'd love an escort, Herr Kohl."

She snatched Marie by the elbow and, together with Zilke, presented Rudi a three-person wall, blocking Karin.

After an instant of aggravation, Karin changed her mind. In fact, she inwardly thanked Elfreda. In thinking she had outmaneuvered Karin, Elfreda had, in truth, done her a favor. Rudi's training would not permit him to refuse Elfreda. And Elfreda's hovering would not permit him to be alone with her.

"On second thought," Karin said, "yes, it's for the best. Herr Kohl's protection will be most welcome."

Marie looked back, and they shared a knowing glance. Karin allowed herself a grin.

"Then let's go," Rudi said.

CHAPTER TWENTY-TWO

Though the street was completely in shadow, the early summer sky held the last moments of daylight when they exited the hall. Trams were infrequent at this time of night, sending many off on foot. Those who waited swarmed the doors and packed the cars to maximum capacity. Rudi used his rank to carve a path through the crowd for himself and the four girls. Worse, he stood at the open door and controlled who and how many entered. When he climbed aboard and instructed the driver to close the door behind him, their car was barely half as full as the others. Yet no one dared challenge him.

Only Elfreda seemed beyond his control. Just after Rudi ushered Karin to her seat but before he could join her, Elfreda pulled him to the opposite side and plopped down. Marie wasted no time and filled the seat beside Karin, leaving Rudi no choice as the tram set off.

"Herr Kohl, you did a marvelous job calming the panic," Elfreda said. "Leading us all to safety, without care for your own. Why, that's the mark of true leadership, don't you agree, Karin?"

Karin knew Elfreda was gloating but didn't care. For once their interests aligned. In fact, Elfreda had saved her. Karin elbowed Marie to watch them. Every bump in the track became an excuse for Elfreda to nudge against Rudi. She feigned embarrassment and looked longingly into his eyes.

Marie leaned in. "Lucky us, yes?"

Karin opened the top of her pocket. "My good luck charm!"

Marie peered inside. "You didn't! Can I see it?"

Karin withdrew the statue but kept it hidden between them. Marie cupped it in her hands while she examined it.

The tram jolted over a rough joint, and the statue slipped from her grasp. It made an audible clunk hitting the floor. Marie reached for it immediately.

"What is this?" Rudi said, retrieving it.

"Give it to me," Karin snapped. Her tone triggered suspicion in Rudi, but he slowly handed it back.

"A gift from a friend," Karin said, recovering. "He couldn't attend this evening's ceremony and wanted me to remember him."

"Sounds mysterious," he said with a smile. "Perhaps even romantic. Care to tell?"

"No," Karin said. "It's neither of those. It's from my grandfather."

She snatched it from Rudi's hand and turned back to the window, sending a clear message: *Leave me alone.*

Rudi seemed to have gotten the message, as did Elfreda, for she started up again.

"I'm sorry," Marie said.

Karin said nothing. She was putting the statue back in her pocket when she noticed the felt had begun to peel away from the cast metal base. In the hollow space inside, she saw the corner of a manila envelope. Her heart jumped.

Open it now and open it later.

The envelope was the kind Opa got from the hardware store for holding tiny screws, nuts, washers, and the like for his many projects. Inside was a slip of paper, handwritten with a message:

H and M, brothers like K and A. Find 211.

"What does it mean?" Marie asked.

Her mind raced. H and M clearly stood for Heinrich and Max. They had certainly been brothers once. But K and A...

She looked inside the statue again and shook it, but it was empty. But her grip was too hard, and she snapped one of the tiny figures from the base.

"Kain and Abel!" she said.

"The biblical brothers?" Marie asked.

Karin nodded. "Fritz never liked the statue. You see, the figures at the base were warriors who fought against Germany, one living, the other dead. They were supposed to evoke sorrow for the sacrifices made, but Fritz made a joke, calling them Kain and Abel."

"Kain murdered his brother," Marie said.

"Just like Schlinge," Karin replied.

"And what is 211?"

Before Karin could shrug, the tram jerked, eliciting a spasm of screams and sending the girls forward against the railing. The wheels squealed and lit the street with a shower of sparks as the wagon skipped and shuddered to a stop in the middle of the block.

Passengers were tossed like chestnuts in a roaster. Shards of light flickered from outside.

Karin climbed to her seat and helped Marie. Rudi was slumped in front of his seat, with Elfreda on top of him, gasping for air. Heads popped up all along the rows. The aisle began to clear.

Everyone's attention turned to the front window, where the driver was pointing at the reason for their sudden stop. In the dim headlight they saw, on the wet cobblestones in the center of the tracks, a baby carriage, only meters away.

The driver opened the door and clomped down the steps. Everyone was watching when he stepped into the beam, stooped over the carriage, and peered into it.

He rose up and rubbed his head. Then, shielding himself from the light, he began to scan the darkness all around. Another moment, another rub of the forehead—then he moved behind the carriage and grasped the handle. He pushed. The carriage began to roll, one revolution of the wheels, and then another.

A hail of dark objects sailed through the light and pattered on the pavement. Something struck the driver in the head, snapping it back. His arms let go of the carriage, his legs gave way, and he twisted slowly to the street with an awful *thunk*.

Elfreda screamed.

Karin climbed over Marie into the aisle.

Rudi's mouth hung open, dumbstruck.

Karin stepped over a boy face down in the aisle, moaning, who had been flung forward from behind. She pulled herself forward and descended the steps to the open door.

Outside, on the pavement, the air was still and foreboding. Darkness had grown in the few minutes since they had left the hall, accentuated by the blacked-out streetlamps, casting an eerie pall over the intersection.

She paused at the door. The driver lay in a heap beside the carriage, arms twisted awkwardly around him. By the light of the tram's beam, she saw the shine of blood covering his head and face. A chunk of brick lay still beside him. Then it all made sense. The baby carriage was empty, a decoy. The Freedom Gang had planned a second attack.

A clunk rang out from behind. She turned in time to see the storm break in a volley of debris that hit the tram broadside, smashing windows, clanking off the metal sides, and terrifying the passengers inside.

It was impetus to move forward. When she reached the driver, he had regained consciousness. She helped him to her knees and gagged. Blood, pouring from the gash on his head, covered his eyes and face while he searched for the source with his hands. They were covered with the sticky dark liquid. He began to shake.

"I've got you," she said, pulling at his arm. He staggered to his feet. If they could get back to the tram, he could get it moving and they would be safe.

Karin turned back to the tram. A second barrage hit the flanks, tearing at the paint and breaking more glass. Screams were followed by another sound—laughter from the shadows.

Then a chunk whistled past her face.

They're on to us!

She spun around in front of the driver and dipped under his arm. She lifted and, using her body as a shield, began to drag him back toward the tram.

Shouts rang out from the darkness. A projectile smacked the pavement behind her and glanced off her ankle. She staggered, wincing in pain, but managed to keep her feet. A voice above the others called out.

"Halt!"

Other voices shouted indistinguishably. A hail of smaller stones rained down on them. More shouts, angry and chaotic.

They reached the door, and she pushed him through. He fumbled for the railings and managed to pull himself in.

She reached inside. Her fingertips touched the shiny brass handrail and slipped around the cool metal when what seemed like the blow of a sledgehammer hit her in the small of her back. The immediate sensation of pain seared a stab of heat through her entire body, and then nothing—no feeling and no strength. Her legs turned to sand, and she fell hard to the street.

From her back she watched Rudi through the open door, bent down in the aisle, tugging at the driver's sleeves as he clambered up the steps.

The damp cobblestones against the back of her blouse brought a strange, cool relief.

Then something new whizzed overhead. A blue flicker, a pop when it crashed against the window frame, and then the smell of burning petrol. Flames dripped down the side of the tram, evoking a new wave of screams, while remnants of the shattered bottle rained down to the street.

Karin's frenzy reached a new fever, but she could not seem to gather enough focus to stand.

Rudi hoisted the driver the rest of the way up and threw him into his seat. "Get it moving!"

The driver blinked through sticky blood and fumbled for the brake lever.

Rudi leaned out to Karin. "Take my hand! Take it!"

Karin pushed up with her arms and strained with all her might to reach him. Rudi's hand was shaking like a dead branch in a storm.

She snatched it. His hand was cold and wet, the bones sharp beneath his skin.

The tram lurched forward, nearly snapping Karin's arm, but the force was too much. Rudi let go. Karin slapped back down to the pavement.

"Stop!" Rudi shouted. "Stop I say!"

The driver obeyed and the tram jerked to a stop. Rudi, still inside the stairwell, called for help while he adjusted his footing. He leaned out again, took hold of Karin higher on her wrist, and squeezed.

He had just begun to pull when the last barrage struck. The projectiles were small, but the volley the most intense of all.

The burst caught Karin in the back, and Rudi took it square in the face. It broke his will, his grip, and he fell back against the steps.

Down for the last time, Karin lifted her head. Rudi was a heap in the stairway. The driver, hunched low in his seat, wore a look of twisted panic on his blood-blackened face. Their eyes met briefly before he looked away. He had had enough. The door closed. The tram whined off.

Karin was left alone in the silent darkness.

CHAPTER TWENTY-THREE

Karin opened her eyes to a dull, gray light. High above, on the iron frame of a broken window, a ragtag group of pigeons jockeyed for position, slapping their wings together, the beats echoing in the cavernous ceiling. For a brief instant, she was unconscious of day and time, simply fixated on the dirty birds.

Where am I?

She swallowed against a desert-dry throat. Every joint seemed clamped in place and moved with sharp, painful protest.

The foul smell of urine penetrated quickly to her stomach. She rolled sideways and retched, the spasm reverberating to the soles of her feet. It yielded but a lone, sticky strand that tethered her mouth to the edge of the mat, leaving her throat on fire.

Corroded iron pillars formed four corners of what was once some kind of interior room within a larger industrial expanse. Most of the plaster of the interior walls had been removed, exposing longer views into what could have been a factory or warehouse, where distant walls of brick were cracked and open in spots to the streets, buildings, and sky beyond. Fear brought her fully awake. *I must get out of here.*

Voices rang out from the distance. In an open space at the heart of the structure, she saw a group of figures standing around a smoldering fire that burned in a shallow depression that could have been hollowed out by a bomb. Their attention was drawn to one of the boys on the far side of the circle and the object he was holding. He lifted it and held it high above his head for all to see—a rifle. Karin froze.

She instantly recognized him—the one called Ziggy—the boy from the tram, and before that, the park. Today he seemed to prefer the rifle to the knife. The others looked to him like a leader, huddled close and pawing at the rifle like a Christmas toy.

Without warning, Ziggy looked up and locked stares with Karin. His eyes swelled with anticipation as if the exhibition of the rifle was simply killing time for something more important. Everyone turned in unison, and all at once, every eye was on her.

Ziggy lowered the rifle to his hip and swept it in a lazy arc across the group. Terrified, they drew back as he laughed. Then his expression changed again. He lifted the rifle to his shoulder.

The sight of the perfect circle of the muzzle turned Karin to stone. She could not even close her eyes.

Click.

Her heart stopped mid-beat.

The blast came in the form of laughter. The boy looked up and widened his eyes at Karin in a crazy grin. Someone slapped him on the arm in congratulations. Others followed.

The adulation continued for a moment while his defiant gaze lingered. Karin, held by some invisible force, couldn't move and couldn't breathe. When the boy's stare finally broke and he joined in the celebration, she took a breath but wondered if she might faint. She had to get up. She twisted on the mat, but her legs were like rubber. Her vision wavered with every throb.

She closed her eyes. Tears welled and fell to the blanket.

Get up!

"Don't mind them."

The voice, close behind, struck like a hammer. "Everyone is brave when the rifle is empty. Time will come and then we'll see."

Gingerly she turned. He sat crossed-legged, balanced on a crate, dabbing a nervous rhythm with his spit-shined shoe. Dark trousers, cut off as with a knife, exposed spindly ankles that matched his white socks. He was lost in the striped suit coat three sizes too large.

"You've got a nasty gash on your head," he observed. "It bled a bit, too. Sorry about your blouse, but the sleeves were the only clean cloth we could find."

Karin threw the musty blanket off and beheld her bare arms and jagged sleeves. She reached up and felt a cloth bandage. They had wrapped the material around her head and tied it off in the back. She slid her fingers toward the source of the throbbing. The lump felt like an egg in the corner of her forehead and sent shockwaves through her.

"Help me get up, please," she said, pushing up from the mat. The iron posts began to spin. She stopped, sat back down, and closed her eyes again, trying to push the dizziness away.

"You're in no shape to get up yet," he said. "Give yourself a minute."

A few moments later, she opened her eyes again. Holding still seemed to help.

Details she had been unable to see that night in the park came into focus. His hair, dyed coal black and shaved on one side, hung like a shroud across half his face, accentuating the chiseled cheek and beak-like nose. A lone eye that peeked out from behind it, dark, sunken, and sad.

"You're Frei," she said.

He uncrossed his legs and cocked his head. "The Jugend Kohl told you."

Karin didn't acknowledge Rudi.

"Frei is an odd name. Why not Frie... like Friedrich?"

"It's Frei, like Freiheit."

"Freedom?" she said. "Here?"

"That's right, and that's what I am—free. No one tells me what to do, and I don't tell them either."

Her memory sharpened—the disrupted ceremony, the tram attack—and then being left behind. The realization struck like a bolt from the blue. The gang had captured her. She had to get out of there. She pushed up once more.

Frei stood up and took her by the arm.

"What's the hurry?" And then, as though he had read her mind, "You're not our prisoner."

With his help, she stood. Her legs were like a newborn calf. She waited, hoping the jackhammer would settle. They had laid her on the concrete floor, softened only by a few yellowed newspapers and thin musty blankets.

"I want to go home," she said.

"Soon," he replied.

"Now."

"Not yet. Not safe."

"From whom?" she asked.

"Settle down, fraulein. You've got a nasty crack on that head of yours, and trust me, I've seen plenty, thanks to your boyfriends in the Hitler Youth. You don't want to rush home just yet."

"I didn't get mine from them, you might recall."

"You should have stayed in the tram, I guess," he said with a shrug.

"Stayed in the tram? You might have killed the driver. I couldn't just leave him to bleed to death outside."

"No one was supposed to get hurt," Frei said.

"Good to know. I feel so much better now."

"That's not what I mean. They were supposed to throw at the tram. Just a volley or two. Just to harass your boyfriend Kohl."

"He's not my boyfriend."

"We didn't expect you to go outside. I tried to stop everyone, but by then, the fever was out of control." Frei's voice changed. "I'm sorry."

Strange as it was, she believed him.

"You know, you've got far more courage than him."

She said nothing.

"Do you have a name?" he asked.

"Karin."

He smiled. "That's nice. Much nicer than the one they came up with."

"Are you going to tell me?"

"Blutchen," he offered. *Little bloody one.*

She let go of him and placed a hand on an iron post. Throbs continued to radiate in a steady rhythm, but the space was no longer spinning.

"How about something to eat?" he offered. "To get your strength back."

Frei bent over and retrieved a broken slat from a crate that he used as a tray. On it sat a dirty spoon, in whose basin sagged a chunk of gray, slimy meat. Accompanying this main course was a piece of broken roll and a brown bottle whose cap was off.

"No, thank you," she said, not masking her disgust.

"Suit yourself. The others will fight over it with gratitude." He set it down on the wooden crate beside him.

"What time is it? And how long have I been here?"

"We are free from the slavery of time around here, but it's early, I know that much. You've been here since last night."

She realized that her red kerchief, BDM armband, and lapel pin were missing. She reached in her pocket, and the statue was gone, too.

"Where are my things? What have you done with them?"

He patted his breast. "They're safe with me, but," he added, tossing a glance over his shoulder, "some among the gang don't like the reminders of, well, *who you are*."

"You have no idea who I am."

Frei began to laugh, which evolved into a coughing rattle.

"I know, I know, you're not like them. I've heard it once; I've heard it a thousand times. You don't have a choice. You must join the Hitler Maidens or Führer Boys." He mocked the names on purpose.

"You're no different from them," she said, trying a step. "Absolutely confident in your own version of the truth. Always talking, never listening. You have no idea."

Letting go of both Frei and the post, she tried a few wobbly steps. He stepped close and took her by the arm.

"You *don't* have to obey them," he said. "You do have a choice."

"I want to go home. Please give me my things and show me the way out."

Just then, she stepped on an uneven place in the concrete. She stumbled and clamped hard on his arm.

"I told you, we can't leave just yet."

"My head will be fine. And you said I'm not your prisoner."

His eyes shifted sideways.

"I thought you were smarter than this. We're not on the best terms with the polizei. So daytime travel is not...convenient."

Karin let go of Frei's arm to test her own strength. The desire to leave had a powerful effect. She took a solo step.

"I don't need you! Just point me in the right direction, and I'll find my own way back."

The commotion drew the attention of the gang. They gathered around her, six or seven altogether, a mix of tattered, multi-colored shirts, blousy trousers, and baggy coats. She presumed they were boys but couldn't tell for sure. Their faces were pale, eyes with blackened circles, hairstyles too similar, too bizarre. Their voices were loud and agitated.

"She can't stay here," said Ziggy, the rifle cradled in his arms.

A figure pushed forward in the crowded space. Despite the oversized clothes, her fire-red hair, cropped short but for two tufts on the sides tied with white ribbons, gave her away. Zara was drilling Frei with piercing blue eyes.

"Get rid of her," she snarled. "Or we will."

Frei stepped forward.

"I told you, Zara, she's been injured. I'll move her when it's safe."

Zara stabbed her finger in his chest.

"It's not safe now. Not with her here."

The others grunted in agreement.

"I was just leaving," Karin said, climbing to her feet. She was still lightheaded but determined.

Zara pulled past Frei and met Karin face to face, standing just shorter than Karin. A field of faint freckles spread beneath her eyes. Something in her aggressive persona didn't ring true.

"It's not that easy, Blutchen."

Frei pulled at Zara's arm. "Don't worry. She has no idea where we are."

Zara snatched it away. "But she's seen plenty. Too much, and we can't risk it."

"Risk what?" Karin asked.

Zara stepped closer and stuck her chin forward. "That's cute, blondie," she said. "Like you don't know who we are, and we don't know who you are. Try again."

"I have no idea who you are," Karin said. It was the truth.

Frei wedged back between them. "Calm down, Zara. I've told her nothing. I'll take her home now. There's nothing to worry about."

Zara twisted her snarl into a sarcastic smile. "That's sweet of you, Frei," she said, nuzzling up to him. "Just walk her down the street and drop her at the door. I suppose a goodnight kiss for your trouble?"

"That's enough, Zara!" he said, pulling her off. "I should stuff that mouth of yours with a chunk of this concrete."

"I dare you to try!"

They came eye-to-eye, only millimeters apart. Her voice was low.

"Since when are you so concerned with taking care of Nazis? Taken a liking to Hitler's girls, have you?"

Frei's face went white. The others exchanged nods of agreement.

Karin stepped forward.

"I'm no Nazi. And I'm not one of Hitler's girls. By that logic, you're Frei's girl. And his, and his, and his too," Karin said, pointing to the surrounding boys.

They burst out laughing.

Karin turned to Frei.

"I want my armband and pin. And my statue. *Now*. And if you don't show me the way out, I'll find it myself."

Her show of strength was mostly a bluff. She was barely able to stand, let alone fight. But Opa would be worried sick for her. The girls too. She just had to get away.

For a moment, the gang seemed off balance. Zara was embarrassed, Frei was caught in a tug-of-war between them, and the boys were content, it seemed, to sit back and enjoy the show.

Zara recovered first. She took a step and had Karin by the blouse. Karin's stomach fell, and her head erupted again.

Frei wedged between them and tried to push them apart. The girls struggled back and forth, Frei in the middle. Zara's eyes were white with rage. She didn't realize it, but her grip on Karin's blouse was what kept Karin upright.

"Calm down, Zara!" Frei said.

"Nobody talks to me that way!" she snapped.

Frei twisted hard on Zara's wrist and broke the grip on Karin's blouse. Karin staggered back, white spots flooding her vision, into the arms of one of the boys.

"Everybody talks to you that way!" Frei laughed. "And you never do anything about it."

A quick nod brought help from a pair of the others. A moment later, they had Zara between them, nearly off the ground, but under control.

Karin squeezed her eyes shut to focus her strength. She did not want to pass out again. She had to get out of there.

"People will be missing me today," she said. "They know where I was last night and where the tram was attacked. No doubt they're looking already. Do you want them to find you?"

Frei took pause at her question. He took a step back, found a flat chunk of concrete, and sat down. With a bony finger, he began to rub his chin.

"Zara, if you can behave yourself, I'd like to ask you a question."

"Let me go."

"Only if you promise to behave."

Zara nodded. Frei tossed his head toward the boys holding Zara and they let her go.

"How long have we been together, you and I?"

"Almost a year. Just after the invasion of Russia."

"Oh, yes," Frei said. "Operation Barbarossa. Named for the Kaiser Rotbart, the red-bearded one. Tried to conquer Italy four times and failed four times. Hitler is on his second campaign in Russia. Mark my words—it won't take four tries before he learns his lesson."

"I'm so impressed. But what does that have to do with how long we've been together?" Zara asked.

"Ah, yes. In that time, have I ever given you reason to doubt me?"

Zara looked genuinely confused. "Every day! You're making no sense."

"What I'm trying to say is that you have my word as a—as a scholar *and* a gentleman."

"You're a rebel and a thief," Ziggy interjected.

Frei grinned. "Fine. You have my word as a rebel and a thief that I'll deliver her back to her kind and leave no trail back to us."

"It's too much of a risk," Ziggy said.

Karin stepped forward.

"I don't know what you're up to here and I don't care," she continued. "I didn't choose to come here. I won't tell anyone, I promise." She looked at the ruins. "There's nothing to tell. Please just let me go home."

"Home?" Frei seemed insulted. "You know what, fraulein, I used to have a home. It might well have been a barracks. Arms high, legs snapping, neighbors snitching on neighbors. Always on the lookout for the slightest hint of disloyalty. You call that home?"

"Please," Karin replied, looking around at all of them. "I don't know what kind of life you live—here. Not everyone could do it, I'm sure. But that doesn't mean I'm a goose-stepper. Like you, I just want to be left alone. I want to survive them and this war. I do what I have to. I'm not like them."

Karin's last sentence rang hollow, even to herself. Frei jumped to his feet like something had bitten him.

"And I suppose that means wearing the uniform, sieg-heiling, and obeying your masters, huh? You're a pretty girl, what else? Everyone knows what the Nazis expect of their women."

Without thinking, Karin drew back and slapped him across the face.

Frei winced and blinked and then drew his tongue across his lips to wet them. Something in his expression changed. It wasn't that he believed her, but he seemed somehow satisfied.

Zara smiled at Karin and then turned to Frei. She put her arms around his neck, pulled him close, and kissed him.

"Let her go," Ziggy said.

On the sidewalk outside, Karin was eager to remove the blindfold. Frei had secured the smelly rag around her head before they left. He led her along a winding path, down some stairs, and through a narrow passage sour with urine and feces. Pigeons flapped somewhere overhead. Between the blindfold and her splitting head, she had no idea of their path. The fresh air and gentle rain were a relief when they came.

She reached up to remove the blindfold, but Frei blocked her hand.

"Not yet," he said. "A bit farther."

He led her by the elbow over a hard surface. The street was quiet.

"Where are you taking me?" she asked.

"Far enough that you don't know where you were," he answered. "Don't worry, I'll find you a tram back to Mittelsdorf."

Karin stopped. So, he had recognized her after all.

Frei laughed. "When I saw you last night, I felt I had met you before. But I couldn't place the face. I remembered just now. That night in the park."

They started up again.

"Why were you there?" Frei asked.

"I might ask you the same," she countered.

Frei paused. "There's a curb—careful now. Look, if you tell me, I'll tell you."

Karin edged her toe over the edge of the walk and stepped down.

"I was just taking a walk," she said.

"Your boyfriend didn't look your type. Very serious."

She jerked her elbow from his grip and stopped.

"I told you before. Not in a thousand years," she answered.

"You too looked, shall I say, very close. And who can blame you—breaking curfew and all."

She cut him off. "What kind of boyfriend uses his girlfriend as a shield against you and your thugs? He was on patrol. I got caught."

"That's good," Frei said, pulling her on. "Then I have a chance with you. And please, in the future, call my people 'bodyguards.' They get a bit testy being called 'thugs.'"

She ignored him. He led her up the opposite curb and they continued.

"So, what were you doing alone in the park?"

After a pause, she answered. "Call it my own version of freedom. Is it much farther?"

Progress with the blindfold was slow. The longer they continued, Karin began to wonder if Frei was leading her in circles. The rain had become steady. Her head pounded mercilessly, and every step sapped more strength.

Although Frei seemed more court jester than gang leader, he was obviously intelligent and his followers dangerous. As they trudged on, she came to a realization: she knew more about the gang than anyone in the Hitler Youth now, probably even the Gestapo.

She stopped and pulled the blindfold down.

"We're not getting anywhere with this thing on."

They were on a deserted street of mixed brick shops, garages, and warehouses. Many looked deserted, not just from air-raid damage.

"You shouldn't have done that," Frei said. "Zara would skin you if she were here."

"I think Zara would skin you if she were here," Karin said, and started on. The rain continued, and a chill had risen in the air. Ahead, far beyond the jagged roofline, the spires of the Great Cathedral swirled among low clouds. They might have been north in Nippes or northwest in Ehrenfeld, Karin couldn't be sure. She wondered if she could find them again, if she wanted to. Perhaps she could. Mulling this over stirred strange feelings inside. Their attack was reason enough to tell Rudi everything, even though she shared none of Rudi's zeal for pursuing this Freedom Gang. She would have been content simply to get away from this awful place. But now, given everything she had seen and learned, she came face-to-face with a sober conclusion: she might need to use this information later.

She was moving faster now without the blindfold, despite the pain. Frei had to increase his stride to keep up.

"What's your plan for the rifle?" she asked.

He stopped and let her carry on a few strides.

When she turned, his stance had changed. His shoulders had dropped and so had his expression. He shook his head.

"You're just like the rest of them," he said.

Rain ran down the strands of black hair and formed into large, tear-shaped drops before it fell. He raised his hand and slowly backed away.

"Go!" he hissed. "Go!"

Karin turned and ran, despite her brain slamming against her skull with every stride. The rain stung her face, as cold as the shame was hot.

Perhaps Frei is right. I am one of them.

CHAPTER TWENTY-FOUR

Doctors wanted to keep Karin in the hospital a full week after her ordeal, but after three days, she had convinced Opa she would escape on her own if they didn't release her. Promising a strict home routine of bed rest, Opa was successful convincing the doctors. Karin had other ideas.

Marie, a welcome visitor during her stay, had their home in a condition neither Karin nor her grandfather had seen since Oma had died. The clutter of dirty clothes, plates, and dishes had virtually disappeared. The smells of spoiled leftovers and scrapings were replaced by the clean aromas of fresh bread, disinfectant, and, at the center of the kitchen table, a bouquet of freshly cut daffodils in a clean vase.

Sitting in the kitchen, Karin asked, "Is there anywhere you didn't clean?"

Marie shrugged with a smile.

"You put me to shame. But I thank you from the bottom of my heart."

Marie wasn't the type to bask in the compliments, because she was already preparing the table for the midday meal. The rich aroma of onions filled the house.

"I had planned a delicious hasenpfeffer," she said with a playful frown, "but the rabbit had other plans, it seems."

Karin found the cupboard stacked high with clean plates, a state she had never accomplished on her own.

"Now don't make me call that doctor," Marie said playfully. "You sit here while I get things ready."

Just then, the doorbell rang.

"Don't move. I'll get it," Marie said.

A moment later, when she returned, her face had fallen. Karin knew before Marie spoke.

"Tell him I'm not well enough to see visitors." Karin broke open a wide grin. "Except you."

Marie complied, only to return quickly, her expression little changed.

"He insists. He says he has something important. It can't wait."

Karin crimped her face.

"Tell him I'm not properly dressed."

Marie raised an eyebrow. "That's like blood to a shark."

"Blast him! What does he want?"

"He won't say, but he looks serious. You'd better see him."

Karin had barely agreed when Rudi appeared in the doorway. To her surprise, he was not in his Hitler Youth uniform but instead wore dark gray trousers, an open-collared white shirt, and a brown, waist-length leather jacket. Karin was struck by the change. In one sense, he seemed less foolish, since to her the uniform was so pretentious. But in another way, he looked more serious, for the garb was much more like the Gestapo men.

"Pardon my appearance, Herr Kohl, but I just returned from the hospital." Karin said sternly, reminding Rudi that his visit was unwelcome.

"No need for apologies, fraulein. It is I who am here for an apology, on several accounts."

Karin gave pause at Rudi's words and demeanor. Without knowing him, she might have mistaken him for a regular boy. He seemed almost humble.

"First," he began, "my apologies for the interruption today. It's just that I have not ceased to worry about you from the moment I regained consciousness after that terrible night. I followed your recovery with great interest and cannot express enough my gratitude for your obvious good health."

Karin stole an unbelieving glance from Marie. Who was this talking? Where was the innuendo, the manipulation, the scheming? If she hadn't known him, she might have thought he sounded *genuine*.

"Thank you," Karin said.

"Second," he continued. "My sincerest apologies for the night of the attack. Reflecting on my actions, I see that I acted in a cowardly fashion. I was—*am*—embarrassed in contrast to the courage you displayed in helping the driver. Had I acted as I should, it would have been me kidnapped by the gang and in the hospital, not you."

For once, Karin didn't hold Rudi under suspicion. She didn't blame him. "It was a surprise attack," she said. "We all did what we could."

"A man of the Reich is a man of honor," he continued. "It is my highest duty to care for those in my charge, especially women. The maidens of the Reich are Germany's flowers and to be cherished. I failed in my duty. I am a disgrace to my uniform. I ask you to forgive me."

Karin was stunned. The words and demeanor were unlike anything she had ever experienced from Rudi. As she quickly replayed the words in her mind, she tried to detect traces of insincerity, a second or third layer of meaning, or a goal beyond her reach that would turn on her. But as the pause lengthened, she came upon nothing but the simple words, spoken with a unique sense of quiet that forced her to a singular conclusion: there was something human inside Rudi Kohl.

"Of course," she blurted, feeling the pause had been too long. "Of course, I forgive you." The words felt more like giving in than true forgiveness.

Rudi nodded his thanks and let out a deep breath. A weight seemed to lift from his shoulders. He turned to Marie. "If only others were so gracious," he muttered with a pained smile.

"Others?" she asked.

Rudi worked the brim of his hat with his hands as he looked down. "I've offered my resignation to Herr Gossen."

An awkward silence stretched between them. Finally, Karin remembered her manners, a notion, up until that moment, foreign to her relationship with Rudi.

"Would you like a cup of tea?" she asked, scarcely believing her own words. She could feel the wide eyes of Marie on her.

The offer seemed to take Rudi by surprise too, for he paused and let his eyes drift to a faraway place. Sadness appeared in his stare, and it occurred to Karin that never in Rudi's life had he been offered a cup of tea as a sincere extension of courtesy, much less friendship. Karin wondered for an instant what kind of person Rudi would have been had he never become a part of the Hitler Youth.

"Perhaps another time," he answered after a moment. "But I must go. And you must rest. Again, my apologies for the interruption. I know my way out. Good day, Fraulein Blik. Good day, Fraulein Kurtz."

He turned to leave.

Karin was more stunned than relieved. She could not imagine him refusing the kind of genuine offer she just made. She had been a target from the day he met her. Now, unbelievably, she almost felt sorry for him. Such a far fall. What would he do if not rule the Hitler Youth? He was like a shark with no teeth.

At the doorway of the kitchen, Rudi stopped. His head lifted and then, touching a hand to the door frame, he turned around.

"I had said before that I had several apologies. I had forgotten the last." His expression carried a sudden coldness and calculation true to form. Karin's sympathy vaporized. Rudi's hand came out of his pocket holding a sheaf of folded paper. He crossed back to the table and placed them in the space in front of her, smoothing out the folds so that its top page showed plainly. Without further comment, he turned and left.

Karin didn't show him out. Her eyes were locked on the header:

OFFICIAL CASUALTY LIST – COLOGNE DISTRICT – WEEK OF 9 – 15 AUG 1942

Her body began to shake. She pushed the papers away.

Marie rushed to her side. "What—?" She stopped.

Karin's eyes drifted over the lines that filled the page. Name after faceless name.

On the third page was an arrow penciled in the margin:

Stube, Willem S. - Korporal, Kompanie F, 192 Regiment, 6 Division. Vermißt. 17 Mai 1942. Kharkov, Ukraine.

Karin dropped the paper and turned to Marie. Her friend's eyes were already full to overflowing.

"I'm so sorry, Karin, so sorry." Marie embraced her and started to shake.

Karin held her friend stiffly. The tears would not come.

She could not escape the word: *Vermißt. Missing.* And she couldn't escape the conviction that although Hitler Youth leader Rudi Kohl had indeed fallen, he was still dangerous.

CHAPTER TWENTY-FIVE

arie flung herself at Karin. She might have thought she was comforting Karin, but the truth was more the other way around. Marie sobbed as though her own brother had been on the list.

As Karin stroked her soft hair, she realized her own feelings were far more complicated. Eventually, Marie realized it too. They sat back down at the kitchen table.

"Why aren't you crying?" Marie asked, blinking through her tears. Karin could not help but be drawn to her childlike appearance—pink splotches on her cheeks and matted eyelashes. She was truly a fawn among the wolves.

"I wish I could. Something must be broken. I just can't."

"Didn't you love him?"

Karin took Marie's hands.

"He was my friend, to be sure. Other than you, about the only one. He wanted it to be more—" Her voice trailed off.

"More? How did you know?"

Karin leaned back against the cushion and let her gaze drift away.

"I could just tell," she said. "In the way he paid so much attention to me. He would make nervous conversation when I got quiet. At other times, I would turn to him and get the feeling he had been watching me—you know, in a fond way."

"Did he ever...kiss you?"

The question drew a smile, and then a pang of guilt.

"No, he was too much of a gentleman for that. I suppose he knew our feelings weren't equal. When he left for the front—at the Bahnhof—I'll never forget. He asked me to wait for him."

The memory seared Karin's eyes.

"What did you say?"

Karin clenched Marie's hands. Tears began to fall like the first drops of a rain shower.

"Nothing," she answered. "The train left. I never answered."

Karin found a hand towel for Marie, who seemed embarrassed by the volume of her tears.

"What is it?" Karin asked.

"I lost my oldest sister Ingrid two years ago."

"The one Elfreda joked about?"

Marie nodded. "She was good, Karin. My closest friend. Kind to everyone, an angel really. On earth and now in heaven."

"I'm sorry, Marie. I didn't know. Why would Elfreda tease you? What a beast!"

"I don't know, Karin. She likes to start rumors. But Ingrid was a good German girl, doing everything they told her. She was in Mecklenburg for her year of service, almost finished in fact, and they told us she drowned in the sea. I never got to say goodbye."

A wave of sobs swept over her. Karin held her close, wondering about *they told us.*

Grief kept Karin awake. She could only imagine what rumors Elfreda had started. Or whether Marie doubted the truth of what she was told. When her imagination raced, she jumped back to

Willem. She replayed the scene at the Bahnhof, but her imagined answers did not bring comfort. Truth was, Willem had only ever been, and was likely only ever to be, a friend. She regretted not making that clear and now was unlikely to have the chance. Missing was like a half-breath, an unfinished sentence, a giant question mark after every thought.

Eventually, exhaustion conquered the sadness and Karin slept. Within the cocoon of her room, in the darkness of the blackout curtains, day and night became indistinguishable. When she finally awoke and peered outside, her body's clock and the sky over Cologne were momentarily at odds until she went downstairs and learned from the kitchen clock that it was evening, not morning. Opa had already retired to the shed, which made her glad, because she wanted to be alone. Alone was the choice she always made when things went wrong, the path she always followed. Willem had warned her against this before he left.

"What will you do when I'm gone?" he would ask. "You can't live like a hermit. You'll be seventeen and shriveled up already, just like your old grandfather."

Willem didn't know how the words stung. He was right, she knew, but he was so blunt, too. Isolation for Karin didn't seem so much as a choice but a conclusion—the inevitable result of experience. Moving all over Europe every year, one learned not to get too close to friends. Two years in Cologne hadn't changed anything. And family? What example did they set for dealing with the unbearable events of life? The part of Karin that was true and alive seemed out of reach to her now, buried deep in a cave, a cave whose entrance had been blown shut and smoothed over, invisible to anyone passing by.

When Karin curled up on the sofa in the front room with her grandmother's journal, she didn't realize how desperate she was. She didn't understand that she was reaching for the one person in the world who had truly loved her. She started at the back, with the last entry, when Oma was sick:

30 Oktober 1941

The garden got the better of me this year. Next Spring I'll see if Karin will help. Perhaps the garden will take her mind off things.

22 Mai 1941

Thanks be to God! His warmth returned to the earth, and I touched it with my hands and fingers today. The lettuce will raise its hands in praise, the beans ring their silent bells in the breeze, and tomatoes will store up his goodness for all to enjoy!

16 September 1936

Thank heavens for the garden. The vegetables keep us alive. But too bad we can't live off weeds. I would never go hungry!

2 August 1934

The man Papi calls "The Little Austrian" has earned a new title: Der Führer. He promises a new Germany. What's wrong with the old one? If the politicians would just leave the people alone.

4 Juli 1925

Joy of joys! Heaven's blessing came today. Karin Elise Blik. A round and red cherub. Max and Ursula are so proud, and Even Papa raised a glass of schnapps. Poor Ursula—the whole process seemed foreign to her. I never imagined her as a mother, but a baby can sometimes change things. And what a beauty she is!

Karin pulled the journal close, nestling it in a warm embrace as she leaned over against the padded sideboard. She let her eyes close.

If only Oma was here now...

Moments later, the sharp ring of the telephone roused her. She leapt from the sofa and crossed to the table near the front door. Despite their strained relationship, Karin still wanted her mother. After the attack, she had hoped Mother would come. As the hours turned to days without her arrival, that hope died. Now, the ringing phone evoked dread.

"Mother, is it you?"

"Hello, dear. What on earth happened?" Mother's voice was clear, but characteristically distant.

"I'm fine," she lied.

"Were you hurt?"

"Just a few scratches."

"Well, nobody tells me anything around here."

"Will you come visit me?" Karin blurted and instantly regretted it. She feared the answer.

"Well, child, I would have been there last week, but the trains are dreadful. Berlin is full of soldiers these days and the army has priority, I'm sure you understand."

"But you'll still come, then?"

There was a brief pause.

"I've spoken to Papi. He says you're fine now. And I have a better idea. Actually, that's why I'm calling. You remember Gauleiter Simon? The Führer appointed him Chief of Administration in Luxembourg at the beginning of the war, and you won't believe this, but he's made our house there his residence! He's making a big announcement next week—actually two announcements—and Heinrich and I are the guests of honor. You could stand the change, dear—the sweet air above the casemate walls instead of that soot you breathe in Cologne!"

"I don't want to go to a party."

"I've never understood you, Karin. I can't imagine a girl your age not jumping at the chance to dress up, mingle with staff and officers, enjoy delicious food and drink."

"That's your dream, Mother, not mine."

"No matter. All you have to do is smile, say hello, and hold out your hand. You can just make an appearance, for our sake—*my sake*—and then spend the rest of the time as you like. Just imagine it, Karin, back in our old house?"

Luxembourg was the place that held her happiest memories and darkest days. The possibility of return had never occurred to her. She was afraid of the memories and yet drawn to them.

"Heinrich has arranged for a car to pick you up on Friday morning. Do you still have that blue dress I sent at Easter? Summer is not quite finished and so it should still work. Perhaps bring a sweater to cover your arms if we get a chill."

The plan settled, her mother filled the silence with dronings about Berlin's social life, who was rising, who was falling, and how she supplemented her food rations by carrying an oversized handbag to official functions and stuffing it full of choice delicacies. Eventually she realized she was the only one talking.

"Karin? Are you still there?"

"Yes."

"You're not saying anything. You aren't in one of your moods, are you?"

"You don't want to come."

"Now, don't jump to conclusions. I didn't say that. You always go to such extremes."

"But I'm right, you don't."

Through the line, Karin heard her mother take a deep breath. She would feel cornered now, but Karin didn't care.

"Frankly, dear, I'm surprised. I mean, after all this time. I thought you liked our arrangement. Ever since your father passed away, we're like—you know—oil and water."

Karin was not defensive. For once, her mother spoke the truth.

"Yes, Mother, I know. It was like that before."

"Before? What on earth do you mean?"

Karin realized the telephone was shaking in her hands. She had to grip it with both hands to steady it. With a shaky breath, she realized just how exhausted she was. Despite everything, she longed to trust her mother, to be taken care of.

"I'm afraid."

"Pardon me? Did you say afraid?"

"Yes, Mother."

"Oh, my goodness, Karin. You've always been so capable. Who on earth are you afraid of? That gang? I spoke with the police. They assured me these gangs are after the Hitler Youth, not quiet girls like you."

"No, Mother. Not the gang." She hesitated.

"I don't understand, Karin. What are you afraid of?"

The knot was now a stone in her throat, growing and pressing the base of her skull, sending throbs of pain up the center of her brain. Could she speak openly? Could she trust her mother?

"The others."

"What others? You're confusing me."

Karin hesitated. "I'm not sure I can say. Please, Mother. I need you."

The pauses between them had grown longer and longer. Karin could barely hold the phone, let alone insert words into the chasm between them.

"My dear girl," Ursula finally said. "Listen, when the term is over, why don't you come to Berlin? Wouldn't that be nice? I'll take you shopping. You'd be surprised at what one can still find if one knows where to look. It's still the capital after all..."

Karin said nothing. Her mother was adept at filling silence.

"I imagine you're quite attractive by now. Willem probably couldn't keep his eyes off you, I'm sure. It's about time you started learning how to move in Nazi society. I'll show you."

Crushed, Karin started to lose her grip on the phone.

"Are you still there, Karin?" When Karin didn't answer she began to speak to herself. "What's wrong with this line? Has it gone down again? For heaven's sake!"

Karin let the receiver slip from her hand. It cracked against the hard floor. Karin wanted to cry, but it was choked by anger. She'd been a fool to think her mother cared.

Static chirped from the receiver for another moment before falling silent. Karin bent down, replaced the receiver on the cradle, and turned away.

That night Karin had trouble sleeping, and so she read Oma's journal again.

3 Februar 1918

Something has to give. The last of the canned tomatoes are gone, but in truth that last jar sat on the shelf in the cellar as a kind of symbol really—a reminder that we weren't starving. There's nothing on the shelves at the stores either. I'm lucky to get a loaf of bread once a week. Haven't had an egg since the fall. Papa doesn't complain, says our sacrifice is nothing next to that of Max. And he's right, but that doesn't make me feel less hungry. But at least I'm warm, and if I must skip tomatoes so that Max can have a hot meal wherever he is, then I'll gladly do it. I'm afraid to look at the potato bin. I only go after dark, so I don't have to see how empty it's becoming. We need a few for seed but what am I to do, boil the furniture?

16 April 1918

Will winter ever end? A few patches of green appeared around the edge of the garden. Please, sun, come! There's almost nothing to eat, but the hope of growth and blossoms lifts me, at least for moments here and there. At the market, everyone was buzzing at the news. The Russians are quitting in the East. Rumors of a Spring offensive in the West. Another promise to end the war. I wish I could share their happiness. When did we learn to cheer death? I ran into Frau Brüggemann, who said that with the Russians out of the war, it will go better for our boys in France. I'm selfish. The only "boy" I care about is Max. I tell Papa. What a mistake. "Not a chance!" he snaps, as angry and withdrawn as ever. "The Yanks are here—and they're fresh and fed!" "Will it ever end?" I moan. "Yes," he replies, "but not the way we all expect." I wish I had never left the house.

Karin closed the journal. Poor woman, how did she endure? And for what? Another generation and another war, but the same situation.

Sleep was on its way now. Karin laid the book down on the table, switched off the lamp, and let the darkness sweep over her. Sometimes the dark felt like a shroud, hiding her from the world. She let it settle over her so her eyes could adjust.

Careful steps later, she was at the window. Open curtains revealed a featureless night. She lifted the window to let the night come in. It was cool, with a faint breeze, and best of all, no bombers. The rush of air brought the scent of clean earth. The same smell Oma enjoyed. Returning to the bed, she let the sounds sweep over her—the rustle of trees, a few young insects. She remembered Oma's last wish:

Perhaps the garden will take her mind off things.

After an interval, a new sound arose above those of nature. A single metallic knock at first, it grew louder and became a tapping rhythm. It reverberated from the downspout to her right. A trapped bird? A squirrel?

Karin sat up. As she listened, she concluded it was neither, for the sounds were too loud, too deliberate, too much like a signal.

And then a voice: "*Psssssst!* Karin!"

CHAPTER TWENTY-SIX

S he padded downstairs and went to the back door of the house, where she pulled back the edge of the blackout curtain. Frei, in his oversized coat, stood at the bottom of the back porch steps as a dark, rectangular shape in the faint moonlight. She wondered about Opa. He was probably asleep in the shed as usual, but she couldn't be sure. If for some reason he woke up, he would be able to hear them if they talked on the back porch. She opened the door and, without a word, beckoned him in. She held the door open while he entered. The stench on him was so fierce that she buried her nose into the crook of her elbow as he passed. Once she had closed the door behind them and smoothed its window curtain, she switched on the kitchen light. In the span of four days since she had seen him, the change in his appearance was shocking.

"Yes, I know. It's a surprise to see you too," he said, tossing the long lock of greasy hair to reveal a grin.

"Sit down," she said coldly, indicating a chair at the table. He obeyed while she put the kettle on the stove. She tossed a few sprigs from a bin into a cup. While the water warmed, she retrieved a half-loaf of bread from the cupboard, a small pad of butter, and a hunk of white cheese.

"I wish I had more," she said, assembling it on a plate in front of him, "but I'm afraid I'm not much of a cook. My grandfather is starving."

It was a bad joke, made worse by the sight of him. He was disappearing in his suit. The ragged edges of the sleeves and hems gave the coat the look of a kind of animal skin, or what she imagined a shipwrecked traveler might wear. Frei's face, always thin, seemed to hang on his bones, with sharp lines at his cheeks and along his jaw. His eyes seemed yellow, set in dark sockets, like horror-movie makeup.

"You look awful," she said.

He seemed hurt. "It's nice to see you too."

"What are you doing here?"

"Wow, I guess you're to the point."

"I'm surprised. How did you get here?"

"Walked, mostly."

She crossed her arms. "No, I meant, how did you know where I live?"

"Not hard, not hard at all. I went to the hospital and told them I had helped you. For good measure, I added that I was your cousin and needed to return something you had left behind."

"It was that easy?"

"Sure. They keep meticulous records. The German way, you know. Looked you up and wrote it all down for me. Very efficient, very helpful. So here I am."

He reached down into his satchel and placed on the table her kerchief, armband, lapel pin, and the Gëlle Fra statue.

"We couldn't get anything for them," he said through a faint grin.

He tried to be polite with the food, but it was evident he had not enjoyed anything so good for quite some time. He ate with a look of suspicion in the corner of his eye, as if on the lookout for a thief. In a way, she felt sorry for him, despite knowing very little of him. She was tempted to scold him for the whole persona—the life of freedom on the streets, rebellion against convention, defiance, everything. Wasn't there a better way to survive in Nazi society? Hadn't she learned how to get along with Rudi, the Hitler Youth, and the BDM? Wasn't there another way to make it through the war?

"This is delicious," he said, finishing the last of the food. "I really didn't expect this, and I do appreciate it." He gulped the rest of the tea and set the cup carefully on the table. She refilled it and sat down.

"I haven't found tea anywhere in over a year."

"It's birch bark tea. My friend Marie's father went to Bavaria on business last fall. He brought the shavings back. We call it the new tea."

"It's a nice change from that sawdust they call coffee nowadays. You are a better cook than you give yourself credit for."

Frei cradled the warm cup with bony fingers, almost black with dirt except for the yellow nails, and took a sip. He let the steam rise over his face. With some color returning to his cheeks, his countenance changed. He seemed relaxed.

"Why did you come?" Karin asked.

"Ah, yes, of course." He pulled open one side of his coat to reach into the pocket, and Karin nearly gasped at the absence of a torso inside. He was focused on something in his pocket and missed her reaction. An instant later, the moment passed, the object was on the table—a piece of paper, rolled into a scroll and bound with a string.

She picked it up and turned it over in her hands. The thick, brown paper, used to wrap a package, had torn edges.

"A message?"

Frei nodded.

"I've had no contact with my family since the war began," he said. "We don't see eye to eye on most things. When I first left, I thought it would only be temporary. It's become a very long temporary."

He hesitated.

"It's time to let them know—it's time to say—" he hesitated. "It's just time, I guess."

"Your poor mother," Karin said, but then thought of her own mother and wondered if Frei had one like her.

"Will you take it to her?"

"Me?" she replied. "Why not take it yourself?"

Frei shook his head and stared past her like he was imagining her suggestion coming to life. "I can't."

"Why not? Surely, you're not afraid of being caught, are you?"

"No, not really," he said with a laugh. And then he grew instantly defiant. "They have no idea where to find me!" And just as quickly, the attitude melted. "But if they did, maybe it would be for the better."

"That's not funny at all."

He rotated his head as if his collar was too tight. "Sooner or later, this all needs to resolve itself. I'd like it to be on my terms, but I may not be able to control that. If it happens, I'll be ready."

Karin was stunned. He wasn't joking in the least. "Don't you know what they'll do to you?"

He leaned back and folded his arms. "No. Tell me, Maiden of the German Bund."

"What they do to anyone in their way. Put you in a camp."

"That would be fabulous."

"You don't know what you're saying."

"Then you say it. Speak the truth, Karin. The Nazis' power is in their secrets. It fuels their fears. So, when you speak in the open about the things they do in secret, you break their power. If you stay quiet, you perpetuate it."

She wondered if the lack of food had gnawed his nerves to their raw ends. Or perhaps the few bites just now had fueled a surge of determination.

"What on earth are you talking about?" she asked.

He stood up, scraping the chair behind him so hard it nearly fell over.

"Say it, Karin! What do the Nazis do to their enemies? Say it!"

She was frightened by his volume, as well as his presence. She knew what he wanted her to say. Her voice was low when she answered. "They mean to kill you," she whispered.

She braced, thinking he would want her to speak it louder, or to shout it. Crazy people could be like that. But Frei seemed satisfied.

"Now or later. Me today, everyone tomorrow. We all must die. At least I'll have the chance to make it spectacular."

"You're not well," she said. Whether she was serious or not, she wasn't sure herself, but after the words came out, it was clear that they hurt him.

He sat back down, let his head fall, and rubbed his face with a dirty, bony hand.

"I'm perfectly fine. It's you who is unwell. You who have been blinded and bound," he added. But then came a deep sigh, as if his energy was spent. He asked again, "Will you take this to my mother?"

She pushed the scroll back across the table at him.

"You should take it yourself. You know I'm right. Speak to your mother."

Mentioning his mother a second time evoked the same response. He seemed afraid.

"I just can't."

Karin shot up, disgusted. "What's wrong with you all?" Opa, Frei—both so locked in themselves. *Why?*

Frei pushed away from the table and stood up. With a sweep of his arm, he snatched the scroll and clamped it in his hand. "I was wrong to think you would understand." He stuck his chin forward. "Thank you all the same for the warning," he added sarcastically. "I have been duly warned."

He turned to leave.

Despite everything, she felt sorry for him. She remembered the moment she first laid eyes on him.

"Give it to me," she said, holding out her hand. "Before I change my mind."

He complied without a word.

As he passed through the door, Karin thought to call him back a second time and refuse to deliver the message until he agreed to take a bath and change his clothes. He would have been too proud to agree, she was sure. Watching him descend the back steps, almost held up by the worn-out suit, she felt only pity. The rectangular shape drifted across her garden and disappeared in the darkness. She felt sure she would never see him again.

CHAPTER TWENTY-SEVEN

The car arrived on Friday morning, exactly on time. Karin had barely slept—partly from anticipation, partly from the sirens that started just after midnight. She and Opa chose to watch from the garden rather than breathe the sour air of the cramped shelter. The flashes and rumble stayed north—Ehrenfeld or Nippes, Opa guessed—more like a distant thunderstorm than an air raid. While he dug, she tried to pick a few tomatoes, but in the darkness she couldn't tell the ripe ones by feel alone. Even after the sky quieted, the restlessness remained. She dreaded the journey—not the distance but the destination.

When they arrived six hours later, the memories flooded back—the iron fence out front, the stone pillars standing guard. *Fritz had saved her here once.*

The marble foyer was much the same, the den still lined with bookcases to the ceiling. Her father's office gave her pause. When she last saw him here, he'd been on the telephone, shouting at someone until he noticed her. When she was very young, such interruptions had been welcome; now her memory was of Father's look of irritation and the flick of his wrist to shoo her away. Later that day, when she and Hansi had seen Max at the tunnels, she obeyed him and went home, hoping against hope her fears were not true.

After a stiff greeting to her mother and barely acknowledging Schlinge, she asked, "May I walk the neighborhood? It might do me good to sweep out the old memories."

Ursula and Schlinge exchanged glances. Schlinge nodded.

"Don't go far," Mother said. "The reception starts at seven."

The street hadn't changed, trees lining the sides, a shrouded canopy overhead. She strolled beyond the diplomatic quarter to the flats and commercial district, and within minutes found herself at the Grand Place. Shoppers filled the Grand Rue—now called *Grossstrasse*—where nut roasters, flower vendors, and vegetable sellers offered their produce. Cobblestone streets, no vehicles—just as she remembered. The church, the gentle slope of the street, the casemate cliffs—where she had met Hansi. *A lifetime ago.* The valley opened beneath her and stole her breath.

"Moyen." The voice made her jump.

A German soldier had come up from behind. He tossed a roasted hazelnut from a paper cone into his mouth and crunched it loudly.

"I'm sorry, fraulein," he said, in German. "I don't know any more than that. We're not supposed to speak their version anyway. Do you care for a nut?"

"Nein, danke," she answered by reflex, which surprised him.

"I'm two times lucky—getting stationed here and meeting you!"

"Excuse me, but I've just realized I'm late for an appointment." She turned and left, almost at a run.

Later, at the reception, Ursula was the queen, adorned with sparkling finery. Despite her protests, Karin wore her BDM uniform at Schlinge's insistence.

"One day soon, I'll buy you a proper dress and everyone will finally see how beautiful you are," Mother said.

Never, Karin thought.

French champagne flowed. Food and delicacies were piled high on trays. At these parties in the past, Karin was always an outsider. Fritz had kept his eye on her, made sure she had proper food, a glass of sparkling wine, and a sweet treat. She missed him—especially now. Ursula was the star, as usual, but remained surprisingly well-behaved. Schlinge wore a crisply ironed suit that he managed to wrinkle in no time. She couldn't recall seeing his sagging, damaged face smile like this.

"Ladies and gentlemen," the Gauleiter said. He was a short man whose pinched face gave him the appearance of a rat. "This evening, we celebrate the triumphs of the Reich. Our armies stand at the threshold of victory at Stalin's namesake town, Stalingrad. General Rommel has the British on the brink in North Africa, and our U-boats have humbled the convoys of America. Here, I am pleased to announce the formal reunification of the German peoples of the Luxembourg region with the greater Reich—one people, one will, one future."

Everyone applauded and cheered. They toasted and drank. Karin felt squeamish. Everything about the evening felt disgusting. She retreated to the kitchen to find some solid food if it could be found—a chunk of cheese, a slice of bread, something, anything reminiscent of the old days under Fritz's care. A light outside caught her attention. Through the wide windows, across the back of the kitchen, a bulb shone down over the double doors of the garage. Memories flooded her imagination—Fritz bent over her father's Mercedes late into the night, washing, drying, polishing, buffing.

Her eyes drifted to the hook by the door where Fritz would hang his coveralls. One day, she had looked through his pockets and found a stash of lemon candy, which she could not help but sample. Soon her raids became a nightly habit. The hook was empty now, but above it was something she hadn't expected. A row of smaller hooks, where keys hung. Above the hooks, brass plates, engraved with the numbers: 210, 211, 212. Karin's heart surged.

She waited until the party was over—well past midnight—then left her room. She crept silently downstairs, still in her nightgown, listening carefully at every turn. She knew every centimeter of the house, even in the dark, and found a candle and matches exactly where she expected to, in the kitchen pantry. At the back door, she lifted key 211 from the hook and slipped out.

The moon lit Karin's way as she crunched carefully to the garage. To her surprise, the side door was unlocked. Her hands trembled with hope and fear as she pushed in. Her mind raced. How had Fritz designed such a plan for her to follow? How would he expect her to return to Luxembourg?

Inside, she steadied her breath and her hands and lit the candle. The garage she remembered was large enough for the Mercedes and, in the back, a shallow workbench, a few shelves, and a trio of steel lockers. On this night, the car was gone, leaving only sunken ruts in the brick floor, pressed by years of a half-ton vehicle. The candlelight danced in rainbows off oil-stained brick. The gray lockers stood guard shoulder-to-shoulder. Having set the candle down on the edge of the workbench, she approached the center locker. Afraid of the sound, she cupped one hand over the tumbler while she inserted and turned the key. The locker responded, but the door protested with squeaks at even the slightest movement. In an instant, the air had become stifling, forming sweat on her forehead. But in another, she determined that the sound couldn't be helped, and so she simply got on with it. The garage returned to silence.

Inside the locker, a rain slicker hung from a hook. At the bottom, a pair of rubber boots were stuffed awkwardly as though there was not enough space for them. *Not Fritz's way at all.* Karin removed them and set them aside. In the shadow of the raincoat sat a lump of canvas. Trembling, she reached in and felt a large, cylindrical object beneath the covering. It was heavy when she retrieved it. The canvas came away easily, revealing a spool of wire the diameter of a gramophone record and as thick as a hatbox. Trapped under loops of wire was something made of paper. She bent down with the candle, unraveled the wire, and freed an envelope, simply marked: *To Karin.*

She let out a small gasp and quickly unfolded the letter inside.

If you are reading this, then my wish has been fulfilled, though I fear yours may not.

That night after I drove you to Berlin, I was told to forget you and your family—whom I had served for so many years—forever. I was warned never to contact you or your mother, and to never mention anything about my years of service to anyone. In exchange for my silence, I was promised a modest pension. Given the shocking change of circumstances, I agreed, but to my shame. As weeks became months, and then years, a painful realization endured.

The afternoon of 14 November 1939, I thought, would live in my memory forever. But as my health faltered, so too did my memory, and I began to fear it would fade.

I knew something that a young girl would one day wish to know. Something that, if she did not learn it, might leave her vulnerable. And yet to know it—and be discovered for knowing it—carries its own danger. Still, I must tell it.

That afternoon, I heard your father and Herr Schlinge arguing in your father's office. Your father insisted Schlinge accompany him into the tunnel to assist with the wiring of the explosives and to keep a close eye on the expert they had employed for the work—a man your father had come to distrust. They quarreled about the sufficiency of the equipment and length of wire required for the operation. Schlinge insisted everything was in order and that he must leave for his appointment with Minister Dupong, what I only discovered later to be a crucial diversion. They argued frequently, and so I thought nothing much of it at the moment, since in the end, they left together.

My duty as a servant was always to remain silent and discreet in household matters, but later that day, I saw Schlinge return alone in a great hurry. He loaded a travel case in the rear of the car. I helped him, of course. When I opened the trunk, I noticed a large spool of wire beside a toolbox.

No one would have known this, but in my youth, I had worked on a construction team in Bavaria, blasting through the mountains. I recognized that spool of wire at once. Again, I am haunted by the fact that I hardly gave it a second thought until later, when your father never returned and I recalled their earlier dispute about the wire.

I am now convinced that Schlinge withheld the spool of wire on purpose, knowing that the final connection would be too short, and the resulting explosion fatal to everyone inside, including your father.

The terrible truth, my dear Karin, is that because the explosives in the tunnel never detonated, then something—or someone—else killed your father that day. Schlinge's goal was accomplished, just not by his own hand. He wanted your father dead, of that I am certain.

But why?

Sadly, the answer lies in another memory, long buried, and soon to be lost forever, but for this letter.

Earlier that same afternoon, I overheard Schlinge speaking with someone I now believe was your mother. "Don't worry," he said. "Everything will work itself out. Just trust me."

I believe he meant to kill your father in that horrible attack, but make it appear an accident.

I am sorry, dear Karin, that I no longer have the strength of body or mind to protect you. My only remaining duty is to the truth—and to you.

Yours,

Fritz

Light blinded her. Instinctively, she raised one hand to block it while she covered her chest with the other. The candle toppled over and sputtered out.

"What are you doing?"

Schlinge lowered the beam. He stood in the moonlight, still in his suit. The letter lay on the ground beneath her feet. He approached, then trained the beam on the open locker door.

"What are you looking for?"

"Nothing. I just needed to breathe."

"In a musty old garage? There's plenty of fresh air in the garden. I heard a noise. You were looking for something."

He came closer and saw the canvas, the spool of wire, and the letter at her feet. His eye twitched with understanding. He bent down, took the letter, and read it quickly.

"It's rubbish," he said, and to her surprise, handed it back to her.

"It is?" Karin replied.

"You're too clever to fall for this."

"Am I?"

"I thought you were, but perhaps I give you too much credit."

"When Mother hears this, she'll be done with you."

He paused. She suddenly felt very afraid and thought to scream.

"She already knows," he said calmly.

"You're lying," Karin said.

"Let me get her now," Schlinge replied. "Or why don't we go inside and talk about it with her?"

"Then it's true?"

"Not in the least. This rumor started not long after your father was killed. Your mother is not naïve."

Karin opened her mouth to protest.

"I am a powerful man, and not without certain rivals. Such is the nature of a competitive organization such as the Gestapo. I've tried to tell you, yet you insist on trusting...untrustworthy persons."

"I trust Fritz," Karin said.

"This is not from your friend Fritz, who is quite incapable of crafting such a letter. I warned you to be careful about Gossen.

He's charming, clever, too ambitious, and a bit jealous. He's been waiting to get at me since university, when Max won the Ursula contest. Now that I've jumped over him, he must be positively outraged."

"You're saying he arranged all of this?"

"It would be exactly like him—trying to distract from his own failures as an officer and a father. He knows that while truth simmers, scandal sizzles. You are useful to him—for now. But be careful, Karin, because you are also expendable. And you seem determined in your refusal to acknowledge that I protect you. The simmering truth here is that this letter proves nothing. Even if somehow this letter was from Fritz's hand, it's conjecture. A spool of wire means nothing, and the word of a broken, damaged man against an officer of the Reich? It means even less."

"You wanted Father to die."

"You're forgetting something, Karin, something quite important. The casemate tunnels didn't blow up. Neither the presence nor the absence of a spool of wire had anything to do with Max's death. And your stubbornness extends to refusing to acknowledge the most logical explanation."

"Hansi didn't do it," Karin said.

"He told you as much? Or do you have a letter from him also?"

Karin burned inside with anger and also despair.

"Go back to bed," Schlinge said. "You have a long journey in the morning."

The next morning, after a perfumed but lifeless goodbye from her robed and bleary-eyed mother, Karin insisted on taking the train back to Cologne instead of the car. She knew Schlinge would not refuse her.

The walk to the Gare Centrale was not as therapeutic as she hoped. While the quiet neighborhoods reminded her of carefree days of the past, the Municipal Park gardens were full of vegetables instead of flowers, and red banners hung from every lamppost. German soldiers were fewer than she expected, but brown-shirted men with VDB monograms on their armbands were reminders that the past was dead. Near the Pont Adolphe, she was horrified to see the gaping space—the Gëlle Fra was no more—only a stone slab.

Karin let the landscape and the rhythm of the rails soothe what they could, but she couldn't escape Schlinge's parting expression, indifference. That expression, indelible behind his scars, went deep under the surface, like a seed. He knew the truth she discovered in a spool of wire and a letter meant nothing without the one possession seemingly beyond her reach—*power*.

CHAPTER TWENTY-EIGHT

With summer at its peak, Karin relished the long afternoons and warm evenings in the retreat she had fashioned in the backyard. Young tomato plants had grown just tall enough to need support from wooden stakes, which Karin secured with strips of old cloth so as not to damage their tender stalks. Green pepper plants stood in tight columns at full attention below the mounds of earth where potato shoots stood watch. Rain was less frequent now, so Karin hauled water in buckets to keep the soil moist. The work was constant, and she loved every second spent in the small space behind their house that was walled off from the world and the war.

Opa's shelter, which was by now a brick-lined hole in the ground, was the only reminder of the war. The longer it remained unfinished, the more Karin began to wonder if the worst was past. The *Kölner Zeitung* made it seem so. According to their daily headlines, General Rommel's Afrika Korps was pushing the British west from Cairo all the way to Tripoli. In Russia, the new offensive was all roses—German Panzers were streaking once again through the flat plains. This summer's major news came from the south, where German forces were approaching the great city on the Volga that took their leader's name—Stalingrad. If the news stories were to be believed, the entire war hinged on the fate of that one place.

Karin tried to keep thoughts of war out of her mind. She didn't care about the strategy or big picture. To her, the war was just one tragedy chained to another, the latest being Willem. She tried not to imagine the possibilities of what going missing meant but couldn't help it. Professor Putz had forced the class to read a pamphlet on the eastern front battles. For the most part, it was full of glowing descriptions of German heroism—vast encirclements of Soviet divisions—thousands of prisoners, endless progress eastward. The photographs showed columns of German tanks, chewing up dust along the Russian plains, leaving burning hulks of Russian tanks and trucks in their wake. Dirty-faced but beaming German infantrymen enjoyed a cool drink of water. All smiles. But one image haunted Karin—German infantry marching past a dead Russian soldier along the side of the road. The soldiers grinned for the camera but were oblivious to the gruesome death at their feet. The fallen Russian was slumped against a broken wooden fence, his head cocked sideways, and his legs twisted in a grotesque position underneath him. He was stiff and ghostlike. Even though he was an enemy, Karin couldn't help but picture Willem in his place. The image was seared in her mind and dreams. Poor, poor Willem.

She felt guilty for letting him go without so much as a smile, much less a promise. He had loved her, she now realized, and although she didn't feel the same way, she could have treated him better. Much better. His going missing fueled not only guilt and sadness, but anger at the waste of such a promising boy. Missing was as terrible as dead and, in some ways, worse, because she would live not knowing. Another broken mother, too. The news of Willem opened a new drain in the sewer of hate she had developed for the Nazis. She had been a fool to think she could get along.

Karin's feelings had become very dangerous. She would have to find a way to hide them, to bury them. The garden was that place in an almost literal way. Amidst the death all around her, it was warm and green and alive. In every stab of the earth, weed pulled, and pail of water, she fought for her soul.

One afternoon, Karin sat in the kitchen with a cup of birch bark tea, watching the garden through the window. A summer shower was just ending, and the sun was seeking a crack between scattering clouds. She heard a knock at the front door.

Karin wasn't expecting visitors. Opa was out back in the shed as usual. She crossed to the doorway and paused, taking a private look at the front-door glass.

The knock came again, and a figure moved in front of the curtains, trying to get a look inside. A Hitler Youth in uniform. About twelve or thirteen, she guessed, probably making a collection for the war effort. Every scrap of aluminum, rubber, and paper Opa hadn't hidden in his shed had already been donated. If she was quiet, he would give up and go on. She retreated to the kitchen and sat down.

A moment later, the boy knocked a third time and rang the bell. Karin stared out back. The sun had broken through and was streaming down on the garden now, illuminating the leaves of the stalks with rainbow crystals. The young plants, caught in the stiff breeze, shivered like young children stepping out of their bath.

A few minutes later, satisfied that the boy had given up, Karin ventured out back. The storm swept in air as fresh as the blue sky above. The soil would be soft. Pulling the few weeds she hadn't gotten to earlier would be easy. She had never imagined how enjoyable and life-giving the work could be. If only Oma was here to share it.

She had just begun to nip a few of the unproductive sprouts on the tomato stalks when a noise from behind gave her a start.

"What on earth? You frightened me!"

The boy had opened the gate and was standing at the edge of the garden. By the expression on his face, he was not embarrassed in the least.

"Why didn't you answer the door earlier?"

"We gave last week. We have nothing new to give."

He tossed his head back in acknowledgment. "I'm not collecting, fraulein."

Karin wasn't interested in a conversation. "Then what do you want?"

He retrieved an envelope from his pocket and glanced at it. "Are you Karin Blik?"

She nodded.

He handed her the note. She recognized the handwriting at once—Rudi.

What could he possibly say that she cared about? Whatever it was, she was not going to let it affect her glorious afternoon. The garden was the one thing she called her own. It was sacred. She would not let him violate that.

She stuffed the letter in her pocket and without another word turned back to her work. The tomato stalks were in fine shape, dripping with tiny, light green, baby tomatoes. She examined each stalk with the care of a mother checking her child for ticks after an afternoon's hike.

Moments later, she glanced back. The boy had not moved.

"I've got it. Thank you. Now go." Her tone grew exasperated.

"My orders are to make sure you read it," he said without flinching.

Karin let out a long, disgusted breath. She pulled out the note. "And if I don't?"

The boy creased his brow and stepped nervously in place. He was looking away, as if for courage, and seemed to find it. "Then I suppose I'll have to report you," he said proudly.

"Report me? To whom? Your district commander?" She was furious now, and her tone seethed. "Always following orders, aren't you? But what if I weren't at home? Or sick? What would you do?" She turned away and muttered an answer. "Wouldn't think for yourself, that's for sure."

"I was instructed to wait."

"You've said that already. Now run along."

"But fraulein, Herr Kohl gave me strict orders. Please."

"And we mustn't disappoint Herr Kohl, no?"

"Please, fraulein. I'm only second class. I should be first class by now. If I fail this task, I don't know what they'll do to me."

In the space of a sentence the boy had shriveled from the teenage side of twelve to a ten-year-old on the verge of tears. With a huff, she opened the note.

Dear Karin,

I hope you are well and rested after your ordeal. We have all wished for your speedy recovery. You are dearly missed, and we are anxious for your return. Sweeping events are underway. Please return to the office for an urgent meeting tomorrow at 16:00. For your convenience, I will send a car.

Warmly,

Rudi

P.S. Please acknowledge the messenger.

Karin held the note in her hands and stared at the words that Rudi had scrolled in his own hand. *Warmly, Rudi.* How disgusting. A sour pain gripped her midsection.

As the breeze rustled the paper, Karin's heart sank. She had been a fool to think Rudi would leave her alone. He was always bound to come after her. She wouldn't be able to hide forever.

She crumpled the note in her hands and tossed it into Opa's hole. It bounced off the concrete wall and came to rest in the puddle at the bottom of the pit, where it absorbed the water and flattened out. Just like she felt.

"Fraulein?"

She waved the boy away. "You saw me. I read it. Tell him I'll be ready."

The boy, visibly relieved, bowed repeatedly. "Thank you, fraulein. Thank you!"

She didn't look at him. "Get out!"

The next day, Karin was watching when, with the precision of a Deutsche Bahn locomotive, a black Mercedes appeared in front of her house. She slipped out the door and met the driver as he was circling around the front.

Her heart dropped when she saw Rudi in the back seat. He had said a car would pick her up, not him.

"Are you well?" he asked. His tone was back to its official flatness, as though their previous encounter had never happened. She nodded.

"Good. I'm pleased to hear it." Rudi's voice was measured, or so he would have thought, and he pretended to be all business—eyes ahead and casual. But Karin knew better. His confidence seemed to have returned, and he was back to his normal, uncomfortable, dangerous state.

As the car bounded through the streets, she never looked directly at him, unwilling to give him the satisfaction of direct eye contact. She was determined to resist him in whatever small way she could. So instead, she looked out the window. Piles of rubble from May's bombing had almost disappeared. Reconstruction of damaged buildings was everywhere. Still, she knew. She could feel his eyes, stealing glances at her every chance he could manage, and she detected that he had edged ever so slightly closer on the seat. She became so uncomfortable she imagined throwing herself out of the car. But they were going too slow for anything but scrapes and bruises, and he would just find her again.

"To what do I owe this special visit?" she finally asked, still staring out the window, her tone just on the border of sarcastic.

"Ah, yes. Indeed, it is. Very special. I'm gathering the district leaders for a critical meeting this afternoon."

"And you need me to take notes? You know I'm not trained in that. Marie is so much better. Is she coming?"

It didn't matter that he was looking right at her. She refused to grant him the satisfaction of eye contact.

"I don't need minutes, Karin. I need your very blue and perceptive eyes. And those tender ears as well."

Out of the corner of her eye she saw his hand lift off the seat. She jumped against the door and twisted toward him. She locked eyes with him, but her brow was pinched. Her message was clear.

You will not touch me.

His hand returned to its place on the seat, and he smiled. *Message received*, his expression seemed to say.

"What do you need me to do?"

"I want you to observe them. Their reaction. And listen."

"I don't understand. You won't be there yourself?"

"Yes, of course, but they will not respond to me in any way but obedience. I will deliver my instructions and pretend to be called away for an urgent call in my office. I will leave you with them. You will pretend to be working on reports. You will listen to their reaction, watch their faces."

"Are they likely to react differently without you? Why?"

Without moving his hand or shifting his body in the seat, Rudi leaned over. Karin sat rigid.

"You remember that important visitor I spoke of at your reception several weeks ago?"

"The Führer?"

"Yes. It is coming true. He is coming to visit us."

Karin had been mistaken about Rudi. The lust in his eyes was for this news, this tidbit of gossip, the visit of his beloved Führer, not her.

"But we have a problem," he continued. "This so-called Freedom Gang."

Karin's ears stretched back.

"My key Hitlerjugend leaders will be at the office. I am going to discuss with them my plan to find and crush the gang, once and for all."

Find and crush Frei's gang? Karin snapped her head toward the window. She could not let Rudi see her reaction.

"Are you all right, fraulein?"

She rubbed her hands together and wiped them on her skirt.

"Yes, Rudi, I'm fine. Just a little sick from the motion of the car is all. Are we almost there?"

Rudi took advantage of the situation and patted her arm. "Of course, almost there. Now I believe that the reason we have failed so far in our efforts to crush the gang is that they know what we're doing before we do it. I further believe one of my own leaders must be sympathetic to the gang and does not act with decisiveness and strength. When I discuss our new plan, I want you to observe their reaction. I want your eyes and ears trained for a response, a reaction, nervousness. Anything that might help me understand who among them is weak. One of them might be an informer."

Karin swallowed hard. "It sounds too much like spying. I'm afraid I'm not very good at that sort of thing." This was not a lie.

She had made a mistake by looking directly at him. Now he had her in his gaze, and he bore down into her. His tone switched to a mix of serious and threat.

"Don't tease me, dear Karin. You know exactly what people are and precisely what they want."

His eyes didn't move. They seemed to take on an evil power that, despite her tactics, penetrated her defenses.

Seeming to know it too, he smiled with satisfaction. "All I want is your observations and impressions."

He didn't say the words, but Karin thought she heard the addition: *for now*.

By the time they entered the office, she was numb. Only five leaders among the seventeen that reported to Rudi were present. Karin scanned their faces for hints of disloyalty. Could one of them know Frei? How could that be possible? How would Frei come to trust a Jugend? She studied them, wondering if she could discern the traitor, speak to him, and get a message to Frei. Warn the gang to disperse or lay low. The Führer's visit would not be taken lightly. There were rumors that attempts had been made on Hitler's life already, but they never appeared in the news. It was against the law to mention such things. Like the off-color jokes, they landed you in prison. Security would be extreme for such a visit. The Hitler Youth would find Frei and his gang and crush them.

Rudi gathered the leaders in the front room to address them, beginning with a review of the gang's activities. He was uncharacteristically candid.

"Our efforts have failed so far. The so-called Freedom Gang has avoided direct confrontation. They've attacked, disrupted, and fled. Herr Gossen is losing patience with us. We must succeed. We will succeed."

One of the leaders, a handsome blonde, probably seventeen or so, raised his hand.

"From the reports I've read, they seem like minor vandals and thieves. What's so important about this Freedom Gang?"

"With the attack on the ceremony, they're clearly working up to something bigger. They have more sinister goals."

"Such as?"

"No one knows for sure, but what I am about to tell you will make everything clear. What we have all hoped for is coming true—the visit of the Führer."

The room fell silent, with every leader's eyes wide on Rudi. Karin watched. Their reactions seemed genuine. Who among them was hiding their true feelings? How could she tell? How did Rudi expect her to know?

He continued, "Security is always at the highest when the Führer travels. I have been assigned to find the Freedom Gang and eliminate them."

When Rudi lingered over the word "eliminate," several of the leaders squirmed.

The same leader spoke again. Was he simply curious, or was there something more?

"Eliminate them? With our sticks and clubs?" The question resonated with the others.

Rudi curled the side of his mouth into a sinister grin and reached behind the counter.

He brought forth a pistol, the Luger, black and oiled.

"I have been assigned this task by Herr Gossen himself. The Gestapo will offer their support, but the job lies with us. Given the importance of the Führer's visit, we will be prepared. The gang is believed to have stolen a hunting rifle and perhaps a scope. We will meet force with force and destroy them. Among the district leaders I have chosen each of you because you are trustworthy and courageous, and I can count on you."

Rudi closed the space between himself and the blonde and locked eyes with him.

"I can count on you, can't I?"

The leader shrank back, struck by the sudden need to dry his palms. "Of course, Herr Kohl. Of course. By my questions, I didn't mean to suggest—"

"Of course you didn't." Rudi cut him off with a cold smile and a rough hand to the boy's cheek, which by now had taken on a ghostlike shade. It was the caress of an executioner. Rudi patted the boy's face several times while he scanned the other faces in the circle. Karin had not moved. Though in a way it all seemed so theatrical, it was nonetheless effective. She sucked in her bottom lip and bit down. Rudi would have his revenge.

He turned to Karin.

"From your excellent reconnaissance work in the past and Fraulein Blik's superb collation, we know the general vicinity of this so-called Freedom Gang." He swung back to the leaders. "Even better, we have an informer. A member of the gang has revealed the location of the gang's hideout. We simply need to move in and crush them."

Relief rippled through the group, except for Karin, who felt sick in her stomach. Rudi said the informer was among their own ranks. What did he mean? Somehow it made more sense that one of Frei's own would betray him. His grip on the group seemed tenuous at best. Could it be Zara? One of the others? Why would they betray Frei? Either way, she knew he was in grave danger.

Her throat went dry, and heat rose through her neck. Without warning, she wretched. Not having eaten since morning, only a little water came out, but even so, she failed to reach the waste-basket before it came.

"My dear Karin, are you all right?" Rudi said. He helped her to a chair. "Some water, quickly!"

He held her hand while one of the boys fetched a glass of water from the bathroom.

Karin took a sip. "My apologies, Herr Kohl. I don't know what came over me."

"Your face is as white as a sheet," Rudi said. He touched her forehead. She knew he was just taking advantage of the situation. "Cold as a stone."

"I'm fine, just a little lightheaded. I guess I'm not used to being on my feet for so long. Not yet anyway."

"Yes, of course, my dear. Of course." Rudi continued to hold her hand and stroke her arm. His touch made her flesh crawl, but she knew she had to be careful.

"Would you care to lie down? There's a bed upstairs. You could rest."

"May I go home?" she asked.

Rudi paused to think. She realized he needed her observation of the leaders' reactions.

"Of course," he answered. "That's for the best. Before you go, could I have a word in my office? There's a report I'd like to ask you about. It won't take but a moment."

He dismissed the leaders and escorted her down the corridor to his office. She didn't like being near him, much less alone with him, but trusted that he was truly engaged in the new mission. Still, she had to be on her guard. Alone, she could do little. But if it came to it, she decided she would scream. She would fight.

"Please sit down," he said, closing the door behind them. He moved around to his desk.

"Did you notice anything unusual? Suspicious?"

"Only that Kamerad Schneider seemed nervous. He asked a lot of questions, that's all."

"Yes, I noticed that." He rifled through a stack of papers on his desk. "Anyone else? You know, sometimes the rat can be right under your nose, and you don't even smell it. I wonder sometimes about Heinemann."

Heinemann was a short boy who had hung back in the circle, avoiding direct view.

"No. I can't say I even noticed him."

"Very well, I see." He seemed uninterested in the conversation. "My profound apologies, Karin, but I'm afraid we need our transport tonight. We'll be reviewing our plan—maps, coordination, a run through—and then off. Can you make it home on your own?"

Karin stood up. "Yes, of course, Rudi. It's no trouble. It's still early and the fresh air will do me good." She took a step toward the door. "I apologize for my... illness."

Rudi returned the phone to its cradle and swept around the desk. He had her hand in his again and caressed it like a concerned grandmother. "Nothing to apologize for, my dear. I appreciate your service, as always."

The words dripped out of his mouth on the edge of innuendo. She tensed but didn't hesitate.

"Thank you," she said.

"See you Thursday."

She shouldn't have been surprised, but the three words hit her with the weight of a crumbling wall of bricks. She should have known the instant she had climbed into the car, and he shared his secret of the Führer's visit. It was as though that conversation with the broken, humiliated boy in her kitchen had never happened.

He seemed to read her thoughts.

"I need you, Karin," he said in a low, soft tone.

She left, dragging the weight of this dread around her neck. But Thursday's worries would have to wait. Quickening her stride up the street, Karin didn't notice the black Mercedes that started its engine at the far end of the street. The detail didn't register because she had a single thought on her mind.

She had to warn Frei.

CHAPTER TWENTY-NINE

The afternoon sky grew threatening with heavy gray clouds and thunder in the distance. Once she was out of sight of the Hitler Youth office, Karin deviated from her normal route home by turning north. Three blocks on, she came to the broad, east-west road to Aachen and found the first tram stop for an inbound line that would take her all the way to the Hauptbahnhof on the edge of the Rhine at the city center. While the stop on the other side of the street was jammed with commuters waiting for westbound trams, Karin stood alone, exposed.

Would Rudi follow me?

She scanned the scene for the signature uniforms of the Gestapo—men in dark leather jackets and wide-brimmed hats. They would have stood out among the commuters. Up ahead, two women strolled arm in arm, their backs to her. The sidewalk behind her was empty except for a handful of pigeons strutting along the curb. A black sedan had just ducked into an empty spot. Karin took in steady, measured breaths to bring her nerves under control and wrestled with the notion that Rudi suspected her. As the minutes passed and the westbound lanes filled with an almost uninterrupted chain of headlights, she concluded that she had nothing to fear. Rudi was shrewd beyond her experience, of that she was sure, but he was blinded too by his own desire. She could see that in his eyes when they were together and in the way he spoke to her. His sense of duty seemed to hold it in check, but she sensed the war within him. Her own power rested in doing what he ordered and not provoking or rejecting him outright. It seemed her only way to survive, though it felt so foreign, and in a way, so wicked.

Most importantly, Rudi's loyalties were clear. He was dedicated to the Führer and to Herr Gossen. The attack at the ceremony threatened his good standing with them both. Finding Frei was his chance for redemption, and he would not disappoint them again.

At last, the tram arrived. With another glance back, she confirmed she was not being followed. The handful of passengers were uninterested in her boarding—men with their noses in newspapers, an old woman cradling a small dog, two soldiers straining out the window for a glimpse of the Great Cathedral. Betraying him was the right thing to do, but still felt wrong to her, as wrong as everything in the world now felt.

At the Hauptbahnhof, Karin disembarked and felt the first drops of cold rain bounce off the dry concrete. She joined the throng of people heading for the terminal. Umbrellas appeared from nowhere, but Karin was unprepared. She dodged the growing throng and slipped into the building just as the skies opened. Sheets of rain drummed against the glass panes of the arches high above, a loud preview of what was coming. Pondering the next leg of the journey, she pulled her sweater close. It would offer little protection against the storm.

She crossed the terminal, found the north side exit, and paused once more. Like her, the crowd had hesitated to face the downpour. The rain sliced at a sharp angle through the light of the streetlamp outside. The skyline was unfamiliar. Frei had brought her here, she was sure, but the view looked different now. Perhaps she could wait a moment for the storm to pass. The pause, however, gave rise to new doubts. The way forward was not as obvious as she had remembered. How long had she been blindfolded? Could she really return to their hideout? Would the gang still be there? And would Frei even listen to her?

Elbowing through the group at the exit, she broke free and let the deluge hit her. The shower brought an instant chill to the bone, so she began to run. She ran with abandon, free from care about the rain, free from fear of the regime, free from the shadows under the bridge.

North of the tracks, the landscape changed quickly. Shops and apartments on tree-lined streets gave way to brick warehouses, boarded up garages, and bomb-damaged workshops. The street was dark and quiet compared to the bustle of afternoon shopping and traveling home from work. This was where she had just removed the blindfold. Frei had brought her this way.

Her energy ebbed, and she slowed to a walk. The rain started to let up. It was still cool, but her body had also warmed up. Walking in the rain reminded her of breaking curfew.

From news reports, she recalled that the district of Ehrenfeld, north of the Hauptbahnhof, had suffered greatly in the British attack. It made sense for Rudi and the gang to take advantage.

A kilometer on, however, the familiarity of the surroundings wore off. More and more buildings lay in ruins and various stages of repair. Craters pocked some streets, and piles of rubble spilled into others. Some areas had been blocked by hastily constructed fences, and new scaffolding appeared in spots. The streets were nearly empty of people, and those she saw took no notice of her.

Another block, and she stopped. She was well beyond the range of her memory. Everything looked the same—dark, damaged, and industrial. Her confidence evaporated. She was lost, and the warmth from her exertion was starting to wear off.

She reviewed the journey in her mind. The part wearing the blindfold had been slow and difficult. Narrow walls and a tight passageway out of the gang's hideout. Stairs, some kind of doorway, and fresh air. Uneven ground—stones, or gravel, stumbling over something like a curb. No! It was metal! She remembered bending down and feeling the cold steel rail with her hands. Abandoned tracks, that's what it was!

She continued up the street, looking for gaps in the buildings or fences. At the next intersection, she had a feeling she should turn right, toward the river. Two and a half blocks later, she came upon an abandoned rail line that split the block in two. She looked north. A hollowed-out shell towered in the distance. She ran again.

The storm had pushed through, leaving a gentle but steady rain, and darkness was gathering fast. Karin followed the tracks north, through abandoned repair yards, past darkened platforms, and along crumbling warehouses. Where it crossed another street, she came to a steel gate, chained shut. The track continued and curved left. The factory—that had to be the one—was just one or two blocks ahead.

Against all hope, Karin shook the gate. The chain and rusted lock held firm. She looked up. The fence was nearly four meters high and glistening from the rain. A fall could be severe, and she was alone. With darkness closing in, she had a growing sense that time was running out. She decided to go around.

She moved left in a perpendicular direction from the track. Running again, the warmth returned. At the next street, she turned right and pushed herself harder. Her heart thundered and her thighs began to burn. Sucking in deep drafts of chilled air seared the back of her throat so that it burned with a metallic blood taste. Yet now the factory rose into view through the fence to her right. She leaned into the rain and pounded her legs harder.

Two-thirds of the way up the block was a crater that had ripped a hole in the street and through the fence to her right. She paused, studied the shadow of the factory across the yard, and turned back toward the city. The spires of the Great Cathedral were encircled by mist. This had to be it!

Grateful, Karin scrambled along the edge of the crater, climbed through the rip in the fence, and flew across the open yard. She met the tracks again, jumped the rails, and found the corner of the factory. Moving north along the familiar brick wall, her heart leapt. There, at her feet, lay the set of stairs cut below ground level. Panting, she bounded down into the hole. It smelled of oil and rain and urine. But there was the metal door, half open at the base. It scraped roughly when she pulled and opened only a few centimeters. The passage was completely dark. She swallowed hard and stepped in.

The passageway was barely the width and height of the door, and the smells pressed in. She stopped, sensing something. *Animal?* The realization came too late.

A shadow moved in the dull light. Hands seized her arm and her mouth at the same instant, and she was slammed against the wall. The crack of her head against the brick sent a burst of sparks through her vision.

"Don't cry out and don't move," the voice said. She recognized it.

Still terrified, Karin managed to nod.

Zara drew close.

"How did you find this place?" Zara hissed. "Never mind, he probably told you. He'll get us all killed the way he talks. What are you doing here?"

Zara drew her hand down and squeezed Karin's throat. She was strong beyond her size.

"They know!" Karin said. "The Hitler Youth know where you are!"

Zara squeezed. Karin gasped.

"And how do you know this?"

"I heard them. There's an informer in the gang. One of them betrayed you. You've got to warn Frei. All of you, you've got to go. Now! They're coming!"

Zara pressed Karin harder against the wall. Her eyes drilled into Karin, panicked at first, and then calculating.

"There's no time, Zara. They might be right behind me! Hurry! You've got to hurry!"

Zara's expression turned cold. She relaxed her grip just a bit and turned to go. But she didn't release her. Instead, she turned back to Karin and pressed close. Her eyes were filled with cruelty. Without warning, Zara jerked and drove her knee into Karin's stomach. The blow knocked the air from Karin's lungs. As she fell, Zara put a second blow to her nose. Karin staggered backward and bent down as bolts of pain spread in throbs from her sinuses outward. She blinked hard and then put her hands over her eyes, fighting to remain conscious. She fell to her knees, and curled into herself, holding her head in her hands and elbows as if in prayer. If Zara came again, she would be defenseless. But she could not move, only endure, and wait for the next blows.

Moments passed without counting. Zara's next attack never came. Karin's pulse slowed, the throbbing eased, and she let her hands fall from her eyes. She was alone.

She heard voices outside. Light flickered through the crack in the door behind her. Karin climbed up from the filth and stumbled toward it. Scraping past the door, she was met by the cool rain once more. When her head came above ground level, she saw clearly. A group of figures was gathered in the yard, positioned in a semi-circle facing the wall to her right, silhouetted by the light of vehicles behind them. Men, no uniforms, no Hitler Youth. Men in plain clothes, leather raincoats and wide-brimmed fedoras. Gestapo. At the center, their leader, Herr Gossen.

At the base of the wall stood Frei, his head hanging down. The rain poured off the long locks that covered his eyes onto that baggy striped suit. It hung on him like wet towels on a hook. His body looked shriveled beneath it. He was alone.

Gossen raised a pistol.

Karin screamed.

Every head turned, and Frei took it as his chance. He broke in the opposite direction, but the attempt was futile. The men on the far side of the perimeter recovered quickly and hemmed him in like a young dog. One of them threw Frei against the wall, and Gossen fired.

Frei's arms went limp, and his head flopped sideways. He sank to the ground against the wall like a half-filled sack.

"*Nooooooo!*" Karin bellowed and flew up the stairs.

She rushed to the circle, but the perimeter closed again. She flailed wildly, but to no effect.

Frei, in his last moment of life, turned his head. Their eyes met.

She wished it was her.

Gossen approached Frei and knelt at his side. He put his fingers on Frei's throat and waited. A strange quiver rippled across Gossen's face, one Karin might have taken for regret, if she hadn't just watched him pull the trigger.

Gossen flicked his head to his men. Two of them left the perimeter and grabbed Frei by the feet. They dragged him like a deer from the middle of the highway. Karin sobbed uncontrollably.

The gravel crunched nearby.

She looked up. Gossen stood over her, his face carrying a blank stare.

She hoped he'd finish her off next.

"Release her," was all he said.

Karin fell back to the ground. She pressed her face into the gravel and mud, tasting it, begging God to let her join it. The cars drove off, taking their lights with them, leaving her alone in the darkness, no stars in sight.

CHAPTER THIRTY

Herr Doktor Kilmer stood over Karin's bed. He stared at her with dark, narrow eyes, trying, it seemed, to penetrate her mind by sheer force of will. Concentrating, a bushy gray eyebrow lifted from its perch.

Karin avoided his gaze as much as she could. This man with stale breath and cavernous nostrils, whose white hairs, thick as his eyebrows, danced back and forth as he twitched, made her nervous.

His unspoken analysis complete, he snapped up straight, removed his wire-rimmed spectacles, and turned to Opa, who was sitting in Karin's desk chair.

"A word outside," he said.

"No," Karin said, pushing herself up. "I want to hear what you have to say."

The doctor's eyebrow, having just settled, shot up again. He looked at Opa.

Opa nodded.

"Very well," he began. "In short, there's nothing wrong with you. Physically, that is. Your pulse and blood pressure are normal. We didn't put you on a scale, but from the look of you,

I'd guess your weight is down. That bruise under your eye will gradually fade."

Karin looked at Opa. "See, I told you."

Opa didn't respond. In times past, he would have taken up the argument, but no more. He looked tired, but he had reason for concern. She had eaten little, stayed home from school, and hid from everyone, including her grandfather. After sleeping for nearly a week, he finally called the Herr Doktor.

"Then what's wrong with her?" Opa asked. His voice was not angry. And though she could not fully appreciate it, Karin knew by his tone he was truly concerned. It was more than a lack of energy; it was as if she had no life in her body at all. She just didn't care.

The doctor thought for a moment more and then sat down on the end of her bed. He smiled, took hold of her ankle, and gave it a gentle tug.

"In my opinion, Dieter, this girl needs a different kind of rest."

"What do you mean?"

"Some warm sun, fresh air, a break from the city. Nothing like the beauty of nature to heal."

Oma's journal came to mind.

Beauty is God's gift to a broken soul and broken world.

Karin was surprised by the doctor's advice.

"The kind of air they have in the south. I know a place in Bavaria. She would get all these things."

"An asylum?" Opa's voice began to rise.

"No, no. More of a rest home, a sanitarium. She would be well cared for. I know a psychiatrist there, Klaus Bormann…"

"It sounds expensive. I have nothing but my pension. Her mother spends…" Opa stopped. "And the Nazis don't take kindly to those places anymore. Children disappear in them."

"Now, now, Dieter. Don't take me for a monster. I'm not talking about one of those places. If I didn't know you better, I'd be offended. She's not deformed; she's depressed!"

Karin tensed beneath the covers. Children with physical and mental deformities were being sent to special hospitals, sometimes with and sometimes without their parents' consent. No one knew for sure, and no one asked or spoke of it openly, but there were stories of strange and sudden illnesses claiming their lives. So, what initially seemed so promising—a rest in the mountains—became all at once terrifying.

Opa rubbed the stubble on his chin.

"What about Berlin with her mother, then? That could be restful."

This time, Karin cut him off. "No. I'll be fine. I can rest here."

"But you've done nothing but sleep," Opa said.

"I've been tired," she argued. "Do you have anything for the pain?"

The question hung in the air. Herr Doktor Kilmer cocked his head, traded glances with Opa, and then stood up.

"There's nothing wrong with you that requires anything more than aspirin, Fraulein Karin. We'll not have you getting hooked on anything stronger."

He stooped over just long enough to retrieve his bag from Karin's bedside and left the room. Opa followed. Outside, she heard them discussing something for a brief moment, after which the heavy footfalls of the doctor down the stairs assured Karin he was gone.

When Opa returned, Karin had gained a sitting position at the top of her bed.

"He thinks this is all in my head, doesn't he? He thinks I'm crazy."

Opa held up a white business card.

"He gave me the name of a local doctor you can see."

"A psychiatrist? No thanks. I'd prefer the asylum."

"Shush, Karin. You know nothing of what you speak."

"Anywhere would be better than here." She didn't mean the words to hurt him, but she had no energy to undo them once they were out.

"What happened, Karin? Something's changed. You were doing so well."

She shook her head. "I tried, Opa. I really did. I'm just not as good at pretending as everyone else."

He got up from the chair and took the doctor's seat at the end of her bed. She knew he really was trying to be kind, but all that had happened was none of his fault and beyond his ability to help.

"Did that boy—what's his name—Kohl—did he...do something?"

The question made Karin want to shed her own skin. Everything she touched—the sheets, the texture of her nightgown, the contour of the mattress and pillows—made her uncomfortable.

"No, Opa. Not that. But in a way, something worse."

"What, Karin? What did he do? I don't care if he is a little Hitler, I'll not stand for it!"

"No, Opa, no! Don't you see, it's all of them. They're killing me, day by day. They'll kill us all. Maybe not with bombs and bullets, but somehow, it happens all the same. Like drowning—just seeing them, just being near them! I don't know how much more I can take."

Karin rolled to her side, but Opa moved forward and took her by the shoulders. She stiffened, but he held on. The longer they sat together, Opa simply holding her, a thaw began, somewhere from the base of her stomach. Karin fought it, willed it to retreat, but the feeling grew. It was dangerous, and she knew if she gave into it, she might never come back from it. A moment longer. Her grandfather was old, but still a strong man from years of good work. And he was determined—most would say stubborn—and so he didn't let go. After a moment, surrounded by the firm grip of the man and his rough cotton shirt and the smell of tobacco and engine oil, she could resist no more. Karin let out a kind of cough, and it was like a glass breaking. Her body shook as she sobbed, but her spasms were safe within her grandfather's strong arms. Her tears burned and then soaked his sleeve. They released a torrent of hot molten steel that weighed more heavily each day.

She was unaware of how long she cried, but eventually, she could cry no more. Truly, something had been released. She couldn't explain it, but the feeling was deep and real. She was grateful and gave him a final squeeze.

When she looked up at him, he looked more worried than ever.

He really does think I'm insane!

She laughed. "I'll be all right. I'll finish the term. It's only for a week. I can make it."

He didn't seem convinced, but she doubted he understood much of what just happened. She squirmed free and climbed down from bed.

The week of neglect showed in the garden. For the better part of the afternoon, Karin found energy to pull weeds and pluck useless sprouts from the tomatoes.

As she worked, Frei was never far from her thoughts. She tried to picture him as she had seen him in the hideout—leaning back on an old crate, the king of his band of misfits. He was troubled, to be sure, but she couldn't help granting him a measure of respect for breaking from the world. She churned up and down the rows with furious energy, trying to work out in her mind how she was followed and how she might have saved him. As hard as she tried, however, one image was inescapable—Frei, looking at her in his last moment—sad, and yet relieved.

Oma! If only you were here to help me.

Oma believed in heaven. She spoke to God like a person speaks to their close friend. Karin missed that. She would know what to say, what to do.

By the time Karin returned to school the next Monday, the weight of despair had returned, as heavy as ever. The week stretched before her like an eternity and was compounded by the cloud of suspicion rising from her for having tried to warn Frei. Open disloyalty toward the Nazis brought swift punishment; but suspicion, especially the kind fueled by rumor, had filled the school with the smell of blood before she had even returned. Karin's only hope was to avoid contact with anyone.

In the first class, when Karin's name was called for attendance, a smattering of hisses rippled through the room. Such interruptions were never tolerated before; teachers would deal swift retribution to the demonstrators. Today the teacher simply paused, narrowed his gaze, and continued with the other names.

Karin endured the rest of the period, a lecture on changes to world geography because of the war, without further disruption. When the class ended, she waited while everyone else filed out. She learned of her mistake when she stepped through the door and found they were waiting in the hall. Two groups of three or four girls each, pretending to talk, flanked the hall, waiting in ambush. When Karin approached, they blocked her way and quickly filled in behind her.

She clutched her book bag and drew it up in front as a kind of shield. Squeezing hard helped to focus her strength.

She counted eight girls in all, whom she recognized from BDM meetings. They avoided her direct stares. They were nearly as afraid of her as she was of them. But they were good Nazis and knew to hunt in a pack.

A red-haired girl stepped forward. She was in Karin's group that assembled the care packages for the soldiers. One of Elfreda's tag-alongs. Her eyes, coal black circles, seemed fixed on a distant spot. Her lip quivered nervously.

"You're a disgrace to your uniform," she croaked. Her tone carried none of the force of her words. This had all the markings of Elfreda, Karin judged. This was some kind of initiation rite, no doubt.

She felt a jab from behind.

When she spun around, four girls stood defiant, locked arm in arm.

Then someone from the front jerked on Karin's braid. White hot pain shot through her head, causing her to lose her balance. She fell, and then came a sharp explosion in her stomach from an unseen kick. She could not breathe.

"What's going on here?" It was the first period teacher's voice.

Karin felt hands pulling her up. One of the girls had her book bag and was slipping the strap back over Karin's shoulder.

"It's nothing, Frau Dunkmann. Nothing at all." It was the redhead who spoke. "Fraulein Blik has been ill. She must have fallen," she continued, a new confidence in her voice. "We were just helping her up."

"Ill? Is that what you call it, Fraulein Blik? Illness? Since when is treason an illness?"

Karin said nothing. The girls exchanged knowing and satisfied glances.

Frau Dunkmann ordered them on to class and left.

The girls dispersed, but not before the redhead shoved Karin into the wall. Karin sank down against the cold bricks.

The girl bent over Karin, her pigtails wagging back and forth.

"Illnesses can be treated," she said, in a whisper. "But treason is fatal."

Her confidence had grown in a short span of time. Her initiation had reached its conclusion, and her transformation seemed complete. She let a wry smile cross her lips until Karin snatched hold of a pigtail and jerked it hard. The girl's eyes nearly popped from their sockets. Gripping hard, Karin squeezed with all her strength as the girl's eyes welled with tears. Karin pulled her close.

"Tell Elfreda you passed the test," she rasped. "But let her know she'll never get what she truly wants. I might be a traitor, but no matter what Elfreda tries, she'll never get Rudi's attention. He only has eyes for me." She jerked a final time. "Tell Elfreda! Tell her!"

She let go of the hair. Red strands were stuck to her fingers when the girl ran off.

Karin dropped her head and closed her eyes, trying to shut out the world.

"Are you all right, Karin?"

The voice, Marie's, brought tears from an empty well. She had hoped to avoid her, not because she didn't want to see her, but to spare her the shame of associating with a traitor.

Marie knelt directly in front of her. Her face was soft and open, like always. Karin avoided her eyes.

"What happened?" Marie asked.

"Just a quick 'welcome back' from some of the girls," Karin said. "I'm fine."

Marie slid over beside her and slipped her arm inside Karin's. Karin tensed.

"We haven't seen you for a while. We're worried about you. *I'm* worried about you."

The bell rang, warning them that they should be in the next class. They had two minutes more before both would be tardy and in trouble.

Karin climbed to her feet and gathered her things. Marie stepped back, her face pained.

Karin began to walk. Marie followed and came alongside.

"I don't care what they say," Marie offered. "I know it can't be true."

Karin kept on. Marie would never understand. She was one of the good girls, the Nazis liked her, and she would never accept any view of reality but what they told her. No, Karin would not explain.

"You shouldn't be seen with me," Karin said. They were going to be late. She quickened the pace and came to the intersection at the end of the hall. Math was to the right. Karin stopped.

Marie took another step and then realized Karin wasn't following. "Aren't you coming to class?"

Karin looked at the doorway where the last few students pushed through the door. Behind her, the front door of the school beckoned.

She had been a fool to think she could make it through the day, much less the week. The math exam scheduled for second period would be a joke—math had become hieroglyphics on the white page. She would surely fail, just like she would surely fail history, grammar, biology, and every other subject. It was no use even trying. A terrible plan suddenly formed in her mind.

"We'll be late," Marie said. "Come on."

Karin smiled faintly. She moved a step toward Marie and gave her a light kiss on the cheek.

"You're a good friend, Marie. You really are. Farewell."

Marie's look of recognition and then panic told Karin she had understood. The bell rang again. Marie turned and ran.

Karin pushed through the heavy outside door. The thin clouds overhead signaled rain coming. But she was free.

CHAPTER THIRTY-ONE

Karin's plan was little more than an idea. By the time she had climbed off the tram at the Hauptbahnhof and left the shadow of the Great Cathedral, it was starting to unravel like the frayed straps on her canvas knapsack. With Frei gone, who would be left? Where would they be?

She moved north from the station into the industrial district, retracing the same path as before. In the sunlight, the landscape had changed—still peppered with craters and rubble—but more alive. Workers loaded broken brick into wagons, swept debris off the streets, and the sound of hammers punctuated the air. Without trouble, she found the rail spur, the gate, circled around to the yard, and came to The Wall.

The sadness broke over her like a sudden storm. Leaving school, packing a quick bag, and running away seemed—if not quite a good idea—at least a way out. The plan provided a sliver of relief from her unbearable school, her unlivable life. Yet standing here, facing the wall, staring at *the spot*, she was consumed by an oil-, smoke-, feces-, and urine-infused despair.

She descended the short stairs and entered the tunnel. The smell was worse than she remembered. She pushed beyond where she had encountered Zara and passed through the doorway of the cavernous factory. It was deserted.

What a fool! Did I really expect to find the gang gathered around their fire singing camp songs?

The sense of shame swept over Karin with a chill. She ran from the spot, not stopping until she was out of the building, across the yard, and back on the street. She ran until she could run no more, and then, nearly spent, ducked into a rundown café.

She slid into a chair at a table along the front glass to catch her breath. The place smelled of bad sauerkraut and industrial body odor, and was dimly lit by a few bare bulbs. A pair of old men in blue overalls were slumped over their beer at a table in the back. They didn't even look up when she entered.

Karin rummaged in her bag and found enough change for an ersatz coffee and gristly mettwurst. Along with the leftover cheese and bread she had thrown in her bag at home, it would be the first decent meal she'd had in days.

Where did this appetite come from?

The coffee was tasteless but hot. Sugar was hard to come by, but she didn't care. As the food filled her stomach, she experienced a kind of rebound. Her thoughts moved beyond the impulse of escaping school to the possibilities ahead. The gang was gone, but the thought persisted.

Can I make it on my own?

She had no money to speak of and hadn't really prepared. She could return home and pack better. With care, perhaps a few tomato plants could live in a spot along the river or a patch of dirt among the ruins.

What do I tell Opa?

It occurred to her she should write him a letter. He would never understand, but at least he would know what she had done. She was not like Frei. She didn't hate him. It was the Nazis. She would live on her own in the world between the worlds. Not a fighter or a thief like Frei—she resolved not to steal—but not a Nazi either. Maybe someday he would come to understand.

In her bag, she found some paper and a pencil.

Dearest Opa,

You don't need to worry about me.

Before she could write any more, a shape flashed across her view outside. Looking up, Karin saw a girl in an oversized coat, too heavy for the summer, moving up the sidewalk. An instant later, she was out the door.

"Zara?"

The girl stopped and then turned only her head. Karin recognized the profile, thin and drawn, and the dark black eye set deep. Seeing Karin, she ran off.

Karin took off after her, and at first, Zara pulled away. Her appearance in the oversized coat made her appear to glide along the pavement like a wraith.

"Zara, please! I want to talk to you."

Karin, surprised at how fast Zara was, wondered if she could keep up. Zara, ten meters in the lead, disappeared around a corner.

"Zara!"

Karin slowed at the corner and turned.

WHAM!

The object, no more than a blur, brought a sharp pain to her midsection. The clatter of wood on the pavement echoed up and down the street. Karin fell to the sidewalk, gasping for air.

She looked up. Zara had abandoned her weapon and was off again, but this time not so fast. Karin felt lucky, as the blow was more surprising than powerful. Karin struggled for breath and watched Zara slow even further. Then she stopped, staggered a few more strides, and collapsed.

Karin stood up and approached her. Zara twitched but had no strength to flee.

"Don't come any closer!" she said, her frightened eyes like those of a wounded animal. Her voice croaked. "I've got a knife! I'll cut you open, I will!"

Karin put her hands up. "Zara, please! Calm down. I just want to talk."

"There's nothing to talk about! I'll kill you, I swear!"

Zara's sleeve hung so long that Karin couldn't tell if Zara had a knife within it or not. She couldn't afford to take the chance.

"Listen to me, Zara, I'm sorry! I'm sorry about Frei. I didn't mean to—I was only trying to warn him, to warn you all."

"Warn him? You led them right to us. I should kill you my-self."

Her voice was weak, but the words hit like stones. "Everyone says you're a Judas. Full of assurances—*I'm not like them*—and yet you led the wolves right to the door."

Zara's energy and strength didn't match her threats. Karin wondered when the last time Zara had eaten anything more than the rotten crusts she saw at the gang's hideout.

"Zara, please. I can find food for you. They tricked me. I didn't know they were following me. Please believe me."

"Why should I?"

"They told me the gang had an informer."

Zara's eyes twitched. "Who?"

"I don't know. But Rudi said the informer would lead them right to the gang's hideout. As soon as I heard this, I came to warn Frei, but the Gestapo must have followed me. I didn't see them. I never would have led them here, I swear!"

Zara's brow creased. "Who's Rudi?"

Karin tried to explain, but Zara seemed unconvinced. The longer she tried, the more she could not escape the tragic truth. *I misjudged Rudi. After all this, he tricked me. What a fool I've been, thinking I was somehow a match with him.*

Karin dug the half-eaten mettwurst and roll out of her bag, edged closer, and offered it.

"I'm sorry," she said, her voice at a whisper. "So terribly sorry."

Zara snatched the food away and tore through it. The effort of eating seemed to exhaust her at first, until the food settled. It revived her a little. She gazed at Karin through the strings of hair that hung over her face like prison bars.

"Why are you here?" she asked, thrusting her chin in the air. "What do you want?"

"I want to get away from them, from everything."

"And you thought you'd join us?"

The idea sounded silly to Karin now. She nodded.

"That's really rich."

"I mean it," Karin said. "I can't live with them anymore. I'll die if I try."

"That's what you deserve."

"Please, Zara, I have nowhere else to go."

Zara had regained enough strength to stand up. She brushed the grit from the sidewalk off her sleeves and trousers. "Let me get this straight. You led them to us, they killed Frei, arrested almost everyone else, and you say you were duped, right?"

Karin nodded again. Was Zara beginning to understand?

"And now you're sick of them and want to join the gang, which, by the way, doesn't even exist anymore?"

"I told you. I can help. I have a little money. Some food."

"It's tempting." Zara said. "You know, Karin, I'll give you something. You're good, really good. And those Hitler Youth sure know what they're doing now. It used to just be the boys. Trained puppets they were. At times, pretty strong—large numbers too. But not real smart. Individually, you could scare them off. But now they've got you. A hero. An actress. You've got a great future ahead of you."

Karin was dumbfounded. Hadn't anything she said made sense to Zara? As she pondered Zara's words, she couldn't look away from those black eyes—sunk deep in ashen sockets. She didn't notice Zara inching closer.

"Something doesn't make sense, Karin. I've had time to think about this. Nothing but time. No food, no friends, no home, no family. Just time under a black sky. If what you say is true, and you really were duped by the Nazis to lead them here, then why are you here, free as a bird, and not in prison? Or swinging at the end of a piano wire like so many others?"

Karin's blood left her. It was the one question she didn't understand herself.

"I don't know," she said, almost in a moan. "I really don't."

It was at this moment, when Karin seemed utterly defeated, that Zara struck. In the spasm of fright and shock, Karin only saw the flash of a blade. She twisted, but only by reflex. Pain seared below her rib cage. She jumped back just in time to miss the second stroke.

The two stood apart, measuring each other's next move. Zara half-crouched, arms spread like a bat. The knife was long and slender and bounced with a threatening rhythm in her right hand.

Zara came again. Karin retreated step for step. Zara's eyes, quivering with doubt, desperation, and something more. Her lunge, when it finally came, was slow and weak, dulled by the effects of hunger.

Karin dodged easily with a step to the side. Zara lost her balance and fell. Her arms came up, spreading the heavy coat like wings, but she hit elbows first. The blade skittered out of reach.

Karin stepped around her and stopped. She slipped the strap of her bag off her shoulder and let it fall. Zara would find the rolls and the block of cheese she packed from home.

Karin ran. The path out of the alley was clear. She would not be living with the gang.

CHAPTER THIRTY-TWO

Karin endured the final days of the school year like a leper. Everyone gave her wide berth in the hallways, although some hissed when she passed them, and a few were bold enough to shout out, "Traitor!" and other insults. Even teachers avoided calling on her, that is, except for Herr Professor Putz. He wore his Nazi Party badge proudly on his lapel and made it his personal goal to bring the prodigal daughter back to the fold of the Reich. But his well-known method—selecting random students for questions throughout the lecture—when applied to Karin became far more humiliation than rehabilitation. Other students got simple questions about the founding of the Nazi party, the Führer's birthday, and key events in the life of the Reich, such as the burning of the Reichstag and Kristallnacht. Karin was pummeled with trivia questions—party leaders' birthdays, hometowns, service and rank in the Great War. Herr Putz made her stand until she answered a question or the bell rang, the latter of which was normally the case. By the end of the week, she bore the assaults with an all-encompassing numbness. She scored a miserable twenty-seven percent on the final exam. The term ended without mercy, for Karin was certain she would be sentenced to summer remediation, or, refusing that, repeat of the entire year.

She didn't care. The long summer days burned away some of the previous persecution. Oma's garden was a green retreat, her own private sanitarium. She worked the soil, soaked the sun, and gazed at the drifting clouds. Oma's journal was never far away, full of tidbits, advice, proverbs, and verse. Often, they were just scrawled in the margins, like,

Pull a weed, say a prayer.

Garden and soul, tidy and clean.

One day, while Karin was searching for rebellious weeds among the rows of potatoes, Marie knocked at the gate. They hadn't spoken since the last week of school. As much as she might have wanted to, Karin didn't dare call. Guilt by association was a powerful Nazi theme, and Karin refused to put her one and only friend at risk. But she missed her dearly.

Marie, dressed in a bright summer dress, her cheeks brown from the sun, had tears in her eyes when she saw Karin.

They embraced—Karin held tight until a doubt leapt up and grabbed her by the throat.

"Did Frau Hingis send you?" she asked, releasing her.

"Heavens no!" Marie answered, stunned for a moment. "But I can see how you might wonder that. I've been dying to know how you are, ever since..." She paused awkwardly. Karin knew what she meant. Ever since Frei.

Marie smiled. "Ever since school ended."

Karin slipped her arm inside Marie's and led her back toward the garden.

"Come see what I've been doing," she said.

They surveyed the rows of vegetables before taking a seat together on the patch of grass.

"Today is the longest day of the year, the start of summer," Karin said, staring up at the drifting clouds. "I'm going to stay up all night to soak in every second."

They chatted for a few minutes about safe subjects—the weather, the garden, Opa's unfinished bomb shelter, Marie's upcoming visit to her aunt in Bavaria. When these topics had run their course, the pauses grew longer, threatening their pleasant visit.

"What are your plans?" Marie finally asked.

"I thought I might visit my mother in Berlin."

Marie's eyes narrowed. "But I thought you didn't—that she didn't..."

Karin laughed. "I know. That's how desperate I've become, I suppose. All I know is I can't take it here much longer."

Marie, seeming to sense Karin's caution, reached for her hand and took it in hers. "I don't believe any of them."

"That's a relief," Karin said, her voice still heavy with sarcasm. "What have they told you?"

"Do you really want to know?"

"I suppose I could guess, but I might enjoy a laugh at the kinds of rumors going around. Go ahead, tell me."

Marie smoothed the front of her dress. "Actually, it's kind of complicated. There's the official version—the one from Frau Hingis..."

"Which means according to Rudi," Karin interjected.

"Yes. Officially, this is another heroic deed. You led the Hitler Youth to the gang."

"Karin the Magnificent, a model for all Maidens," Karin scoffed. "Funny, but if that version is true, then why hasn't she come to congratulate me? Why hasn't she insisted I return to the BDM meetings?"

"Only the youngest girls believe the official version," Marie said. "And Elfreda. She's green with jealousy."

"Poor thing," Karin said, chuckling. "Give her my regards when you see her. And a piece of advice."

"What's that?" Marie asked, genuinely curious.

"Wolves like to hunt. Quit barking after them like one of their pups. They want a challenge, and will come to you if you're patient. Quiet down, and eventually they'll come to see you as prey."

Marie tensed, her eyes wide.

"I'm sorry," Karin said. "Poor Elfreda doesn't know what she's wishing for." She moved on. "And the unofficial version?"

"I know you couldn't have led the Hitler Youth to the gang, Karin. You would have never done that knowing they would kill that boy."

Marie's tone suggested a question behind her statement. Karin judged she was looking for confirmation of her faith.

"Be careful," Karin said with a wink. "That kind of talk sounds like treason. You don't want to align yourself with me. Don't get me wrong—I really appreciate you coming over today, Marie—but it's a big risk for you."

"A big risk? What do you mean?"

Poor Marie. Her innocence would die a quick and painful death, sooner or later. After a moment, Karin regretted the thought. If Marie was naïve, then Karin was stupid, for she had led the Gestapo right to Frei.

Karin looked around the perimeter of the fence before lowering her voice.

"You and I think we are having a private conversation, right?" Marie nodded.

"And for now, it is. But if Rudi or the police or the Gestapo learn that you were here, then you fall under suspicion. And if they question you, then whatever we discuss, *eventually,* will no longer be secret. And anything I tell you that doesn't fit with the image of Karin the Magnificent—anything I tell you that you don't share with them—makes you as guilty as me. So, the less I tell you, the safer you are."

Marie looked horrified.

"I'm sorry, my dear, but it's come to this. Even for teenage girls."

Marie's face showed her struggle with the reality Karin described.

"Then why did you go? Why did you try to find him? Why risk your life for that boy?"

Karin looked down and pulled on a sprig of grass.

"I've been avoiding that question, Marie." Karin said with a smile. She took Marie's hands as tears spilled down her cheeks. "Leave it to you—my friend, my one and only friend. The only person in the world who cares about me."

They held each other for a moment and let the tears come. Karin had misjudged Marie. Her innocence was the strength of love.

Karin started at the beginning, sharing the basics of her encounters with Frei. How his personality didn't fit his nickname. How there was something unusual about him that she couldn't put her finger on. Frei was weak and yet, to Rudi and Gossen, so powerful. When Frei was caught, the encounter was terrifying, but odd. Gossen seemed so... so rattled by Frei. What was it that made the boy so dangerous?

"I suppose after everything, I felt sorry for Frei. And curious as to why. Why did he leave his family for the sake of this notion of freedom? He wasn't the least bit free. He seemed tortured by something, I have no idea. And still, he was freer than you or me."

Marie pressed her lips together. "How do you figure that? He had the whole world chasing him."

"Look at us," Karin replied. "We dress up like Nazis and do what they say. Be good girls for the Führer. Bear a child when the time comes. Fight the war in the kitchen. Don't speak up or speak out. We can't even enjoy a quiet afternoon in the garden. They are with us everywhere. They want us every moment. That's not freedom."

"Was he planning to assassinate the Führer?"

Karin chilled for an instant. Was Marie asking on her own? Was this still just a friendly visit?

"You see, Marie? Even that question shows how they are in our minds! They come between the secrets of friends and cause us to doubt. Don't you understand?"

Marie's expression told Karin she didn't. She had leaned back, inserting a slight distance between them. Her eyes showed worry. But Marie's reaction served as all the confirmation Karin needed. Marie was not thinking about freedom. She was still concerned for her friend.

Karin let out a breath, shook her head, and answered Marie's original question.

"I don't think Frei was planning what you asked about. For everything Frei was, I don't think he could have brought himself to do it."

"How do you know?"

"I don't. It just seemed like he wanted to be, somehow, normal. Just like me, in a way. But there's no such thing as normal anymore."

"I've missed you," Marie said.

"And I'm sorry, Marie. Please forgive me, will you?"

Marie shook her head. "Don't be silly. What's to forgive?"

"I'm sorry I got you involved with the Hitler Youth office. With Herr Kohl—*no Fraulein, I insist—call me Rudi*," she mocked.

"There's nothing to forgive."

"Be careful, Marie. You're a beautiful girl. You shouldn't let him get you alone."

Marie blushed.

"Don't worry about me," she said. "I'll be fine. It's you I'm worried about. If, like you say, you were, let's say—sympathetic at least, to Frei and the gang, and you were trying to warn him, why don't they arrest you?"

"That's the one question I can't figure out. Especially with the Führer's planned visit. You'd think they wouldn't take any chances, even on someone like me."

Karin got up from the grass.

"Wait here," she said.

A moment later she returned with a small brown envelope.

"Some weeks ago, Frei came here to visit," she explained. "He gave me this letter and asked me to deliver it."

Marie's eyes were as round as the garden's green tomatoes.

"A letter? To whom?"

"His mother. I understand now. He seemed to be hinting that it was his goodbye." Karin was turning the letter over and over in her hands.

"Why didn't you take it?"

"When Frei was killed, I became afraid. I don't know what to say to her."

Marie stroked Karin's arm.

"You don't have to say anything. Let the letter say it."

Marie was right. She had promised Frei she would take it. As painful as it might be, his mother needed to know, she needed to have the letter.

"Will you go with me? Right now? I think I might be able to if you come too."

Marie stood up first, brushed off her dress, and pulled Karin to her feet. Linking arms, she pulled Karin toward the gate.

"Let's go," she said.

Nearly an hour later, they disembarked the tram in a section of Cologne that neither of the girls had ever visited before. Along the way, they asked a mailman for directions. They marveled at the tree-lined streets, stately mansions behind iron fences, and manicured lawns. The neighborhood reminded Karin of hers in the diplomatic section of Luxembourg City.

She double-checked the address Frei had scrawled on the brown paper and wondered for a moment if he had staged some cruel hoax from beyond the grave. But the written number matched the chiseled digits on the stone column of the entrance, and they had come too far to turn back now.

Through the arched iron gate—opened but not inviting—they ascended the slight rise of the circular stone drive.

Karin knew this kind of place—grass, shrubs, trees, flowers all groomed to such an unnatural level of perfection that human presence seemed alien to it. Even the crunch of gravel beneath their shoes seemed a violation.

Under the portico of the entryway Karin reached for the buzzer and pressed. The sound was swallowed by the vast interior. Her resolve suddenly wavering, she retreated, clamped her arm inside Marie's, and waited.

Uncomfortable seconds later, the door swung open, and they were greeted by a housemaid in a gray dress, white apron and gloves to match, whose severe pinpoint eyes, looking down over a bird-like nose, told them they had better have a good reason for disturbing her.

Karin suddenly realized she had no idea who to ask for. She didn't know Frei's full name.

"Excuse me, please, may we speak with the lady of the house?" she finally managed.

The maid paused and then pursed her lips. "And whom shall I say is calling?"

Karin introduced them, and then added, "Would you please let her know that I knew her son."

A look of alarm flashed in the maid's dark eyes.

"What do you want?"

Marie stiffened. "It's for the lady of the house, only."

The maid's eyes darted to Marie, and all at once her severity changed to fear. She asked them to wait and disappeared behind the great door. The girls' grip on each other tightened.

A moment later, a tall, slender woman came to the door. Karin knew at once this was no hoax—the woman's gentle features and pale skin were the source of Frei's. Her eyes carried the same uncomfortable distance as well as his sadness. The only thing out of place in the presentation of exhaustion and grief was the string of bright pearls around her neck that matched her silver hair.

She did not invite them in.

"One of you knows—pardon me—*knew*—my son?" she said, her voice breaking at the mistake.

Karin curtseyed. "Yes, Frau. I did. A little."

"What do you want?"

Karin nibbled her lip. "May we come in, please? I have a letter he wanted me to give you."

The woman staggered back and was caught from falling only because of the maid nearby. She blinked away sudden tears and trembled.

"Is this some kind of joke?" she stammered.

"Nein, gnädige Frau. He wanted me to deliver this before," Karin replied, showing her the note. "But I was afraid."

The woman ran inside, leaving them alone with the maid, whose expression had softened.

"Wait here," she said, and disappeared inside.

Karin and Marie looked at each other nervously.

Moments later, the maid reappeared and ushered them in. She led them down a marble-tiled hall to a set of French doors on the left, which opened to a sitting room full of light from the patio behind it. The plush decor—carpet thicker than grass, finely detailed antique furniture, glittering ceramic cherubs, fresh-flowered vases, and gold-framed Renaissance art on the walls—awakened another long-lost memory of Karin's home in Luxembourg.

The maid had them sit down on a red-velvet sofa, of the finest quality, Karin was sure, but not at all her idea of comfort. The memory of her own mother flooded back: *Sit up straight, knees together, soles flat on the floor, hands folded on your lap. Don't speak unless spoken to.*

A minute or two later, Frei's mother appeared. Her face was red and blotched, and she clung to a white handkerchief. She sat down on a chair opposite the sofa.

The maid left, only to return a few moments later pushing a dark wooden cart, which bore a large silver tray. It featured an enormous brass samovar, blue and white Dutch teacups with thin edges and handles, a plate of sugar cubes, and stacks of triangular sandwiches. The speed of production seemed to Karin a minor miracle.

The housemaid poured the cups, dropped the sugar cubes, and stirred the milk without even asking. The entire operation had been executed with the precision of a military operation rather than a social gathering. With a flick of her glance the maid was gone, leaving the three of them alone.

The woman took the teacup to her lips. Everything was thin—the edge of the cup, the dark blue lines depicting windmills, canals, Dutch maidens and tulips, the woman's fingers, the wisps of hair that refused to obey the others, her gray lips. She was a violin whose strings were tightened far too often, Karin judged, and at her breaking point.

"May I see the letter, Fraulein Blik?" she asked, unable to contain the rattling of the teacup on its saucer.

"Of course," Karin answered. When she handed the note to Frei's mother, she took one look, curled her nose, and held it between her pinched fingers like it was a dead rat. She struggled for a moment with the knotted string, unable to focus her nerves on the task.

"May I?" Karin offered. The woman forced an embarrassed smile and obliged. Karin quickly freed the scroll and gave it back to Frei's mother.

The woman's entire body trembled, and the tears returned to her eyes. She pressed back against the sofa and clutched her arms together, shaking her head.

"I can't," she said. "I can't read it. Please, will you?" Her voice shook like her body.

Karin shared a nervous glance at Marie, then spread the note out on her lap and read:

Dearest Mother,

If you read this letter, then my heart is glad, for that means that Karin was successful finding you.

Please give my regards to all in the house who remember me. And please give Fritzi a good scratch behind the ears for me. I hope with all that is in me that you are well and in good health.

As for me, I am well, as are all my friends. We are safe, well fed, and happy. And most of all, free. I don't expect you to understand nor agree with me as to why I have chosen this path, but I want you to know that if there was any way I could be with you, I would. Perhaps soon it will all be over, one way or another, and we can be together. That is my sincerest wish and fondest hope. But in the meantime, please know that I think of you always, and always keep you close in my heart.

If fate decides it, we will be together again, perhaps even in happy times. But perhaps not. Evil prowls too close and keeps us apart.

Please forgive me.

Your beloved son,

Friedrich

By the time Karin finished, Frei's mother was rigid but quaking, the tremors growing more pronounced by the second. Karin stood up, walked around the cart, and took the woman in her arms. She seemed shocked at first, drawing back, until she could help it no longer. She leaned into Karin and sobbed. Karin held her gently, as the woman seemed little more than a skeleton beneath her fine clothes. The emotions washed over the woman in great waves, and Marie was in tears, but Karin herself did not cry. Something darker boiled inside.

Karin wanted to go. She had kept her promise, and there was nothing more to say.

"Thank you for the tea," she said, standing, and returning the cup to the tray. "We'll go now."

Frei's mother stood up with them. She looked embarrassed from her emotional lapse and was fiddling with her hair, pearls, and the fit of her dress. Then she realized she was still holding the letter. She froze and then thrust her arm forward like it was infected with spores, but she didn't drop it.

Then, an idea flashed in her eyes, and she retreated to a cabinet on the far side of the room near the patio doors. She snatched a portrait that was propped there and returned to the girls. Carefully removing the back of the frame, she folded the letter and inserted it behind the photograph. Karin wondered why Frei's mother wanted to hide the letter until she replaced the back and turned the portrait face up. Karin's heart froze in her chest.

At the center of the picture, Frei's mother sat with a proud smile. At her knee, the young son with sad eyes. Behind them the charming father in a crisp suit: Heinrich Gossen.

CHAPTER THIRTY-THREE

Karin flew out the front door and ran straight for the gate, leaving a wake of flung stone in the perfect carpet of grass. Her momentum carried her between the stone columns and into the street, where she turned and sprinted down the middle like an animal freed from a trap.

Her body could not sustain its fury. Within a minute, her heart racing and throat scorched, her legs went rubbery, and she faltered. Two steps later, staggering sideways, she managed to reach the curb and the soft grass under the shade of a maple tree. She fell on hands and knees and let go the eruption of bile.

Every strand in her body clenched to expel the rage and disgust. Her stomach wretched again and again, the sounds more beast than human—as if to expel not only the contents of her stomach but something more, something deeper.

When Marie caught up, Karin still shuddered with grief. Marie took her in her arms and held her like the child she was.

The next day, the city was invaded by swollen clouds along a wide front from the west. It blanketed the city and let loose. Karin's midsection ached from the previous day's strain, but the soreness was minor compared to the bitterness in her soul. She alternated—one moment enraged at the vile man who had killed his own son, the next turning on herself for letting him and Rudi entangle her in their scheme to destroy him. She had gone from naïve to fool in the space of weeks. And that's how it would end. The regime did not permit one to continue the journey from fool to wisdom. She would remain forever a fool. They would extract her obedience day by day, drop by drop. She would soon forget how it had come to this. Like everyone else, she would simply go numb and fall in line. The rain only contributed to the feeling, stretching from one day to the next and the one after that. The shroud over the city was a heavy, dull gray that matched the despair she sucked in with every breath.

Eventually the rain stopped, but Karin's numbness did not. Using the excuse with Opa that she was ill, she hardly left her bed in the days that followed the revelation. Not that she slept—most nights were spent tossing in the space between sleep and consciousness—seeing either Frei's young face in his mother's picture frame or the twisted one on the street at the base of the brick wall in Ehrenburg.

When Karin finally ventured out into the backyard one steamy afternoon, the smells of damp earth and the sun upon the fresh leaves had lost their power. Although the tomatoes, peppers, peas, and potatoes seemed to have exploded in the space of a few days, along with an insurgency of new weeds, she had no heart for the battle. Her desire for the garden seemed to have washed into the muddy pool at the base of the hole Opa called a shelter.

On top of it all, Karin's survey of the backyard changes uncovered, in the strip of grass in the far corner, her grandmother's journal, left open to the onslaught of weather. She picked up the swollen, smeared mess that was twice as heavy as before. Most of the pages were an unrecognizable wash of blue and black ink.

It was the last straw. She dropped it where she found it and returned to the house, devoid of any feeling but the desire to disappear.

She was on the edge of an abyss, she knew, one that threatened to swallow her forever. She had not sought this place and had tried everything she knew to avoid it, and yet here she was, staring into a bottomless pit.

Rain returned the following day. Karin watched from the kitchen as Opa, visible from the chest up, bailing the rain from his hole, one futile canful at a time. Who knew how long he had been working at it, but his face was red—from exertion and surely frustration too. After a time, he gave up, slamming the can down, which sent a great brown splash out the hole. This struck Karin as both darkly funny and utterly ridiculous. Opa still believed in solutions, and despite his present setback, seemed determined to defeat even the rain.

If only I were more like him.

Instead, the shovel reminded her of the pistol she had dug up in the garden. Surely it was hidden in Opa's shed. A dark idea slithered up from the abyss and wrapped around her ankles.

That night, once Opa had retired to the shed and darkness had covered the world, Karin slipped outside. Like she did when breaking curfew, she waited on the back step to let her eyes adjust and then, under a starless sky, crossed the garden.

She paused at the shed door. Opa was snoring lightly.

She slid open the door, a few centimeters to test for squeaks, but the crack revealed too much light from inside. Neighbors or a local patrol might see it. Better to go quickly even if it makes a noise. Opa could sleep through bombs, she reasoned, and so perhaps he would sleep through the scrape of a door. She was right—he didn't even stir.

Once inside, Karin almost gave up at the start. The interior of the shed was a junkyard in itself, worse than she remembered. Once she had offered to organize it for him, but he refused.

"It's organized already," he had said, tapping his forehead. "In here. I know where everything is."

She tried to make sense of the chaos. Long boards hung in the rafters, scrap wood in a metal bin. A pile of bricks merged with a half-finished floor. String in bundles, string loose, wire on spools, wire in a basket. Nuts, bolts, screws, nails, hinges, doorknobs, hooks—filling old soup cans and glass jars. Tools everywhere and half torn-down typewriters, fans, irons, a telephone, and other unidentifiable machines. Enough metal for a tank, and she wondered how it had escaped the eye of the Hitler Youth scrap drives.

Karin pushed and poked at the tangled mass, checking each move for signs of him stirring. She could have torn the structure down around him, it seemed, and he would have snored on.

The search seemed hopeless, and she was about to give up when Opa snorted. Shifting in his chair, Karin noticed an unusual bulge in the corner of the seat cushion. Bending over the wooden arm of the old office chair, she looked closer. The seam along the bulge was stitched with a piece of cotton string rather than thread, and stuffing from the cushion lay in clumps on the dirt floor. Most telling, however, was the dirty burlap that showed from inside.

Karin knelt and tugged at the seam. Despite the mess Opa had made of the repair, the string held. But she could feel the hard steel inside the burlap. She felt a twinge of shame—he must have anticipated this moment and deliberately stashed the pistol where she would never think to look.

She nudged him and pulled at the edge of the cushion at the same time. Soon she had maneuvered him enough to make out the triangular shape of the burlap.

A pair of scissors would take care of the stitches. Having not seen any during her previous search, she focused her efforts on the workbench. In the shadow below the lowest shelf, she found them among a spilled jar of pencils and the metal box the pistol had been buried in.

The box made her curious, and so she pulled it forward into the light. The lock was no barrier now. She opened the lid and learned why the box was still heavy—inside lay her grandmother's journal, in a bed of uncooked rice. The volume was still swollen and the pages wrinkled, but it was nearly dry, and perhaps not beyond all hope.

Carefully she lifted the book and placed it on the workbench. She opened it to a random page, a list of vegetables planned for the garden of 1918. The date triggered a memory. One day the previous February, Karin thought she would maximize the vegetable ration by bringing turnips home from the market. Proud of herself, she showed Opa her haul. He calmly took the basket, walked to the curb, and threw them down the sewer.

"I don't care if I starve, but after the winter of 1918, I'll never eat turnips again," he said.

Karin smiled at the memory of his stubbornness and closed the journal. Opa had settled over the pistol again. Even asleep he was trying to protect her.

The dark idea suddenly let go. She did not pick up the scissors. The pistol would stay where it was, safe under Opa.

She had just slid the box back on its shelf when it caught on something. Bending down, she reached into the narrow space and withdrew a small bundle of envelopes bound by a string. Even in the faint light, the circular ink stamp was clear: *Feldpost.* Her breath caught. The familiar handwriting—*Karin Blik*—went through her like a blade. For an instant, anger flared that Opa had hidden them, but as she set the bundle atop Oma's journal, it passed. He had only been trying to protect her.

Each envelope bore the same postmark, two days earlier, which was no surprise. Mail from the Eastern Front was notoriously delayed, though no one dared complain.

Worried that Opa would wake up, she read only the first one:

2 Juli 1942

Dear Karin,

Hello and pardon from the back of a truck—the bumps cause my pencil to bounce but the ride is a welcome break from km after km marching. Only time for a quick word, but spirits are high among us all. The horizon stretches forever. I wish I could bring this sky to you!

Don't forget to look up and remember me,

Willem

The letter stung her eyes. She would need strength to read the others.

Before leaving, she placed a kiss on the crown of Opa's head.

Outside, mist was rising in the garden. She held the letters and journal against her chest and waited for her eyes to adjust. A rabbit moved between the rows and began to nibble on a leaf. She smiled and let him eat his fill. Overhead, the clouds obscured all but a few of the brightest stars. For the first time in weeks, she slept hard.

CHAPTER THIRTY-FOUR

The next day, Karin's mind was made up. She would not go into the shed again. But she would not sit in her room, staring into the abyss either. Opa could not protect her. The garden could not save her. Schlinge's indifference—the seed he planted in Luxembourg—had sprouted in soil watered by Gossen's manipulation. Neither cared for truth, only image and power.

Karin had worried that trying to warn Frei would bring retribution, but she had been looking at it the wrong way. Gossen's wayward son Frei, she realized, had been an embarrassment, and worse, a threat to his reputation and authority, a secret to be kept at all costs, including murder. A man like Schlinge could use that secret as a weapon. Now so could she. She would turn Gossen to dig Schlinge's grave.

She left after breakfast while Opa had already retreated to the shed. Clouds had returned, sinking to rooftop level before pummeling the city with sheets of rain.

The EL-DE Haus was a nondescript, three-story office building that nonetheless carried an intimidating aura in its starkness. As Karin approached, she noticed that people avoided passing directly in front of it, choosing to cross the street instead. When

Karin stepped over a sidewalk grate, whispered rumors among boys at school came to mind, which she had discounted until this moment. They said that if one drew near after dark, you could hear the cries and screams of interrogated prisoners through the sidewalk grates. Her pulse quickened, but she pushed through the revolving door of Gestapo Headquarters.

Inside, the foyer was polished marble and surprisingly free of red banners and swastikas. All business, the inhabitants were dressed like ordinary clerks, secretaries, and managers. Even the man at the reception desk greeted her with a smile.

"May I help you, fraulein?"

"I'm here to see Herr Gossen," she said as confidently as she could manage.

The man's eyebrows jumped.

"Do you have an appointment?"

"Yes," she lied. The opposite answer would never have worked.

"Just a moment." He picked up the telephone and consulted a directory.

Realizing that permission was unlikely, she headed for the stairs behind him.

"Fraulein!" he called, but she was already gone.

She took the stairs two at a time, heading for the top, where she guessed Gossen's office would be. On the first-floor level landing, a sign blocked the ascending stairway: Closed: Use the Elevator. Two workmen in gray coveralls were rolling a pale coat of paint over a ceiling once filled with constellations in a midnight blue sky.

She paused and looked behind. Two officers had entered the stairs below, sure to intercept her on the way to the elevator.

She stepped over the barrier and kept climbing, her shoes slipping on canvas drop cloths. Halfway up, she had to crawl through the scaffolding. A crossbar caught her foot; she stumbled, striking her knee. One of the painters shouted down at her, a flick of his brush splattering her hair and sleeve like bird droppings. She didn't stop.

Gossen's office, as she guessed, occupied the front corner. Another secretary sat guard.

"I'm here to see Herr Gossen," she announced.

He looked up from his pad, his annoyance plain.

"I have an appointment," she added.

"One does not make appointments with Herr Gossen," he said.

As before, she stepped around his desk and crossed to a large, paneled door.

"Fraulein, I insist..." the secretary called, but Karin pushed through.

Herr Gossen was at his desk, pen in hand. He looked up without surprise.

The secretary appeared in the doorframe. "I'm sorry, sir."

Gossen raised his hand. "Fraulein Blik is welcome anytime."

The secretary retreated while Gossen ushered her to sit in the padded leather chair across from his desk.

"Are you well? Your face is quite flushed."

Karin became conscious of her feverish cheeks and thundering heart.

"To what do I owe this...happy surprise?"

The script she had pondered escaped her. Her confidence faltered like something in the rain.

"Forgive me," she began, trying desperately to settle herself.

He poured a glass of water from a cabinet, and she drank.

"Nothing to forgive, fraulein. You've had a great shock. We try our best to protect children from the dangers and evils of the world, but alas, fate thrusts itself upon us at times and in ways we do not choose. To test our resolve, our strength, our determination. I don't expect you to understand now. But one day I think you will."

She handed him Fritz's letter.

"I have evidence now," she said. "Schlinge wanted to kill my father."

He took a moment to read it, in which she studied him for hints that he knew its contents already. His expression revealed little but suggested that he had not seen the letter before.

He placed it on the desk and smoothed the wrinkles with his hands for a moment.

"Well done, Karin, and thank you for bringing this to me. Does anyone besides Fritz and you know of the existence of this letter?"

She explained the discovery in Luxembourg and her encounter with Schlinge.

"I see," he replied through a characteristic smile. "You've done very well for yourself. I need investigators like you on my staff."

"This is enough—you can expose him now and take him down."

Gossen stood up and circled to the window, where the rain streamed over the pane. "Your determination is outstanding. But let me ask you something, Karin. What do you make of Herr Schlinge's lack of concern that you found this letter?"

"He says it's all lies, just an old rumor, and blames you. He told me not to trust you. You're just a..."

"Go on."

"A smooth talker."

"No doubt he claims that I'm jealous of him, now that he is engaged to your mother."

She nodded.

"Dear old Heinrich never changes."

"He's not worthy of his office," Karin pressed. "He's a traitor and a coward."

Gossen continued to stare out the window.

"And I've never said a word to him about Frei. I came to you first!"

He turned back suddenly, his expression flashing something fierce, but only for an instant.

Karin's face ignited again. "Oh no! I didn't mean it that way! I would never tell him anything. Never."

"I'm glad for that, fraulein."

She swallowed hard. "Then you can take him down?"

He forced a calm smile. "As I've told you, Herr Schlinge is a powerful man. This information must be used carefully. It will take time. But you must leave it with me."

He had returned to his desk and pressed a button. His secretary appeared and ushered her out, leaving her in a new torrent.

CHAPTER THIRTY-FIVE

The Hauptbahnhof was busy with men and supplies, soldiers, and businessmen. Karin waited in line at the ticket counter, all at once aware that she, as a young girl alone, stood out among the travelers. The station seemed empty of children, parents, students, and tourists. But her mind was made up. She needed a change, a new start, a new life. Perhaps she could convince Mother to help her.

The woman at the ticket counter gave her a strange look when Karin approached the window.

"One Second Class ticket to Berlin on the 11:30," she said, sliding the Reichsmarks under the cage. "One way."

The woman shook her head. "Not today."

"Is something wrong?" Karin asked.

The woman looked over her glasses at Karin. "Special restrictions are in effect until further notice. Didn't your BDM leader inform you? All efforts are being focused to support the soldiers in the east."

The woman shoved the money back.

"How long will it last?"

The woman shrugged. "Who knows? But you must have prior approval. Reason for travel. You don't look like a soldier and are too young for business. When you're one of those, come back. Next!"

Karin staggered back, stunned.

Can I never escape this hell?

She wandered around the station for a while, mulling the options in her mind. Could she hop on a train at night? Hitch a ride on a truck? She remembered the first days of the war, when she tried to travel from Berlin to Luxembourg to warn Hansi. She managed to convince Schlinge to issue her a pass.

I have to get out of here.

She found the row of telephone booths near the center of the terminal. She dug the coins from her pocket and dialed the number.

Please, God. For once, let her answer.

Her prayer was answered. Mother answered. Karin began to cry.

"Karin, dear, what's happened? Where are you?"

"Please, Mother. I need you."

"Calm down. I'm sure everything will be all right."

"No, Mother. Not this time. Please, I've got to leave. I can't bear another minute here."

She told her about trying to buy the ticket.

"I know you can get me a ticket. *Herr Schlinge.*"

"Now, Karin, we've discussed this. You can come in August, before school starts again. It's only a few weeks."

Karin cradled the phone in both hands. Her body trembled as she spoke. The line seemed to be the last thread holding her at the edge of the abyss. Her voice grew low.

"Mother, please listen. I'm begging you. I don't ask you for much, but I need this one thing. This one thing. I know we don't get along, but if any part of you ever loved me, or ever loved Father, then you'll do this for me."

She sank to the floor, still clinging to the phone.

The line was silent for a moment.

"All right, Karin. Enough with the theatrics. I'll make the arrangements."

Two hours later, the woman at the ticket counter wrote up the ticket.

"Your mother must know some pretty important people," she said. "This kind of thing usually takes days, if not weeks."

Karin did not want to think about it. She took the ticket and left with the only thoughts that mattered: Mother had kept her word, and Friday, two days away, she would be leaving Cologne. For good.

The next day, Karin used all the ration coupons she could to buy a ham bone, stripped of all but a few shreds of meat. She boiled it with some potatoes and the first harvest of young green beans from the garden. It would last Opa a while, after which he would have to fend for himself. She felt some guilt over leaving him, but not that he would starve. The seat cushion in the shed and the bomb shelter project were evidence enough that he could rise to the occasion. More difficult was the idea that she was leaving for good when he thought it would only be for a week or two.

In the afternoon, she turned to packing. She was in her room, filling the suitcase covered with stickers from all the places she had been—Oslo, Paris, Luxembourg. As she had so many times before, she had learned to keep things to the bare minimum. Clothes and shoes could be replaced. Attachments only made things more difficult. She was sure to leave room for Oma's journal. Otherwise, the feeling was different. This time, she was desperate to leave. She was folding the last blouse when the phone rang.

For an instant she tensed, wondering if her mother was calling. Or the station.

We're sorry, but there's been a mistake. Your ticket is not valid.

She let it ring, hoping the caller would give up, but it was no use. With every ring, her anxiety rose. She could not bear it.

"Hallo?"

"Good afternoon, fraulein."

It was Rudi. His voice was weak and almost slurred, she thought. Not like him at all. She regretted answering at once. But strangely, she was not afraid.

"What do you want?" she asked.

"Are you well, Karin?" He seemed put off.

"I'm fine."

"You haven't been to the office lately."

A strange and obvious observation, she thought.

"I've quit, Herr Kohl."

"After all this time, Karin. Back to Herr Kohl?"

"I've quit, *Rudi*. I'm not working for you anymore." She realized she could have lied and simply told him she was visiting her mother in Berlin.

"Now, now, Karin, you sound so...so final."

"I am."

There was a pause on the phone, some shuffling of paper or something in the background. What was wrong with him?

"One just doesn't quit, you understand."

"Well, I have. I can't do it any longer."

"Of course you can. Karin! I need you! Pardon me, forgive me." One moment he was shouting, the next he was back to his normal monotone. "You must return. The place is a disaster without you."

Karin's anger was heightened both by the surprise and his determination to pretend like nothing had happened. No doubt he was giddy over Frei's death, but had he forgotten that she betrayed him in the process?

"Rudi—do you hear yourself? Why do you want me? You know I didn't hate Frei. I was trying to protect him. I wanted to warn him! Don't you understand? I'm not like you. I hate you. I hate all of you!"

"No, Karin, please." His voice—*he sounded so desperate.* "Don't speak that way, Karin." There was another pause, and then his voice turned suddenly sober again.

"You cannot talk to me that way, Karin. I am your superior. Surely you remember our agreement."

"What agreement? You and Herr Gossen agreed, but did I? Did I really have a choice?"

"It was an arrangement any other girl would envy," he countered. "To be honored by the Reich, to be favored with a job such as yours. Do you hear yourself, Karin?"

He was right. A girl like Elfreda would have died to trade places with Karin. If only they could have. But at what cost? It was too terrible, and Karin was finished. She refused to argue.

"I'm certain you remember the terms. You would stay in school, join the BDM, and work for me in the Hitler Youth office. Sadly, you have failed in all three areas. Frau Hingis tells me your final grades are an embarrassment. You've quit attending meetings of the BDM, and—"

"I know this! Why are you repeating it?"

"There is still a way out, Karin."

"I don't want it."

"I can reverse your scores. I can fix things with Frau Hingis. I just need you to come back to the office."

"No, Rudi! I told you—I'm not coming back! I'm never coming back! Send me to Poland, I don't care. Anywhere but here."

The phone went silent again. Was Rudi—*hurt?*

When he finally spoke, his voice quaked with rage.

"Don't you realize, Karin, that with a phone call I can have you arrested?"

There it was. She had expected it earlier in the call. Even now it made her tremble, forcing her to hold the phone handset with both hands for fear it might fall.

"Then why haven't you?" she asked.

"A perceptive question, to be sure. It's part of the reason we haven't. You are very clever, very valuable to me. To us," he quickly added. "Sending you to Poland would be a waste of a girl such as you. By the way, I would not be so eager to go there if I were you, because, given our rapid advance, it's more likely you'd be sent farther East. Ukraine I would guess, maybe even Belorussia, who knows? The Bolshevik collective farms are a disaster. And a pretty girl like you will be quite an attraction to those starving, lice-riddled POWs working there now."

The images made her shudder. She had seen pictures in the newsreels and magazines. The conquered territories seemed lost to modern progress—tumbledown wooden shacks against barren landscapes. Squat and shriveled women bound in scarves slapping their clothes against the rocks of a river. Dirty-faced children whose ribcages pushed through their pale skin. Misery from sunrise to sunset.

The ticket in her bag gave her hope and courage to finally stand up to him. This vile Rudi, who thought he had her, but did not. He was nearly as vile as Gossen. She should have stood up to them both, long ago. She would show them now.

"I don't care what you do to me, Rudi, I don't. Just leave me alone!"

Karin slammed the phone down and returned to her room. She looked at the ticket one more time: Köln to Berlin—tomorrow morning at 7:21. Once she explained to Mother everything that happened, Mother would be surprised, but only a little. And she would rise to the occasion. Her considerable charm could be put to good use for once. She would transfer Karin's residence papers to Berlin. Perhaps Opa could sell the house and join them. Karin could start over. And if Rudi's or Gossen's arm proved long, Mother could rekindle the flame with Schlinge, leveraging the memory of Karin's father, his old friend. And if Schlinge turned cold, she could find another official in Berlin higher than them all. Mother would do all of this for her daughter, especially if Karin showed interest in Berlin society like Mother had suggested.

Karin clutched the ticket to her breast. Rudi had called her bluff, but she had changed the game. The exhilaration brought tears to her eyes. She might finally be free.

CHAPTER THIRTY-SIX

With the slam of the receiver on its cradle, Karin's anxiety broke like a fever. The pressure of her life seemed somehow finally lifted. And for the first time in months, she felt the full sense of herself, the full weight of her body on the floor, and the full depth of each breath. Passing a hundred history exams could not have done more.

She had hardly turned away when the phone shook again.

Like all Nazi leaders, Rudi was not accustomed to defiance. Truth was, she was not accustomed to it either. Standing up to him brought a sensation of freedom. But the fever of doubt was stubborn and rose again. She had gone too far, and she knew it. The phone kept ringing. She reached for the receiver, her hand shaking.

Stick with the plan, came a quiet voice from inside. *Write the letter.*

Karin broke away from the telephone stand and ascended the stairs, leaving the phone to drone on. In her room, she closed the door behind her to shut out the noise and knelt beside her bed.

The suitcase was full. The ticket still said *Freitag, 07:21*.

The phone rang a few more times and then stopped. The silence was chilling. Rudi, she knew, would not give up.

Keep going.

She took a seat at the desk and retrieved a sheet from the tall stack of stationery paper intended for letters to Willem. The crisp edges and smooth finish of a blank page normally gave Karin a sense of hope and possibility. Now she saw only its emptiness—each sheet a testament to the loss, each page a conversation that would never take place. The ink would stay in the pen, the words never written. Willem—in the ground somewhere far away, and silent.

Dear Opa,

Please forgive me for not telling you, but I had to leave this way for your own sake. I could not bear you trying to talk me out of it. Explaining any further would only put you in danger when they interrogate you.

When you find this letter, I will be on the train to Berlin. I am going to Mother's. For good. Perhaps you can join us later, but for now, it's the only way, as I can no longer pretend as they want me to. I am not their hero. I am not my father's daughter.

Liebe,

Karin

P.S. Be sure to burn this after you read it.

She folded the sheet, slipped it in an envelope, and let her head fall to the desk. The same strange mix of release and exhaustion accompanied the completion of even small tasks.

She closed her eyes and pictured herself on the morning train. She would nestle up to the window among soldiers, business-men, and bureaucrats. There would be very few like her, and she might stand out among them. But she had the approval, the ticket to prove she belonged there. The train would slip out of the shadow of the terminal and slide across the Dom-Brücke, the

Cathedral Bridge. Below the great steel arches, long coal barges would plow the muddy waters of the Rhine. She would watch the old City of Cologne melt away into farmland and let her eyes close. The rails would rock her to sleep. She would leave it all behind. There would be time to get ready for Mother. They would have to adjust to each other. But somehow, it would work. It had to.

The doorbell made her jump.

She had been dozing. The clock by her bed read almost 9:30 PM, about twenty minutes after she had looked at it last.

It rang again before she had crossed the room. Opa was surely in the shed, unable to hear it.

The bell rang a third time, the interval filled with sharp raps on the door. Karin rushed to the stairs and bounded down. The blackout curtains prevented her from seeing the porch.

"Open up! Open the door!"

"What do you want?" she managed before Rudi pushed through the cracked door. His face held no color. He was panting and looked like he had just outrun a ghost.

He pointed at his throat urgently, mouthing the word "water." She hastily went to the kitchen and returned with a glass of water. He was sprawled on the sofa and was loosening his collar.

She had always observed him as someone under control. And ever calm, like he had just awoken from a restful night's sleep. In front of her now, he was neither. His appearance confused her.

He downed the water in a single draft, letting the last half-gulp stream down his chin. His eyes darted about, and he was shaking.

"What's happened to you?" she asked to her own surprise.

He shook his head as he tried to settle his breath and leaned forward.

"Not me," he said, pointing. "You."

"What about me?"

"It's over."

He fell back against the sofa and let his head sag.

Are those tears? Her surprise and confusion turned to fear. She forced herself to think. Rudi didn't know her plan. Whatever he intended to tell her didn't change that. She would play it out and see.

"I know," she said. "You told me. Poland, Ukraine. I don't care."

He shook his head again.

"No. That's out now."

On the phone, Rudi had been upset, but still confident, and certain. He always seemed to be playing a game, toying with her. He especially enjoyed issuing commands or passing a sentence. All that was gone now.

"I don't understand," she said.

Rudi finally caught his breath. He edged even further forward on the sofa and took Karin by the hands. She jerked away, but he held tight. His hands were cold and sticky. His eyes were open, almost sad. She was as curious as repulsed. He was different somehow. He was *afraid*.

"I spoke with Herr Gossen," he said. "The year in the East is no longer an option. No year of service, no housemaid for a German general, no farmhand."

He stared at the floor, taking his breaths in gulps, bracing himself, it seemed.

Karin couldn't wait.

"Prison? Concentration camp? Where?"

He shook his head and then snapped it straight at her. His eyes, spidered with stress, found hers. He spoke just above a whisper.

"They're coming for you."

The British might as well have dropped a bomb through the roof of her house. The room began to spin. She snatched her hands from his grip and staggered back. Rudi jumped up and guided her to the sofa, where he returned to his seat beside her. She closed her eyes.

"I haven't seen him this way since..." Rudi paused.

He didn't have to finish the sentence. Karin knew what he meant. *Since Frei disrupted the ceremony.*

Her blood went black. She had seen firsthand what Gossen would do.

She had been a fool. A man willing to kill his own son wouldn't hesitate to dispose of her in the same way. But why? Why now?

A moment on the sofa settled her vision but not her thoughts. Things didn't make sense.

"I thought everything was settled. I know I didn't hold up my end of the agreement. But Gossen got what he wanted. He got the gang. He got Frei."

When Karin opened her eyes, the once confident leader of the Hitler Youth had vanished. Before her sat a frightened boy, much like the orphan with wet pants on the edge of the bombed building.

"The Führer's visit has been cancelled," he said. "Schlinge is on his way from Berlin. It will not be a friendly visit. And if I know Gossen, he will not go without a fight. He will take as many with him as he can. You and I are on the top of this list."

CHAPTER THIRTY-SEVEN

Karin pressed back against the cushion. Rudi slid off the seat and picked up the glass from the side table.

"May I have some more water?" he asked. She took it to the kitchen and refilled it. The action broke a kind of spell. Her mind began to race. She could still leave for Berlin. The distance, if not her mother, might protect her. Gossen was high-ranking in Cologne, but not Berlin. If she could escape long enough for Schlinge to deal with him, perhaps that would be enough time. Her mother could speak with Schlinge. Karin would say she loved her father. He was a hero. She missed him and was simply misguided. A poor girl, after all. They loved submission, oaths of loyalty. She would say whatever they wanted.

The plan will still work. Just make it until morning.

Rudi downed the water with unusual urgency.

Karin's voice was calm. "Why did you come here?"

His eyes flashed the old Rudi. "I came to warn you."

"Warn me? An hour ago, you were ready to send me away," she replied. "You couldn't have been happy I hung up on you. You don't like being told no. You've gotten your way from the moment we met. So why the change of heart?"

He took a step sideways, averting her gaze.

Karin moved with him.

"Come to think of it, that's not the real question. The real question is this: why, since Gossen killed Frei, and you and everyone else knew I tried to warn him—why haven't I been arrested before now?

Rudi didn't answer.

"You know something," she pressed. "There's something you haven't told me! What is it?"

She was standing face to face with him now. The force of her words had drawn his eyes back to her. The confrontation seemed to revive the old Rudi.

He crossed to the corner of the room opposite the sofa, where, on the small cloth-covered table, the portrait of Karin's father stood. Her chisel-chinned father, watching over her with a proud but stoic stare. Rudi ran his finger along the frame.

"From the moment we met, Karin, that night in the park, I learned all I needed to know about you. Disrespectful of authority. Sympathetic and vulnerable to rebellion. Your rescue of the boy in the bombed-out apartment was certainly brave. The daughter of a national hero—a hero herself! The perfect story—and necessary after such a massive raid. But I knew. Without the Fatherland, there are no heroes. If you were not willing to join us, you could not be thought of as a hero. I knew you couldn't bear the idea that your father was a hero, because you think of his death as betrayal. I knew the real reason you had avoided joining the BDM all these years, making excuses. You hate the regime; you hate us all." And then, with expert timing, he added, "You hate me."

He let the words have their effect. But she knew his tactics. He expected her to crumble. She sucked in her bottom lip and bit down hard. The pain brought tears but focus. She would not yield.

"And yet you took me on." she said. "If you were so perceptive from the beginning, then why did you do it?"

His ears stretched back in a flush of anger. But, true to form, only for an instant. The smile returned. The game was still on.

"Herr Gossen thought you would be useful. I disagreed. But a good soldier obeys. I took you on. Your work was acceptable once the other one joined you."

"Your office was in shambles. You needed us."

Rudi let a grin turn up from one side of his mouth and began to pace the room. His tone lightened.

"You know, Karin, some people think that we who are the true believers are so rigid in our thinking. We listen only to what we want to hear, and force everything and everyone to our will. It's not always so."

He stopped and turned back to her.

"You, for example. Despite your obvious disdain for your father and the cause he died for, I learned to respect you. You are not like the other girls. You are not constantly primping, are not prone to fits of giggling, nor do you elbow your way for attention."

Elfreda.

The lightness left. His chin was tilted down slightly so that his gaze had become serious, almost sinister. "You are very dangerous," he said. And then, taking a step closer, "And also exciting."

His smile faded. "Do you know why I came tonight, really?"

Karin said nothing.

"Herr Gossen spoke with Herr Schlinge on the telephone," he went on. "They agreed it was time to solve their common problem—you. Schlinge said, *too many weeds have grown up in your garden.* Gossen did not disagree."

Rudi looked down. "So he sent me. Said I might find a gentler way."

A tremor reverberated through Karin's spine.

As soon as he had finished the sentence, he turned away. "It became a challenge, I suppose, that intrigued me. The more I realized your capability, the more I thought I could somehow convince you to join us. I wanted to."

All consideration of Rudi's plans and motivations had vanished. The warning behind his words overwhelmed any meaning in his statements. Karin no longer cared why she hadn't been arrested. Had tonight's show of pity been simply a new level of performance? Whatever the truth, it no longer mattered. His violent intention was finally unmasked. She was in grave danger, as every breath and heartbeat told her. Opa, asleep in the shed, would never hear.

"Are you all right, Karin? You look like you've seen a ghost."

Her expression betrayed her. Rudi was within reach.

He let go of the frame.

She watched it fall, wondering why he had done it. A corner hit first with a crunch; the frame bounced and spun a few times before coming to rest on the edge of the rug. Splinters covered her father's face on the floor.

And Rudi, taking advantage of the distraction, had Karin by the waist.

"Your capture by the gang was a blessing," he hissed, now so close she could taste his stale breath. She flexed, but he was stronger than he looked. Her arms were helplessly clamped at her sides.

"Rudi don't!" she begged, trying to stay calm.

"We knew you were sympathetic to him, that coward! But he was clever. He always managed to slip through our fingers. But then, the idea came to me as a revelation. I took it to Herr Gossen. He was impressed."

"I don't know what you're talking about. Please let me go!"

Karin twisted with greater urgency. Rudi countered, rage in his eyes.

"I had only a faint idea where the gang was, but I told you we did. I baited the trap, and you took it. You took us right to him."

Rudi seemed disappointed when Karin did not react. She found it hard to believe Rudi came up with the idea on his own, but it didn't matter. She had not proved clever at all. The truth remained, she led them right to Frei and the gang. It was all her fault. Without her careless flight to warn him, he might be alive today. She was wrong to suspect Zara. She had just been trying to protect him.

The betrayer was Karin.

Oma's verse came back:

Weeds and lies sprout
and grow quickly without
Truth and good soil
Care and long toil

Karin had let the weeds overrun everything.

Rudi was squeezing the air from her lungs—but truth was crushing the last of her hope. She was responsible for a needless death. She had no right to escape to Berlin, no right to live while Frei lay dead in an unmarked grave. Her body relaxed. She no longer cared what Rudi intended.

He shuffled her toward the sofa, and she felt the cushions against the back of her calves. Then without explanation, Rudi paused. As if reading her mind, his expression changed. He let go and shoved her down onto the sofa.

"You disappoint me, Fraulein," he said. "Did you think I would—?"

She fought for air.

"Herr Gossen thought the same thing," he said. His speech became garbled by his tongue moving around in his mouth like he was distracted by a sore tooth. "He considered you a favor to me for finding his son. I was given his permission to keep you as long as I wanted to. *However* I wanted. But now that Schlinge is on the way, the clock is ticking."

He sat down on the other end of the sofa. Karin saw it as her chance. She could beat him to the back door. Opa would help her. Gossen or not, she would bear Rudi no longer.

She leapt from the sofa.

To Karin's surprise, Rudi was quick. He dove at her as she was almost out of the room. His arm caught her at the ankles, sweeping both legs out from under her. She landed hard—elbow, hip, and cheek to the floor. One step more, and she might have made the hallway. Instead, writhing on the tiled floor, Rudi had her by the legs as he clambered to his knees.

"No, Rudi! No!" she howled. While he corralled her, she clamped her eyes shut and kicked her legs with a fury. One leg broke free. She pulled forward on her elbows. He leapt forward, clamping down on her leg with his own. Her hand slapped near the base of the front window. She grabbed the hem of a blackout curtain and pulled. It snapped from its mooring and came down on them. But he had her. An instant later, he had climbed across her waist and was pinning her down.

Face down on the cold tile, she couldn't breathe even to scream.

He put his full weight on her back and drew close to her ear. He took hold of her face and twisted it toward him. She was near to passing out.

"I'm not going to hurt you, Karin, no," he said, his voice a rasp. "Whatever I am, I am not that. You see, I have it all planned. I know the way out. We can escape, you and I, don't you see?"

She was not looking at him. Her eyes were clamped shut, focusing everything on escape.

"Look at me! Look at me!"

He shook her face in his hands.

She squeezed a look. His face was bright red, lathered in sweat that pasted his hair across his forehead. His eyes were swollen with crazed desperation. His lips were parted, and his yellowed teeth stretched in what seemed a strange and wide kind of grin until Karin saw what had been occupying him these last few moments. A small glass capsule, no larger than a pill, was wedged between the upper and lower teeth.

"We can go together, don't you see? Gossen gave me two hours. He said he would come here. He would find us dead or take care of it himself."

He jerked at her face and spoke like a slithering snake.

"The doctor prepared a dose large enough for the both of us. Take it with me!" he pleaded. "Bite down! We'll escape together!"

He leaned further in and pressed his lips on hers. She flinched but could not twist away. How long since her last breath? She felt the capsule against a tooth. If it snapped, it would be all over.

Rudi strained her neck upward, pressing harder. Karin's head was in a vice. A day before, she might have considered this kind of plan. His way was not unheard of. Stories circulated, whispered in the hallways or around the campfire, of British spies, parachuted from above, carrying vials of cyanide to use in case of capture. To young people with so much life ahead, despite the war, such an option seemed unthinkable. Had Karin space to breathe, she might have wondered. But now, the world and its darkness had shrunk to the space between Rudi's teeth and the space between them both. She knew only the will to breathe.

As panic took over, her entire body began to jerk. Her chin, stretched up to the limit of its range, had only one direction to move. The convulsion brought it down. In the spasm, Karin felt his lips scrape up her face and glance off her nose. There was a faint crunch, and Rudi sucked in a surprised breath. An instant later, he let go and fell back, coughing and spitting. The smell reminded her of almonds.

By the time she looked up, it was too late. Foam ringed his mouth, and his eyes were in the back of his head. A shudder of twitches, and he was gone.

Karin's first instinct was to replace the blackout curtain. She found the top of it in the mass of cloth at the door and stretched it across the window. The rod was intact, but the mount was broken. The curtain was heavy, and after a moment's struggle, she let go. She was not thinking clearly. The rod could not be fixed.

She remembered breaking curfew with Willem and switched off the light.

She bounded up the stairs. She would get her things and leave. The night air was sure to be cool, and the usual curfew was in force, but perhaps she could hide in the park until morning.

She closed her suitcase and buckled the strap. The ticket was safe in her knapsack. A coat from her closet would ward off the cold tonight. As she slipped it on, her thoughts turned to Berlin and her mother. *We'll make a new start.*

Reality opposed her downstairs. The body of Rudi was up against the door. The blackout patrol might have seen the light from the window.

Even in death, his presence was unbearable, but his words echoed in the darkness: *Gossen gave me two hours.*

She paused to think. In her desperation to leave, she had been foolish. If the blackout patrol arrived and peered through the window, they would see Rudi's legs. They'd break down the door and call the police. If she was gone, Opa, though unaware, would be held responsible. Gossen would arrive. He would use Opa to find her. Even in Berlin, she could not hide for long.

The cathedral of her plan began to crumble, as under a hail of bombs. She fell to the floor where she stood and began to cry. The way to her mother seemed closed. Perhaps Rudi's way had been better after all. Perhaps even now, there was enough poison left in his mouth...

CHAPTER THIRTY-EIGHT

There was just enough light to see the top of the garden fence against the morning sky. The strip of grass that framed the beds glistened with morning dew. Steam rose from Karin's head and neck, and her breath formed a cloud around her. Her body was covered in soil that smelled of rain and worms and hard work. Dirt caked under her fingernails. Her limbs were warm, loose, and ached with satisfaction.

The tomato stalks in front of her jiggled like children startled from their sleep. She pushed the earth around each one, mounding and smoothing it. She hoped the transplanting had not disturbed them too much. Time would tell. The fresh fruit, still green with youth, was hungry for long summer days. But they smelled minty and alive.

Karin stood and looked at the last stars of morning.

A verse from Oma's journal came to mind:

The morning dew, the promise of heaven.

Karin might have been in a dream. But the garden, whose surface was substantially higher than it was before, was proof that she was quite awake.

Earlier that night, Gossen arrived as Rudi predicted. She heard the car stop outside, the door open, then close, and faint steps on the landing. The door was unlocked. He did not knock, expecting no one to answer.

The latch clicked, and the outside sounds passed through the doorway. More steps, careful ones, assured Karin that, as Rudi said, he was alone. She dared not look.

The door closed. The floor creaked with more steps and then silence.

The click of a switch and faint light beneath her eyelids told Karin he had found the switch in the hallway. She hoped he would notice the missing blackout curtain when he came to the front room, fear that light was spilling outside and turn it off again. Darkness would aid her deception.

He left the light on. The footsteps drew nearer. They crunched on glass from her father's portrait.

Karin wondered what went through Gossen's mind when he stepped into the room. What expression crossed his face when he saw them? Was he shocked? Did he smile?

She would never know. She only knew that when he turned from the hall, he would see two figures, together, it seemed, in an eternal embrace.

There hadn't been time to move Rudi to the sofa like she had wanted. He was too heavy. Instead, she just propped him up against it in a kind of sitting position. It was impossible to tell how natural it looked when she curled in a ball and rested her head in his lap. The soap was a last-second idea—it left an awful taste in her mouth, but she hoped the lather looked like the foam in Rudi's mouth.

The switch on the lamp clicked. Anticipating that Gossen would want a closer look, Karin had unplugged it. The light from the hall would have to do. Too much light, and he would certainly see her chest slowly rising or her heart hammering in her neck vein.

The steps drew closer. She could feel his weight through the floorboards underneath. He was being careful.

The plan had come to Karin in a flash, driven by desperation more than intelligence. There was no time to think, no time to calculate—only to act.

Leaving Rudi where he had crunched down on the capsule, Karin had flown out the back door and crossed the garden to the shed. She was not worried about waking Opa. Like before, he would not be disturbed by the scraping of a flimsy door. Inside, she was met by the familiar smell of old oil and ancient machines, and, tonight, the scent of a new ration of schnapps. Opa was slumped in his old rocking chair, snoring.

The pistol was just where she had left it the time before. It took a moment to find the scissors—they were tucked under a wooden and leather bellows Opa was fashioning out of scrap. Seeing it days earlier, she had asked about his invention.

"A ventilation system for the shelter." He said, and proceeded to explain how it would provide air to the shelter even if they were buried alive.

She freed it from the stitching and wondered what Opa would think when he discovered it was missing. It was a loose end, quite literally, with no time to tie up. The gun's cartridge was stashed deeper in the cushion. She could see at least two bullets. In Luxembourg her father had shown her once how to insert the cartridge and flip off the safety.

Turning to leave, she looked at Opa in his chair. If this went wrong, she would never see him again. Even if it went right, she might not for a very long time.

She bent down and kissed his forehead. The smell of schnapps was heavy on him. She blamed the war and the Nazis. She closed the door behind her and left.

The expression on Gossen's face, the only one she got to see when at last she opened her eyes, told Karin that her plan had worked to perfection. He was frozen in a stare just above her, a mix of shock and horror. She had waited until the last possible second, feeling him near and at the limit of her ability to hold her breath.

Her arm, previously hidden under Rudi, snapped up. At such close range, it would have been difficult to miss. She pulled the trigger—the sound rattled the walls—her arm jerked sideways.

Gossen staggered back. He looked confused and began patting himself like he didn't know which pocket held his pen.

Karin fired again. This time, he felt it hard in his midsection. His eyes were wide in realization.

Not sure it was enough, she hoped the cartridge held more than two bullets. When the third shot spun him around, she felt a kind of relief.

The fourth shot probably missed because he was already going down. Opa would find the hole in the ceiling one day and scratch his head.

The fifth and sixth were only empty clicks.

Given the choice, she would have preferred it had been Schlinge at the end of the barrel, but Gossen deserved it too.

Karin let her arm fall. The soap tasted awful in her mouth.

As she dug the trench in the garden, Karin felt a strange pity for Rudi. Like Frei, he likely had a mother who would wonder what happened to him. Perhaps a brother or sister, or two, though he never spoke of them. Maybe his father was off at war—France if he was lucky, Russia if he was not. Maybe he was already dead. Maybe he was another Gossen somewhere.

Using Opa's shovel, Karin dug as deep and wide as she could manage, practically transplanting the entire garden. She worked all night. The bodies went in on top of each other, Gossen first and then Rudi, and then the dirt. Dragging them through the house had nearly exhausted her. Once she fled, she knew, if Opa expanded his shelter, he would be sure to find them. She counted on the project stalling like so many of his others. She would have to take the risk.

The sun had just broken through the gap between the houses across the street when Karin finished inside. Opa would never notice the dark stains left behind from the blood that wouldn't clean from some of the cracks of the tile in the kitchen. He might crunch on a rogue piece of glass but would never realize it was missing from Father's picture. Could he tell the difference between the lingering smell of the pistol and the grease and oil on his hands? The broken blackout curtain, which Karin couldn't fix, would give him pause. In the end, he would simply shrug his shoulders like always and fix it.

When Karin left using the kitchen door, she did not look back on the house. She held no fondness for it. But pausing at the gate to the alley, for a last glance at the garden and Opa's shed, the sadness was overwhelming. She sucked in her lower lip, where a lump of raw flesh was still unhealed, and bit down. Leaving was the only way. The Gestapo would come looking for her. Berlin would give her time, if not space. Mother could help. Mother had her ways.

CHAPTER THIRTY-NINE

Six Months Later

Karin crunched across the frozen path and lifted her eyes to a ribbon of stars burning above the barren treetops. The night was as still as the statue of Friedrich the Great watching from the courtyard behind her. Tonight would be a cold she had never known. They had warned her that in Berlin there was winter, but in the east, there was winter's winter. Somewhere beyond the horizon—at the edge of her imagination—Opa shivered in his shed, and her unharvested stalks stood frozen.

She pulled her gray woolen coat tighter against the chill and felt the lump of her nurse's medallion, awarded only hours earlier, against her breast. A token of survival, if not atonement.

An unspoken prayer ascended with her frozen breath. To the heavens, to God, to Oma—she wasn't sure, but she was grateful all the same.

A voice pierced the cold silence.

"Ingrid? Is that you?"

Karin turned. It was the Mother, silhouetted against the bright doorway of the dormitory, where the celebration was winding down.

"You'll catch your death out here. Come to bed. We have a long journey tomorrow."

She stole one last glance at the stars.

"Coming!"

Karin reached for the Gëlle Fra in her pocket, felt its cold weight against her palm, and went inside.

HISTORICAL NOTE

In the spring of 1942, the Nazi regime stood at the zenith of its power. Most of Europe and North Africa lay under German control, and U-boats stalked Allied shipping across the Atlantic. In the east, after surviving the Red Army's winter counteroffensive, the Wehrmacht was once again on the move—this time toward the Soviet leader's namesake city, Stalingrad. Across the Third Reich, expectations for victory had never been higher.

Great Britain sought to puncture that confidence. Just after midnight on May 31, 1942, more than one thousand Royal Air Force bombers took off to strike Cologne, a key industrial city in the Ruhr region. The "Thousand Bomber Raid," as it became known, demonstrated the Allies' growing ability to mount large-scale attacks. Though damage to the city was extensive, it was scattered, and the Nazi regime quickly mobilized citizens to clean up and rebuild. Nevertheless, the raid marked the beginning of an aerial campaign that would continue until 1945 and ultimately reduce Cologne to a shattered, nearly empty ruin.

Cologne itself—industrial, Catholic, and pragmatic—was compliant, if not a stronghold of Nazi fanaticism. Still, outright resistance remained rare and dangerous, confined largely to small youth groups such as the Edelweiss Pirates, whose defiance took the form of nonconformity, sabotage, and mockery of official institutions.

The **Freedom Gang** in this story is a fictional counterpart to those groups: young people who lived among the ruins, rejected Nazi conformity, and sought not heroism so much as freedom from lies.

Like most adolescents of her time, **Karin Blik** would have tried her best to get along. She would have shared in the ordinary tragedies common to that world—friends sent to the Eastern Front, letters arriving months too late, teachers arrested for careless jokes, disabled children and the ill "sent away" and never returning—and accepted them with weary resignation. Only Karin's years in Luxembourg—away from German propaganda—gave her the distance to see her world differently and the courage to choose another path.

The **Grand Duchy of Luxembourg** occupied a peculiar position during the war. Though neutral before the war, once invaded it was treated by Germany not as an occupied country but as a province destined for annexation, partly on account of its linguistic and cultural ties to Germany. When that annexation became official in August 1942, Luxembourgish men were conscripted into the Wehrmacht, and its symbols of independence were suppressed. The **Gëlle Fra** monument—erected in gratitude to Luxembourgers who had died fighting for the Allies in the First World War—was torn down in 1940 as "anti-German."

Finally, this story was sparked in part by an elusive thread of history, perhaps a lost record or just a rumor, of a Gestapo chief assassinated by resisters. Whether or not such an event occurred remains uncertain—but its possibility was enough to ignite the imagination.

ACKNOWLEDGEMENTS

I n war, all children are victims.

The trauma of Holocaust children is well known, as it must be, always and forever.

In The Garden At Midnight touches on the experience of a German girl whose life was poisoned by the Nazi regime, and on how difficult it was to recognize that evil for what it was.

Boys and girls in the Hitlerjugend or Bund Deutscher Mädel found friendship and purpose—qualities tragically twisted toward destructive ends. Many believed they were living normal childhoods, only to be horrified later by what their nation had done when the war returned home in 1944 and 1945.

Resistance was rare and often fatal, yet many who defied the regime were young themselves, showing extraordinary courage and paying the ultimate price. Those who did not resist still bore deep wounds—from the bombs that fell and from the moral reckoning that followed.

This book is written in remembrance of those children—victims and bystanders alike—whose lives were shaped by a system that betrayed them.

I am grateful to the teachers, curators, and archivists whose work preserves this era's memory. Their care makes it possible to glimpse ordinary life amid extraordinary times.

Writing is solitary work, but a family endeavor. To my wife, Mary, ever faithful in support and encouragement—my deepest love. To Megan and Peter, for your cheer; David and Liz, for your enthusiasm; Erik and Amie, for your sharp eyes; and Chloe, for friendship beyond measure—this book exists because of all of you.

And to the real young people of that dark era—may your stories remind us that innocence, once corrupted, demands both remembrance and renewal.

QUESTIONS FOR FURTHER DISCUSSION

1. How was Karin different from the other characters in the book? How was she like them?

2. Had you grown up in Karin's world, how would you have navigated the pressures of the war and the youth organizations or gangs?

3. Which of Karin's relationships affected her life the most in both helpful and damaging ways?

4. What is Karin's most important value in life?

5. Where do you go when you need refuge from the world? Do you prefer to be alone or with others?

6. Who are the people in your life that have encouraged you to be strong, courageous, or faithful?

7. When did you first begin to wonder if the world was different from what you were led to believe?

8. When have you stood up for yourself or your beliefs in the face of opposition or isolation? What was the result?

ALSO BY TIM BYERS

LUXEMBOURG WAR STORIES

The Order Of The Red Lion

On the eve of war in 1939, fourteen-year-old Hansi Broussard's world shatters when a bomb rips through the train station. With his friend Karin, the daughter of a German diplomat, Hansi follows a trail of clues that threaten both his family and the gentle Grand Duchy. Will courage be enough against the gathering storm?

The Vianden Deception

As German forces pour into Luxembourg in May 1940, fifteen-year-old Hansi Broussard volunteers with the Luxembourg Resistance for what is supposed to be a "routine mission." When the world shatters beside a lonely bridge in the Ardennes Forest, Hansi makes a promise he might die to keep.

www.ingramcontent.com/pod-product-compliance
Lightning Source LLC
Chambersburg PA
CBHW010607310726
48969CB00010B/2605